FAST AND LOOSE

Books by Fern Michaels

No Safe Secret
Wishes for Christmas
Fancy Dancer
About Face
Perfect Match
A Family Affair
Forget Me Not
The Blossom Sisters
Balancing Act
Tuesday's Child
Betrayal
Southern Comfort
To Taste the Wine
Sins of the Flesh
Sins of Omission
Return to Sender
Mr. and Miss
   Anonymous
Up Close and Personal
Fool Me Once
Picture Perfect
The Future Scrolls
Kentucky Sunrise
Kentucky Heat
Kentucky Rich
Plain Jane
Charming Lily
What You Wish For
The Guest List
Listen to Your Heart
Celebration
Yesterday
Finders Keepers
Annie's Rainbow

Sara's Song
Vegas Sunrise
Vegas Heat
Vegas Rich
Whitefire
Wish List
Dear Emily
Christmas at
   Timberwoods

The Sisterhood Novels

Point Blank
In Plain Sight
Eyes Only
Kiss and Tell
Blindsided
Gotcha!
Home Free
Déjà Vu
Cross Roads
Game Over
Deadly Deals
Vanishing Act
Razor Sharp
Under the Radar
Final Justice
Collateral Damage
Fast Track
Hokus Pokus
Hide and Seek
Free Fall
Lethal Justice

Books by Fern Michaels (Cont.)

Sweet Revenge
The Jury
Vendetta
Payback
Weekend Warriors

The Men of the Sisterhood Novels

Double Down
Fast and Loose

The Godmothers Series

Classified
Breaking News
Deadline
Late Edition
Exclusive
The Scoop

eBook Exclusives

Desperate Measures
Seasons of Her Life
To Have and To Hold
Serendipity
Captive Innocence
Captive Embraces

Captive Passions
Captive Secrets
Captive Splendors
Cinders to Satin
For All Their Lives
Texas Heat
Texas Rich
Texas Fury
Texas Sunrise

Anthologies

When the Snow Falls
Secret Santa
A Winter Wonderland
I'll Be Home for Christmas
Making Spirits Bright
Holiday Magic
Snow Angels
Silver Bells
Comfort and Joy
Sugar and Spice
Let It Snow
A Gift of Joy
Five Golden Rings
Deck the Halls
Jingle All the Way

Published by Kensington Publishing Corporation

FERN MICHAELS

FAST AND LOOSE

ZEBRA BOOKS
KENSINGTON PUBLISHING CORP.
http://www.kensingtonbooks.com

ZEBRA BOOKS are published by

Kensington Publishing Corp.
119 West 40th Street
New York, NY 10018

All Kensington titles, imprints, and distributed lines are available at special quantity discounts for bulk purchases for sales promotion, premiums, fund-raising, educational, or institutional use.

Special book excerpts or customized printings can also be created to fit specific needs. For details, write or phone the office of the Kensington Sales Manager: Attn.: Sales Department. Kensington Publishing Corp., 119 West 40th Street, New York, NY 10018. Phone: 1-800-221-2647.

Zebra and the Z logo Reg. U.S. Pat. & TM Off.

First Kensington Books Hardcover Printing: May 2016
First Zebra Books Mass-Market Paperback Printing: September 2016
ISBN-13: 978-1-4201-4063-7
ISBN-10: 1-4201-4063-9

eISBN-13: 978-1-4201-4064-4
eISBN-10: 1-4201-4064-7

10 9 8 7 6 5 4 3 2 1

Printed in the United States of America

Prologue

Philonias Needlemeyer was many things. First and foremost, he was rich. Some said if he spent a million dollars a day until the day he died, he would never run out of money. Philonias was thirty-nine years old. Others said he was richer than God, but could not offer up proof that it was so. There were so many rumors about Philonias, it was hard to tell what was real and what wasn't, all of which suited Philonias just fine.

Philonias was also a philanthropist. He gave to every worthy cause, and some that were not so worthy. He never stinted when it came to donating money. Philonias was a pillar of the community of Las Vegas, albeit a very reclusive pillar. What that meant was he was a stand-up guy and could always be counted on for whatever the community needed or wanted as long as he didn't have to put his person on display, speak, or give interviews—and he never allowed his picture to be taken. Ever.

And there was a reason for that. Philonias Needlemeyer was a giant among men. He was seven feet three inches tall and weighed 360 pounds. Some said he was a big ole cuddly teddy bear. He was not a big ole cuddly teddy bear. Others said he was a gentle giant. Whatever else he was, Philonias was *not* a gentle giant among men. What he was, simply put, was a large man with a strange name who happened to be incredibly, obscenely rich.

Philonias was a kind man. A gentle man. A generous man. At least that was how he thought of himself. And he never argued with himself. Why not? Because he knew that he would win in the end, and what was the fun in winning all the time?

He lived in a ten-thousand-square-foot penthouse apartment at Anna de Silva's Babylon Casino and Hotel. It was a penthouse he had inherited from his parents. Because he was such a big man and required such massive furnishings, he had purchased the adjoining ten-thousand-square-foot penthouse and had combined the two apartments into one massive unit that was the envy of every other resident at Babylon, as well as anyone else in Las Vegas who knew about it. He had a gourmet kitchen with every kitchen appliance, tool, gizmo, and gadget with a plug known to man, because he loved to putter in the kitchen. He thought of himself as an *almost* gourmet chef. He also knew how to clean his living quarters, how to do laundry, and how to shop for nutritious food. Philonias Needlemeyer was a man of many talents. But only because he valued his privacy, and the only way that worked was to do everything himself.

His digs, as he referred to them, had six fireplaces, all wood-burning. He had installed a surround system that would make Hollywood cringe in shame if they knew he had it. He had wall-to-wall television sets. The carpeting was ankle thick, because he liked to walk barefoot. But most of all, he had a perfect view of the city he loved. Oftentimes, at night he would sit by the hour, with all the lights extinguished, and stare out at the city, with its magnificent illumination.

All of the above was the public version of Philonias Needlemeyer. What no one knew or even suspected was that there was another Philonias Needlemeyer. That Philonias Needlemeyer hung his second hat in his adjoining penthouse, where he spent half of each and every day playing Robin Hood. Philonias Needlemeyer, aka Robin Cool Hood, was a cyber thief, or, as he liked to say, hacker extraordinaire. Not for himself, since he clearly did not need the money. It was the challenge. Because he didn't approve of gambling, he loved to help himself to the Vegas casinos' money and use it to do good for others. And he loved doing it right under all the noses of the casinos' owners, including the Countess de Silva and her head of security, Bert Navarro.

Straight arrow Philonias Needlemeyer had many cyber acquaintances but no real flesh-and-blood friends. He liked it that way. The Robin Hood version of Philonias Needlemeyer had one real cyber friend, the kind of friend you would trust with your life and your money. And that person was Abner Tookus. Abner was his best and only real cyber friend because he had been the one to train the sixteen-year-old Abner when he was just a long-haired geek with magic in his fingers. They'd met at an underground convention of cyber geeks in New Jersey that he had wanted to explore but had never quite got up the nerve to because he was afraid he would be the eight-hundred-pound gorilla in the room. The thing was, to his relief, not one of the geeks or their promoters gave him a second look. All they were interested in was his fingers and what he could do on a computer. And that all worked for him. He'd never attended another convention.

In some ways, the relationship was a bit one sided, what with Philonias knowing everything there was to know about Abner, while all Abner knew about Philonias was his cyber name of RCHood. And Philonias planned to keep it that way. Forever, if necessary. Philonias had spent many enjoyable hours watching Abner try, to no avail, to ferret out his real identity.

Each and every time Abner was about to crack the code, he threw up a happy face. To Abner's chagrin.

Philonias Needlemeyer was also a brainiac. He had two doctorate degrees and MBAs from three different Ivy League schools—Harvard, Yale, and the Wharton School of the University of Pennsylvania. He also had total recall on each and every event in his life from the age of five. His parents, even at that early age, had recognized that they had given birth to a genius who had no equal.

From that day on, the man and the teenage boy were fast friends, not flesh-and-blood friends, mind you, but cyber friends. Each saw something in the other that allowed them both to swear to secrecy as to their professions. It was a rule neither of them had ever broken, because it was sacrosanct. Like doctor-patient confidentiality or lawyer-client privilege. Neither knew nor cared where the other lived. They communicated only through computers and only by using their cyber names. No matter how much depended on one of them locating the other at a moment's notice, even if it was a life-or-death matter, doing so was impossible. Philonias was simply RCHood, which stood for Robin Cool Hood. Abner was TRIPLEM, which stood for Triple Mister Magic Money.

The man and the boy had met face-to-face only once, at the aforementioned cyber fair. And that was years and years ago, too many to even remember these days. The boy of sixteen with fire in his eyes, ragged jeans, and stringy hair was now a grown man who wore Armani suits and John Lobb shoes and worked at legitimate jobs. And some that were not so legitimate. Talking about one's achievements, along with bragging rights, was allowed as long as no names were mentioned. TRIPLEM was also wealthy these days, though not as wealthy as RCHood and not because he had inherited anything of value. No, his wealth had come from special jobs he did for private individuals. Philonias was very proud of his one and only star pupil. Just as Abner whooped and hollered when he saw a cyber message attributed to RC-Hood that said something had gone down that was not to RCHood's liking, to which he had replied, **Screw this up, and I will wipe out your entire bloodline**. That simple, succinct response put him at the top of the cyber pole. Or in layman's terms, "Never mess with RCHood."

RCHood was a legend among the men and women of the cyber world.

The legend among men stared at the wraparound computer room, which rivaled NASA, with all its computers and monitors, as he tried to decide what he wanted to do. It was early in the day, not quite seven o'clock Vegas time, and he'd already had his hourly workout in his private gym and eaten a manly breakfast that he prepared himself—eggs, bacon, pancakes, and a whole melon, along with three cups of coffee. He'd showered, shaved, and read three newspapers online, and he was now ready to start his day. This was the time of day he loved best, because he knew he was clicking on all cylinders. Today, though, he was out of sorts, and he hated the feeling. He hadn't slept well. Normally, he slept a full ten hours of deep, peaceful sleep. Last night he'd tossed and turned all night long, and when he did finally drift off into a fitful sleep, he had awful dreams, which he could not remember on awakening.

Philonias flexed his fingers, gave his neck a workout, then rotated his massive shoulders in preparation for a long stint at the keyboard. Something wasn't right; he could feel it in every fiber of his body. Something here at Babylon. Something he had missed, which was unlikely because he knew more about the inner workings of the casino than the security firm and the owners knew. He had all their banking records on file, encrypted, of course, all the private e-mails between Bert Navarro and Dixson Kelly and, of course, the entire security force. He knew what was going on minute by minute. He even knew everything there was to know about the entertainers, the regular dancers, and the showgirls. Right down to every last penny of their bank balances. He knew who was in arrears, who was up to date, who was dodging bill collectors, and whose vehicles were about to be repossessed for lack of payment. He knew every high roller to enter the doors of Babylon, knew if they could afford to gamble or were just winging it on a hope and prayer.

Knowledge, Philonias Needlemeyer told himself daily, was the most powerful aphrodisiac in the world. He loved the power. He loved that he could choose to crush a reputation the person with the reputation deserved to have destroyed. He also loved to make one soar to unbelievable heights if the universe was moving too slow to suit him. He also loved that he was never wrong. And yet, somehow, someway, he knew the day would come when he would make a mistake. He tried not to think about it and worked extra diligently to make sure he covered his tracks.

His neck and shoulders at peace with each other, Philonias hit the keys and brought his world within view. He scrolled and tapped and pecked for ninety minutes, just long enough to let him know nothing had gone wrong during his sleepless night. He was about to exit Dixson Kelly's Babylon e-mail account when something caught his eye. He sat back and eyeballed a message that, on the surface, was innocent enough at first glance. **Call me. We need to talk**. That meant ASAP. Philonias scooted his chair to another computer, where he brought up a new screen that logged Kelly's in-house in and out calls. No calls to Macau, where Bert Navarro was living these days, while overseeing the building of Babylon II. He moved to yet another monitor to check Kelly's personal Verizon cell-phone account. Also no calls to

Macau. He knew Dixson Kelly had nine burner phones that he used for his dating life. As always, he had at least three women on what he called his love chain. The reason for the burner phones was so that none of the women knew they were part of any daisy chain. He wanted to keep it that way, too. Phelonias checked those, too. No calls to Macau.

Philonias nibbled on his lower lip. When Bert Navarro spoke, Dixson Kelly hustled. A call had been made; that was for sure. Otherwise, there would have been a storm of incoming calls from Bert, but there had been none following his initial call. That had to mean Kelly had gone outside Babylon's doors to make the call. But why?

Philonias moved his chair to yet another in-house monitor to check the entrances and exits at the casino for the past eight hours to see if Kelly had left the premises. It took him a full ten minutes before he spotted the temporary head of security leaving the casino sans jacket and tie. His shirtsleeves were rolled up, and he was wearing a Boston Red Sox ball cap. Just another customer hooked on gambling. Philonias blinked. He'd never seen Dixson Kelly in anything but his Hugo Boss suits, of which he had twenty-two. To anyone else, it would have been a dead end. Not for Philonias Needlemeyer.

Philonias moved back to computer number three and pressed more keys, which would show him the traffic on the street. He was able to track Kelly all the way to the Wynn resort and casino, where he entered through the massive front doors with a gaggle of people, even though it was three o'clock in the morning. Vegas never slept. And it was true, there were no clocks in the casinos. Deliberately so.

Another program suddenly filled the screen, one that, had he known about it, would have sent Steve Wynn, the owner of the Wynn Las Vegas, screaming to the authorities.

Philonias continued to track Kelly across the main floor, never losing sight of him for even a second. He acted the part of a customer, stopping here and there to drop a coin in the slots or to stand and watch someone else waste their money. Ten minutes later, after winning thirty-seven dollars, he made his way to the men's room and entered a stall. Now he was off-limits to Philonias, who cursed ripely. Within fifteen minutes, Kelly was back on the main floor. He dropped another coin in one of the slot machines and was about to walk away when it pinged and clattered to life. He'd won another seventy-three dollars. He cashed in, settled his baseball cap more firmly on his head, and made his way to the nearest exit. From there he returned to Babylon, checked with his assistant that all was well, and retired to his apartment. Actually, Bert's apartment, which he was using until Bert's return.

"Crap!" The single word flew out of Philonias's mouth like a gunshot. He worked his neck muscles and settled down to what he knew was going to be an even longer day at the keyboard than he had originally thought. He'd had days like this before, and he welcomed the challenge. After all, he had all the time in the world to figure out what was going on.

And he would figure it out. He always did.

Chapter 1

Jack Emery, Cyrus on his heels, walked aimlessly from room to room in the old farmhouse that he and Nikki had recently purchased from Judge Cornelia Easter. Nikki, along with the other girls, had been gone only two days on a special project for Interpol that was so NTK, she wasn't even able to tell Jack *where* she was going, much less why. All she could tell him was that she and the sisters would be gone for at least a month, possibly longer.

Jack looked down at the massive German shepherd, which, in his opinion, was more human than animal, and said, "A month, maybe longer! Do you have any idea how long that is, Cyrus? It means you have to make your bed probably forty-five times. With our luck, it will turn out to be two months. We have to cook for ourselves, clean, do laundry, plant the garden, go to the office to check on things, and try not to be lonely. It sucks! I don't mean that Nikki did all that stuff. We share everything, you know that. Here's the straight skinny. I'm pissed that Nik wouldn't tell me anything. I'm her husband, for God's sake. Like, who am I going to tell? If you can't trust your spouse, who can you trust?"

He dropped to his knees and cupped the big dog's head in his hands until they were eyeball-to-eyeball. Jack was so close that he could feel the dog's warm breath on his cheek. Cyrus whined until Jack hugged him and whispered, "It's going to be okay. We're going to survive. We did the last time Nik and the girls went away."

This time, Cyrus reared up and let loose a shrill bark, which Jack took to mean that Cyrus was in agreement.

"Okay then. I say we head into town and hang out at the BOLO Building and get caught up on our paperwork. We can always plant those flowers when we get back. The weatherman said it might rain later this evening, so that will work. While I get my stuff ready, it's your job to fold the towels, so get cracking, pal. And . . . get your gear ready. Two things, Cyrus, and not your security blanket."

Jack grinned to himself as he watched Cyrus head to the laundry room, where he slapped one massive paw on the dryer door, stood back, then nudged it all the way open. Then he dragged the four towels out onto the floor. He barked once, a shrill sound, to let Jack know he'd done his chore before he trotted off to the family room, to his basket of treasures. Jack quickly folded the four bath towels and set them on top of the dryer.

A year into ownership of the big shepherd, Nikki had heard that a dog whisperer was in town, and she wanted to take Cyrus because she thought he was acting depressed. Jack had gone along with her and had watched, absolutely amazed, as man and dog seemed to communicate with each other. The end result was that, according to the dog whisperer, Cyrus was depressed because he had no duties to perform and didn't feel worthwhile. "He needs a schedule, praise, and a time-out when he doesn't hold up his end of the bargain." The expert had gone on to say they both needed to sit down with Cyrus and lay it all out for him as to what they expected. Which they had, and to their amazement, Cyrus now made his own bed, took the towels out of the dryer, picked up after himself, and answered the phone by knocking the receiver off the hook and barking once. The only other rule he had to obey, apart from performing his duties, was that though he was allowed to chase the squirrels, he was not allowed to catch them.

Jack opened the back door to let Cyrus out. "Don't take all day, okay?"

Cyrus looked over his shoulder, as much as to say, "You're kidding, right?"

Jack shrugged; the dog had it down to thirteen minutes. While Cyrus was doing his thing, he spent the time checking and packing up his briefcase for the trip into Georgetown. He heard the sound then, one that was familiar, one that he hadn't heard in a long time. The ringtone of the special encrypted phone Avery Snowden had supplied to all of them, the sisters and the boys, too. Where was it? Somewhere in the bottom of his briefcase, buried in a mound of papers. Finally, he found it.

Cyrus let himself in the kitchen door and ran to the table the moment he recognized the strange sound coming from Jack's briefcase. He forgot all about the treat he always got when he came in from doing his business, because he knew that when he heard that particular sound, it meant *action*. He sat back on his haunches as he listened attentively to what Jack was saying.

"Bert!" Jack's trouble antenna went straight up in the air. "Talk to me, big guy!" Cyrus was on his feet, his tail between his legs, his ears flat against his head at his master's tone of voice. Jack listened, frowned, grimaced, and finally said, "Yeah, yeah, I get it. I'll call a meeting. We're on it! You do know the girls are off on some mystery mission that Interpol requested. Except for Maggie. She's holding down the female fort, so to speak. No, no, no communication until their return. Six weeks, possibly longer. Yeah, yeah, we're on our own here! That's not a bad thing, Bert!"

He listened again and said, "Abner will be my first call. I'll get back to you sometime later, after I call a meeting. Other than that, how are things in Macau?" He listened again to a detailed progress report, then broke the connection.

Jack stuffed the encrypted phone into one of the pockets in his cargo pants. He looked down at Cyrus, knowing the big dog wanted an explanation. "Trouble is looming, buddy. Gotta call the guys for a meet at the BOLO Building. You know that old saying, 'Be careful what you wish for, because you just might get your wish.' Well, ten minutes ago, I was wishing for something out of the ordinary, and here it is. Saddle up, Cyrus. Get your gear, and let's hit the road."

Cyrus didn't need to be told twice. Within minutes, he had clutched in his teeth a tattered, whiskerless yellow tabby named Goldie and a pink-and-purple dragon with half the stuffing missing that Nikki had sewn and resewn, a gift from Lily Wong that was the dog's pride and joy and that Nikki had named simply Dragon. He was good to go.

There was a lilt in Jack's voice and a spring in his step when he ordered Cyrus to the kitchen door that led to the garage and his brand-new farm pickup truck. Cyrus was as excited as a six-month-old puppy. In dog language he noted that at last he had something to do besides make his bed, fold towels, and chase squirrels he wasn't allowed to catch. Life was good, he thought as he hopped into the F-150 and secured his seat belt. For now, along with his owner, he was king of the road. Yep, life was good.

* * *

An hour later, Jack parked in a no parking
zone at a deli across the street from the BOLO
Building. The name BOLO, an acronym for "be
on the lookout," was a law-enforcement term.
He ran in to pick up the order he had called in
en route. Ham, cheese, and roast beef on rye,
along with a tub of pickles, for himself and the
guys. Yogurt and salad for Maggie, and three
all–roast-beef sandwiches for Cyrus. He paid
for his order and sprinted back to his truck at
the curb, grateful no diligent cop had stuck a
parking ticket under one of the windshield
wipers.

Jack unlocked the security door, which had
a special, one-of-a-kind lock, and entered the
building, turned on the lights, and reset the
thermostat. He moved around, getting out
paper plates and utensils, something Maggie
usually did, but since he was the one who had
brought the food, he'd decided to save her the
trouble. He then prepared the Bunn coffeemaker, which would give him and the others an
almost limitless supply of coffee for the meeting
that was about to go down.

Everything under control, Jack knew he had
at least a good ten minutes, so he used them
wisely by watering the huge banana tree in the
foyer, a gift from Maggie when she had been
stalking them and trying to find out what he
and the others were up to back when he and
the boys had just been getting organized. In
the end, because she'd been so relentless, they
had taken a vote and had allowed her to be-

come a member of the Men of the Sisterhood.
But that had been during a time when the girls
didn't know what the boys were up to when
they traveled off-site on a mission. They knew
now, and everyone was okay with Maggie being
a member of an all-guy team. Cyrus was also
okay with it, even though Maggie always arrived
smelling like her cat, Hero.

The hands on the nautical clock in the
kitchen were straight up at noon when the last
member arrived and took his seat at the huge
plank table where they ate and discussed business. They all ignored Charles's edict not to
discuss business while eating, simply by saying
he could say and do whatever he wanted when
he was at Pinewood, the Sisterhood's head-
quarters, but here in the BOLO Building, he
was just one of the guys, and no one person
was in charge. Charles acquiesced gracefully.

The questions came hard and fast.

"What's up?"

"Is this an emergency? A mission?"

"Where? When?"

"Does it have anything to do with the girls?"

Cyrus decided it was time to voice an opinion, and besides, he had just wolfed down his
three sandwiches and was trying for a little
extra from those at the table. He barked his
one, two, three bark, which meant all of the
above.

Jack eyeballed Cyrus and warned him, "You
eat any more, and it's thirty minutes on the
treadmill tonight and one solid hour of yoga.
You know how you hate doing yoga with Nikki."

Cyrus growled and walked away.

Maggie got up and cleared the table. "Don't any of you get the idea that it's my job to clean up after all of you. It is not. I'm doing it so we can get on with it. Looks like we might need another pot of coffee. Raise your hand if you want more."

Every hand in the room except Harry's went up.

"I'm making you tea, Harry," Maggie told him.

"Good, good. I think we're going to be here awhile, so until we're all settled, let's just sit here and chitchat," Jack said. "The reason is that I'm going to need your undivided attention when I tell you all why I called this meeting."

The group talked about the weather, the possibility of rain later in the evening, the newest updates on the latest plane that had gone missing out over the Indian Ocean on the 24/7 news channels. The moment Maggie signaled that the coffee was ready, they made a beeline for the pot, filled their cups, and were back at the table, their eyes expectant at what was to come.

"Spit it out, Jack," Ted said. "Whatever it is, we're ready."

Jack withdrew the special encrypted phone from his cargo pants and placed it in the center of the table, then pressed the PLAY button. Bert Navarro's voice in China was crystal clear as he started to talk. The amenities over, he got to the point of his message.

"Jack, I want you to listen to me carefully, and then I want you to call a meeting with the guys, at which point I want you to call me back. What I'm going to ask you to do involves everyone, and we all have to vote on it. Here it is in a nutshell. As you know, while I was at Babylon, I ran the whole show, the security, the banking, the hiring, the firing, the whole ball of wax. I did that for the nine years I worked there prior to coming here to China, where it looks like I'm going to be spending, at the very least, another year.

"Dix is running Babylon. By running it, I mean he is in charge of everything except the financial end of things. I am still doing that from here. I have a lot of free time on my hands over here, so I've been going through the financials and have been in touch with the accounting firm that handles things. Something is wrong. We'll talk about that when you return my call. For now, I want to ask if you, the boys, and Maggie can head to Vegas and do a little recon for me. Dix doesn't know you guys, but he's smart. He might figure it out. Make a plan and get back to me.

"Jack, this is about as serious as it gets. I haven't even told Annie, and I'd like to keep it that way, at least for now. I know they're off on a mission that doesn't include any of us. Hopefully, you guys and Maggie can get a handle on this and settle it before their return, which I understand can be anywhere from one to two months down the road. Call me when you're all together so I can explain better."

Jack reached across the table and turned off the encrypted phone. He looked around at the serious expressions on everyone's face. "Okay, you heard him. I'm sure you all have questions, so let's get started."

Before anyone could speak, Cyrus let loose with a loud bark to weigh in and show he could follow instructions.

"Count me in. I can come up with several scenarios that will allow me to be in Vegas. I think Ted, Esposito, and Dennis fall into that category along with me. We do work for the *Post* and Annie, and Annie owns Babylon. What could be more natural? Good PR, and we can throw Bert in there, along with what's going on in Macau. We can make it work, Jack," Maggie said.

Jack nodded. "Sounds good to me." He made a note on the legal pad in front of him.

"With the girls gone, Fergus and I are at loose ends. Count us in," Charles said.

Fergus nodded in agreement.

"Sounds good to me," Abner Tookus said happily. "My problem is that I can't fly, so I'll drive. I've got some colleagues who live near and around Vegas. Good chance for me to hook up and compare notes. It's a whole new security cyber circus out there these days."

"Do you mean your hacking buddies?" Dennis asked.

"Yeahhh," Abner drawled.

"If you get caught, you could endanger the mission," Dennis said fretfully.

Abner's jaw dropped. He looked at Jack. "Tell me he didn't say what I just heard him say."

Jack laughed and stared down Dennis. "Yeah, he said it," Jack drawled, "but he didn't mean it. Did you, kid?"

"Guess not," Dennis mumbled.

Jack turned to Harry. "Can you get away, Harry? With Yoko gone, who is going to look after Lily?"

"The nuns at Saint Teresa's. That's where Lily goes to school these days. She stays there during the week and comes home Friday night. The nuns will look after her, and she will love it. If I have to, I can take the red-eye on the weekends. I don't see a problem. We're at our spring hiatus at the dojo, which means we're just doing maintenance and refresher work. Quon and Chin can handle things. I'm in."

All eyes turned to Jack Sparrow, the current director of the FBI. "Count me in. I owe Bert big-time. I have a bundle of vacation time due me. I just have to put it through, and that will take at least three days.

"Okay! That means all nine of us are headed for Vegas, as per Bert's request," Jack said.

A loud bark from under the table caused Jack to correct his mistake. "All *ten* of us are going to Vegas, per Bert's request." Cyrus barked his thanks for the correction.

"Let's talk and firm it up before we make the call to Bert. We need a plan. Charles, it's what you do best, so let's hear your thoughts," Jack said.

Charles toyed with his pen, pushing the point in, then out. The clicking sound irritated Fergus, who grabbed the pen and stuck it in his pocket.

"I can't hatch a plan with so little information. I need to know more," Charles said. "Assuming this concerns the millions of dollars that wash through each and every casino every day, we still need to know what specific thing triggered whatever it was that put Bert on this path. Is it a sudden happening, or is it something that has been going on that he just became aware of? How privy are we going to be to the accounting firm? Or are we depending on Abner to get us that information, or is Bert going to provide it? Maggie's suggestion that the four of them go as a team carries weight. I think it's plausible, as well as credible. What happens in Vegas doesn't *have* to stay in Vegas, not when there are five-star investigative reporters milling about."

"Anyone else have any questions or comments?" Jack asked.

Harry raised his hand. Startled, Jack just stared at him. Harry never asked questions. "What?" Jack asked.

"If you recall, Jack, my pictures were plastered all over Vegas when we were on that Chinese caper with Wing Ping. I've attended martial arts trials and participated in the ones held in Vegas. Customers won't recognize me, but the heavies will, and the security will for sure. Right now, I'm the number one in the whole country. That carries some publicity. How do you want to play that? Dude me up with a disguise? You know how I hate that crap. Let me go in as a shill? I'm all for going. I just don't want to compromise the mission by being so exposed."

"Harry's right," Dennis said boldly.

"You're right, kid. Charles will figure something out. He always does. We are not going anywhere until we have a foolproof plan of action," Jack said.

"Should we perhaps give some thought to alerting Lizzie Fox and Cosmo Cricket?" Maggie asked. "They're Nevada residents, and Cosmo is the lead attorney for the Nevada Gaming Control Board."

"Not just yet, Maggie. If Bert wanted to involve Cosmo and Lizzie, he wouldn't have contacted me . . . us. He would have contacted them. That tells me we need to keep a lid on this, even from Cosmo," Charles said.

"I can assign some extra agents to our Vegas field office," Jack Sparrow volunteered. "I have to tell you all that Vegas security is ten times better than the security they have for the White House, what with those Secret Service guys who keep getting into one sort of trouble or other. To say it's top-notch would be an understatement. As much as I hate to admit it—and Bert and I have been around and around the bush on this—his people are better than my best-trained agents. So if Bert has some bad apples in his crew, those bad apples know what they're doing. If any of you are thinking this is going to be a walk in the park, adjust your thinking right now."

The table went silent when Sparrow had finished speaking. It was Dennis who finally broke the ice by saying, "I think we're up to the challenge!"

"Well said, kid, well said," Ted announced, clapping the young multimillionaire reporter on the back.

Jack reached for the encrypted phone. "Anything else before I place the call?" No one said a word.

"No? Okay. Here we go, then! The next voice you will hear will be that of Bert Navarro, coming to you all the way from Macau, China."

Chapter 2

"If we're sure we're all okay with this, then here we go," Jack said, hitting the number two on his encrypted phone. He turned up the volume and hit the SPEAKER mode. The short burst of sound was as loud as a buzz saw on a still morning in the quiet room.

Bert clicked on after two rings. "I'm listening," he said curtly.

"Jack here, Bert. We ran it up the flagpole and everyone saluted. That means we're all here. We're good to go. Abner is going to drive cross-country, because he can't fly. Dennis will allow us to use his Gulfstream, so we can fly out at a moment's notice. Charles is working on a plan. That's our end of things. Oh, there is one thing, before I forget. Notify Dixson Kelly that I'll be bringing Cyrus, and we'll say he's a service dog. I don't want to have to jump through hoops when I get there. It's a game changer, Bert. If Cyrus doesn't go, we don't go."

"Not a problem. I'll take care of it. When do you think the rest of you can get under way?"

Jack looked around at the others. Almost as one, they shrugged, which meant they could go at a moment's notice or they could wait until Charles came up with a plan. If necessary, they could wait three days, until Jack Sparrow could begin taking his vacation days.

"It's Charles, Bert. To be on the safe side, I'd say we'll be good to fly out of here in three days, give or take a few hours. Abner will probably arrive before we do if he leaves today, even though he's driving cross-country. From what Jack has told us, this is not a time-sensitive matter, which means we will use the coming days to formulate a plan and, of course, run it by you for your approval before we commit to it. Will that work for you?"

"It will. Okay, let's get to it. Like I said earlier, I have a lot of time on my hands over here and no social life at all to speak of, so I've been running numbers, checking over bank statements, talking to the accounting firm, reading reports, doing everything I always do when I'm at Babylon, but with a little more thoroughness. I can't explain what it was or what triggered something in my head, but once I started the review, I knew in my gut something was *off*. I use the word 'off' because I am not sure something is *wrong*. My gut is telling me yes, something is very wrong. Gut instincts in this business are just as credible as seeing something in black and white.

"When I took over Babylon nine years ago, everything was in perfect order. With the changing of the guard, I hired on a new five-star accounting firm and a new legal team. I wanted to start clean and fresh. The lawyers and accountants told me that we were in good shape, and that the previous guys had done a good job. I had no cause to doubt any of that, and I still don't doubt it. Whatever is at play here is insidious. I do not use that word loosely.

"I think someone is tapping into or hacking our accounts. I think . . . Now, bear with me while I try to explain my thoughts, because right now I cannot prove anything. Let's just say someone like Abner, who excels at hacking, manages to get into the account and alters the deposit by, let's just say by thirty-three dollars or even one hundred thirty-three dollars. Who is going to pay attention to revenue being down thirty-three dollars or one hundred thirty-three dollars? But if the next day revenue is down, say, one hundred nineteen dollars, no one is going to pay attention to a loss of one hundred nineteen dollars. Then maybe nothing for a few days, and everything is back to normal, no glitches, no penny shortages.

"And then it starts all over again, with small amounts for maybe a total of five days a week, to the tune of let's just say five hundred thirty-two dollars for the week. It could be more, or it could be less. Multiply that by four, and you have two thousand one hundred twenty-eight dollars. Certainly not a fortune by Vegas standards, where the casinos operate in the millions every day of the year. Multiply that two thousand one hundred twenty-eight dollars by twelve, and you have a tidy little amount of twenty-five thousand five hundred thirty-six dollars. Remember now, these are just rough numbers. If this has been going on for the past nine years, the amount would be somewhere around or close to two hundred thirty thousand dollars for that time period. Give or take a few thousand. Who knows how long it has been going on, or if I'm even right. No one caught it, because the amounts were so small.

"As I said, the industry deals in millions daily, and this is pennies compared to that. In the scheme of things, we can afford to lose that much and not blink an eye. Since it has gone unnoticed, that should tell us all something. If I'm right, and I'm not saying I am, this is one very clever son of a bitch we're dealing with here. It would have to be someone who has an in to this business, and no, it is not Dixson Kelly. He simply doesn't have the stones to pull off something like that. Could you, Abner, with all your expertise, do what I've just described?"

Abner looked suddenly like a deer caught in the headlights. "As much as I hate to admit it, the answer is no."

"I realize you travel in . . . um . . . different circles, have an eclectic set of friends, fellow hackers, and I mean no offense here by saying that, but is there anyone you know who could pull something like this off?"

Abner's brain raced. He didn't trust himself to speak and just shook his head before he realized Bert couldn't see him shaking his head. "No!" he blurted.

"Well, then, it's your job to check things out once you get to Vegas, nose around, see what the inside information is, if any. Pay out some serious money. I'll reimburse you. Shake the tree. Hard. Something might fall out."

"Yeah, sure," Abner said, his eyes suddenly going glassy.

Jack wondered if anyone but he was picking up on Abner's offbeat behavior. He casually looked around, and sure enough, Maggie and Ted looked worried. Dennis was openly staring at the hacker, but thankfully, no one said anything. They could figure out later what, if anything, the hacker's strange behavior meant.

"Okay, folks, now let me get to the rest of the story here. In case you don't know it, there are roughly one hundred seventy casinos in Las Vegas. Granted all of them are not of the same caliber as Babylon, Wynn, Bellagio, and the rest of the big ones, but they still rake in millions every day. Otherwise, they wouldn't be in business. Now, having said that, take that number two hundred thirty thousand dollars and multiple it by one hundred seventy and tell me what you get."

"A little over thirty-nine million dollars," Dennis chirped.

"But you said all the casinos are not on par with Babylon, so the amounts would not be the same for all casinos, and this is over a nine-year period," Fergus said as he pressed digits on the calculator in his hand.

"You're right, Fergus. Regardless if it's twenty million dollars or only ten million dollars, that's a lot of money to be skimming off the casinos. And we do not know how long it's been going on. I used conservative numbers when I did my calculations. The truth is a loss of only five hundred dollars wouldn't raise any eyebrows at any of the casinos. It would be just chalked up to a miscount, a clerical error. I'm talking daily here."

"Is there a way to prove your theory? Forensic accountants, that kind of thing?" Charles asked. Then he looked at Abner, who just shrugged.

"I suppose, but I don't want to rock any boats. I believe I have the best of the best. Vegas, as you all know, is a closed shop. We like to take care of our own business, even when we're paying and jumping through hoops for people to take care of said business. If this were to get out, every Tom, Dick, and Harry who can add two numbers will try to take a crack at us. The bottom line is that to have even one small iota of this getting out is not good for business. In fact, it could be a disaster."

"I see your point," Charles said. "Are you thinking along the lines of the time the MIT graduate students hit the casinos with their card reading?"

"No! That was child's play compared to

this. This is big-time. Doesn't get any bigger or more intricate than this. This is someone or some group that is homegrown, that lives and breathes hacking, and carries it to a whole new level. They're an underground operation unto themselves. That's why I thought Abner could get us on the inside track, and we'll take it from there. You guys up to this? Or should I just bide my time until the girls come off the mission they're on? I mean, I've waited this long, so a few more months isn't going to make that much of a difference."

"That's a real low blow coming from you, Bert," Esposito barked unhappily.

"I didn't mean it that way. This is some pretty big stuff. It could be dangerous. The girls are fearless. We all know that. I just want to be sure you guys are up to this."

"We are," Harry snapped out of the blue.

Bert had his answer, and that was the end of *that*.

The call ended. Fingers drummed on the tabletop. Cyrus barked into the silence. Dennis got up and headed to the coffeemaker.

Abner yawned and stood up. He waved and said, "I'll see you in Vegas."

The others waved good-bye.

"What's this all mean?" Dennis asked. "Are we pinning all our hopes on Abner coming up with some clown smart enough to rip off one hundred seventy casinos nine years straight and not get caught?"

"Kind of looks that way at the moment," Ted said. "I repeat, at the moment."

Jack homed in on Charles. "What do you need us to do, Charles?"

"Get in touch with Avery Snowden while Fergus and I try to come up with something. If Avery has committed to the girls, then he is useless to us, and we're on our own. If that turns out to be the case, ask him if he can put us in touch with the top hackers. I'm sure he knows a few. If the girls haven't laid out any up-front monies to Avery, I can wire a down payment to his account the moment he agrees to sign on. As we all know, Avery goes where the money is. Even though his first loyalty is to me, he still likes working for the girls. If he doesn't come on board or recommend anyone, we're going to have to rely solely on Abner."

Jack remembered the strange look on Abner's face and wondered how that was all going to work out as he tapped in the numbers on his cell. Snowden picked up on the second ring. Jack concisely stated his business and within three minutes had his deal locked down. Two minutes after that, money was flying through cyber land to the Antilles and Snowden's account. A minute after that, Snowden confirmed they would meet up at the Tiki Bar at Babylon in three days. He ended the conversation with, "Yes, I know a few people known in the business for helping themselves to other people's money."

"Done!" Jack shouted to the room at large.

Cyrus barked to back up his master's announcement.

*   *   *

All the way back to the loft he shared with
his wife, Isabelle, Abner's mind raced as he tried
to make sense of everything he'd just heard in
the BOLO Building. His mind was still racing
as he threw clothes into two duffel bags. Not
knowing how long he'd be gone, he made sure
that all his appliances were unplugged, that
leftover food in the refrigerator went into the
garbage disposal, that trash was taken out to
the Dumpster, and that the alarm was set. At
the last minute before he exited the loft, he
made sure that he had his credit cards; his
driver's license; his car registration; cash; his
special gold shield; an exclusive cell phone
that only Isabelle had the number to; his regular cell phone, with its hundreds of apps; and
his special encrypted cell phone, compliments
of Avery Snowden.

Once inside his Range Rover, he clicked on
his GPS, punched in the address, then sat back
to send off a mass set of texts from his address
book. He asked that all recipients call him on
his cell phone and, with a twinge, used his and
Isabelle's private number. He explained that
he was driving cross-country and could not e-mail
or text for the next several days, but he could talk
hands free with his Bluetooth earbud. Satisfied
that he'd done all he could for the moment,
Abner put the turbocharged Rover into gear
and drove out of the underground garage.

Hour after hour, mile after mile raced by as
Abner kept playing and replaying in his mind

the two hours he'd spent in the BOLO Building with the guys. He tried everything he could think of to relax, to get rid of the knots and the sick feeling in the pit of his stomach. He wasn't sure, but he rather thought he'd kept his cool when the subject of supreme hackers had come up. Just as Harry had been the number two martial arts expert until the nominal number one was killed at an old rival's command, he, Abner Tookus, had been . . . *was* the number two supreme hacker, right after RCHood, who had taught him everything he knew and who continued to be his mentor. RCHood was the only one who could do what Bert and the guys thought had been done. Not only was he, in Abner's opinion, the only one, but RCHood could probably do it with his eyes closed and one hand behind his back. That was how good he was.

Loyalty. Where did it lie? With the boys or with RCHood? He was where he was on the ladder of life because of RC, as he thought of him. Without his tutelage, he wouldn't be the real-estate mogul that he was, not that he advertised that fact, but he did own millions of dollars' worth of prime oceanfront property. He would never have met Isabelle and married her. He wouldn't be part of the sisters and brothers whom he admired so much. For the first time in his life he had normal friends, friends who were human, face-to-face friends, not faceless letters on a keyboard. Yes, yes, he had hundreds, thousands of male and female novice hackers as friends, because they all belonged to the same underground organizations. They cared about each other, but in a very different way. Any one of them would drop what they were doing if he asked for their help. That was loyalty, too. Where did he draw the line? And wherever he drew it, which side of the line did he come down on?

Abner wished he had a companion sitting in the passenger seat. Even a dog would be good. Someone to bounce his thoughts off.

As the Rover continued to eat up the miles, Abner ran one scenario after another through his mind. Should he have mentioned RCHood back at the BOLO Building? Should he have told them right then and there that RC was the only hacker, in his opinion, who could do something like what Bert suspected? Why hadn't he spoken up? It wasn't that he was afraid of RC, even though RC probably already knew what was going on if he was the one responsible. No grass ever grew under RC's feet. If it was RC, then he knew everything there was to know about Bert, and that would lead him to the sisters and the brothers. Would RC expect him to confide in him because he was his mentor? Hell, yes he would!

Abner was so intent on his thoughts, he almost bounced off the ceiling when a slew of fat raindrops hit the windshield. To his troubled mind, they sounded like gunshots. He clicked on the windshield wipers. Then he fumbled around in the glove box to see if Isabelle had left any of her cigarettes behind. His wife didn't smoke much, maybe one cigarette a month, but she always kept a pack somewhere in case she felt the craving for one. He himself had quit smoking years ago, but right now he needed *something*. He didn't know if a cigarette would do the trick or not, but, by God, he'd give it a shot. He needed to calm down. His hand groped inside the glove box. *Aha!* He wondered how old the cigarettes were, how long they'd been in the glove box. Were stale cigarettes worse for you than fresh ones? Like he cared at this point. He fired up a cigarette and almost choked, but that didn't stop him from puffing away. He cracked the window, then opened it farther, not caring if the rain soaked him or not.

To tell or not to tell. If he wanted to, the next time he stopped at a roadside gas station, he could e-mail or send a text to RC to try to feel him out. He could do that. But it was probably not a very good idea. That would let RC know he was losing his cool. No, better to keep quiet. No need to get in touch with any of the guys, because unless he wanted to share his information, his worry, there was no reason to get in touch.

Abner let his mind travel back in time. When was the last time he'd communicated with RC? A while ago, because nothing was coming to mind. Was it before Christmas or after New Year's? A holiday greeting? Off the top of his head, if he had to pick one over the other, he'd go with sometime around New Year's. Had he returned the greeting? Probably, but maybe not. It was coming up to the end of

April now. After four months, give or take a week or so, it was not unusual to hear from RC. Or for him to communicate with Abner, which, when he did so, was to ask a question about something or other. They rarely made small talk. "State your business. Time is money," was the way RC thought, and who was he to test that edict?

Abner let his mind travel farther back in time, to when, at the age of sixteen, he was already hacking into government offices, banks, and anyplace he thought could do him some good. He'd saved up $338 mowing lawns and shoveling snow the year he first heard about a get-together in New Jersey. With the permission of one of the many foster parents he had had, none of whom cared what he did as long as he got As in school, he had hitchhiked to Jersey, found the underground meeting place, and had the time of his life for three straight days. If he slept, it was only an hour or so at a time in some corner, because he didn't want to miss anything. On that trip was when he'd met RC.

Abner tried to bring the man's face into focus, but he couldn't. He was big. Big compared to Abner. Lots of curly hair. Nice smile. Superintelligent. Respectful of the other attendees. Willing to share his knowledge. And out of all the attendees that day, RC had chosen him to mentor. He'd been so grateful, still was. Even though he'd never set eyes on RC from that day to this. All communication was over the Net.

Abner fished around for another cigarette.

Funny how puffing on one of the hateful sticks helped him to think more clearly. But he was missing something; something was niggling at his mind. What the hell was it? In frustration, he blew one perfect smoke ring after another and watched out of the corner of his eye as they floated out the window.

Ah . . . he had it, that elusive tidbit of information that didn't mean a thing. Just another little link in the daisy chain of information. Goldie@hotmail had sent a text to all the names in her address book around the end of the year that said RCHood was pissed off that in the movie *The Gambler*, which was coming out, one of the characters used his most famous line, which was, "Screw me over, and I will wipe out your entire bloodline." He was asking everyone if he should sue and went on to say he was referring to a cyber bloodline. The overwhelming response had been a resounding no. Abner himself had voted no. He had gone to see the movie after that and had been satisfied his vote was right. RC had printed those words long before John Goodman uttered them in the movie, and RC's utterances carried more weight. Especially for people like himself and his cyber buddies.

His cigarette finished, Abner tossed it out the window, knowing he was littering—but then again, he rather thought cigarettes were biodegradable. He fired up another one and puffed. This time he blew a perfect double smoke ring, which floated right out the window.

Abner's thoughts turned toward his wife. He wished there was some way he could call or get in touch with her, but there wasn't. He always felt lost when she was gone. She'd promised never to leave for a job like she had when she'd gone to England and they had almost gotten divorced over the whole mess. Thankfully, they had been able to talk it through and get back on track. This leave of absence was different. The sisters always came first, and he knew and accepted that. A mission took precedence over everything and anything. Isabelle's bottom line when she left was, "You'll see me when you see me. I will think of you every day, and I will miss you. Love you." Then she'd called over her shoulder, "Don't get into any trouble while I'm gone."

Abner snorted on a mouthful of smoke. There was trouble, and then there was *trouble*, and he knew in his gut he was looking at the worst kind.

Screw me over, and I will wipe out your entire bloodline.

Chapter 3

The BOLO Building was quiet now since the others had all left, and it was just Jack and Cyrus holding down the fort. Jack opened the plantation shutters and looked out at the miserable late-afternoon weather. The promised rain, which had held off until now, was a steady downpour that almost obliterated his view of the Bagel Emporium across the street. Did he really want to drive all the way back to the farm in the downpour? Or should he just hunker down and spend the night in the BOLO Building? He looked down at Cyrus and posed the question to the 140-pound shepherd.

"Here's the deal. Either we drive back to the farm, which in this weather will take us well over an hour if we leave now, or we call Mr. Domingo Lopez across the street and order one of his specialty dinners. One bark for going to the farm, two for calling Ding."

Cyrus barked twice.

Jack laughed. "Okay, that means we need to decide what we want to eat. We can chow down and feel guilty, or we can eat healthy. I vote for chowing down and working out twice as hard tomorrow."

Cyrus barked once.

Jack pressed in the digits of the Bagel Emporium and placed his order—a double hot roast beef sandwich with coleslaw and cranberry sauce for himself, and a triple order of chicken nuggets and a double order of the vegetable medley, which consisted of carrots, zucchini, and string beans, for Cyrus. For dessert he ordered apple pie for himself and a large pumpkin custard for Cyrus, because pumpkin was good for dogs' stomachs. He was told the food would be delivered in forty-five minutes.

"Time for us to get the files in order, make some notes, and catch the first of the evening news. While I do that, you can tidy up," Jack said, tongue in cheek.

Cyrus tilted his head to the side, as much as to say, "Get real here." The shepherd bent down, picked up Dragon, and headed for his favorite spot under the long conference table.

All day, Jack had felt a sense of unease, and he didn't quite know where it was coming from. He frowned as he ticked off possibilities on his fingers. Nothing to do with Nikki—he was okay and understood her absence. The weather? No, rain had been predicted, with the rest of the week to be typical spring weather. The guys? Everyone was okay with Bert's request. And anxious to get on with it. No anxiety there. Charles and Fergus leaving to go back to the farm? No, they had to take care of the dogs, so no concern there. Maggie creating a legend, as they said in clandestine jargon, to explain the reporters' presence in Vegas? Perfect scenario for the reporters, so no problem. Certainly not Harry. Actually, Harry had surprised him by his easy acceptance and the traveling to Vegas. That left Abner. Bingo! Abner's less than enthusiastic response to this new mission. This was right up his geek alley, so to speak, and yet . . . and yet he had acted almost like he didn't want to be part of it.

What's up with that? he wondered. He thought about calling or texting Abner, but he was already on the road. Maybe later, after he gave it some more thought. Right now, though, his gut was telling him that Abner knew something he hadn't seen fit to confide to the others. Assuming he was right, why was that? Abner had always been an up-front, stand-up guy. He was the last person whose loyalty to the guys and the sisters would come under scrutiny. Until now—because Jack couldn't shake that deer-in-the-headlight look he'd seen on Abner's face. He was glad he hadn't mentioned it to the others, but he was aware that both Maggie and Ted had caught the look on Abner's face. Like him, they hadn't commented on it, and like him, they were probably trying to figure out what, if anything, it meant.

Jack's gut churned. Maggie was like a dog with a bone. Once she got a sniff of something that didn't sit well with her, she went after it full bore. Same with Ted. Espinosa brought up the rear. Young Dennis, if he had noticed Abner's reaction, probably hadn't put it all together. Abner was entrenched long before Dennis became a member, so Dennis wasn't as tuned in to Abner as he himself and the others were. But the kid was intuitive, and Jack knew that he had picked up on something, because his face was an open book. At least to Jack.

Jack knew this all was really going to bother him if he didn't come to some kind of resolution where Abner was concerned. What could he do other than call or text the hacker and reserve some talk time, then come right out and ask point-blank? Or should he contain himself and wait out the three days until he got to Vegas and scheduled some real face time? Another ten minutes of worrying rushed by before Jack made the decision to wait for face time. Face time so he could look into Abner's eyes and read the truth.

Jack came to his decision just as the doorbell rang at the front of the building. Cyrus tossed Dragon in the air and made a beeline for the front door. Jack arrived right on his heels. The slicker-clad delivery boy, one of Ding's sons, held out two shopping bags. Money changed hands, and Jack added a robust tip, which brought a smile to the waterlogged young boy's face. He waited at the door until he saw the boy safely on the other side of the road before he closed and triple locked the massive mahogany door.

"Supper's here, Cyrus."

Back in Virginia, Fergus looked at Charles and said, "You sure you don't mind my staying here at Pinewood? It's just that Annie's farmhouse is so big, and there aren't any animals to keep me company. I just rattle around there by myself. I thought I could be of some help if I stayed here."

"Of course I don't mind. I'm grateful for the company. Lady and the pups adore you. Like you, even with the dogs romping around, I am still alone here. I don't like cooking for just myself, so with you here, at least we'll eat good food, not the fast food we buy on the fly and eat in the car.

"I also suspect you want to discuss Abner's . . . um . . . I don't quite know what to call it. It was just a fleeting expression. For all I know, he could have been having a gas pain that made him wince like he did," Charles said.

"It was no gas pain," Fergus said, authority ringing in his voice. "That young man knows something he didn't see fit to share. It might be nothing. Then again, it might be something, something important. He might be troubled over whatever he thinks he knows and how it would reflect on all of us. I believe he is a wonderful young man and loyal to all of us. I think he knows something, and he's trying to sort through it before he mentions whatever it is. Did what I just said make sense, Charles?"

"Of course it made sense. I was just dancing around the whole thing because I think like you do. While I start dinner, I'd like you to either text or call Avery and ask him who the number one geek hacker is. I don't even know if there is such a thing, much less a title to go with it. My gut is telling me that yes, there is such a person and that we need to know who that person is. Male or female."

"What's for dinner?" Fergus asked as he scrolled down on his cell phone's list for Avery Snowden's number.

"Chicken Marsala with fresh peas from the greenhouse, which you are going out to pick and will shell once you get off the phone with Avery. My special cheesy butter scones and a spring lettuce, tomato, and cucumber salad, the ingredients for which you are also going to fetch from the greenhouse."

"It went straight to voice mail, Charles. I'm sure he'll call us back," Fergus said as he donned a yellow slicker hanging on the coatrack by the kitchen door. Charles handed him the vegetable basket, and off he went.

Charles's nimble brain raced as he worked robotically, pounding out the chicken fillets, uncorking the wine, and readying the fry pan to sear the chicken. Scenario after scenario flowed through his brain as he tried to figure out Abner Tookus's mind-set. He liked the

young man; they all did. And he had saved the
day on many occasions with his uncanny ability
to hack into places no one had gone before and
to cover his tracks. There was no more valuable
asset to the group than Abner Tookus.

Abner had sworn his allegiance to the group,
as they all had. He couldn't see the young man
tossing that all away and betraying the group.
There, he'd given space to the ugly thought
rushing through his head. *Betrayal* was such an
ugly, ugly word.

Even though he missed Myra, Annie, and his
chicks, as he thought of the girls, he was glad
they weren't here, because, without a shadow of
a doubt, they would have pounced on Abner in
the blink of an eye, and that included Isabelle,
his wife.

Charles slid the seasoned chicken cutlets
into the fry pan and was rewarded with an im-
mediate fragrant sizzle just as Fergus, carrying
a basket of vegetables, opened the kitchen
door. He was setting them in the sink to be
rinsed when the phone rang. Both men looked
at each other for a second before Charles
clicked the mobile on.

"Good afternoon, Avery. Thanks for getting
back to me so quickly. I'm here at Pinewood
with Fergus. We have a question for you. Not
sure if you know the answer or if it's outside of
your purview. I know in your line of work you
are privy to a host of underground activities
that I and the girls can't begin to know about.
Who is the number one hacker, the go-to guy

when you want something done that you don't want anyone else to know about?"

"And you want to know this why?"

Why indeed? Charles swallowed hard and relayed what had happened at the BOLO Building. "It wasn't my imagination, Avery. Fergus saw the panic on Abner's face. He knows something, but for reasons known only to him, he elected not to share it with the group. He is, as we speak, driving cross-country to Las Vegas. I'd like you and your people to hit the red-eye tonight and get there before him so you can scout around and follow him or see what you can find out before the rest of us get there. So . . . who is the number one person, if you know?"

"Contrary to what you may believe, Charles, I do not know *everything*. I've heard rumors over the years, but I can't be specific or pin anything down for you. Those computer brainiacs are a breed unto themselves. They meet in underground locations, and you could waterboard any one of them, and you'd get no information out of them. I've heard three handles, or cyber names. For whatever good they'll do you. One is RCHood. All indicators place him at the top of the list. There's another one called PIP, which I once heard stood for Pretty in Pink. Oh, yeah, RCHood supposedly stands for 'Robin Cool Hood.' The third one is TRIPLEM. Someone said it stands for 'Triple Mister Magic Money.'

"As I understand it, there is no way for some-

one like you or me to get in touch with any of
the three. You have to know someone in their
exclusive group, and they pass the word up the
daisy chain. And they cost big-time. RCHood,
it's said, is seven figures just for a consultation.
PIP is six figures, as is TRIPLEM. Is it true? I
have no idea. Could be myths the three of
them have perpetuated to drive up their
prices, but I did hear that they give an absolute
guarantee if they take on a job.

"Think of it this way, Charles. At last rumor,
there were thousands of hackers who belong
to the same club or organization, or whatever
you want to call it. Let's just assume, for the
sake of argument, one of them is on a job and
makes a mistake. Oops. All those thousands of
hackers in the group swing into action and
screw things up so badly, the screwup gets fixed,
and no one is the wiser. I personally do not
know if that ever happened. It was just a scenario presented to me. A hypothetical of sorts.

"I know a couple of mid-level hackers. I can
put the word out if you want to hit on one of
the top three. My advice would be to wait till
we are all in Vegas and can talk this through.
With or without Tookus. That's your call to
make, Charles."

Charles shook his head at what he was hearing as he expertly flipped the cutlets in the fry
pan. "I pretty much thought that was the way it
would work. I agree, there's no sense in stir-
ring up something right now. Better to wait
until we are all together and can hash it out. I

don't suppose anyone anywhere has a clue to the identity of the top three."

"Not a clue. Several years ago, I spoke to a top-notch hacker, and he shared a few things. I asked him if he'd ever met the top three, and he said he *thought* so. I asked him where, and he said at a convention in Pittsburgh. Now, this guy was forty-something years old, a graphic artist by profession, and a good one. He said he had no clue. Nor did the other three guys he put me in touch with. All these guys and a few females care about is what you can do with a keyboard. You could be buck-ass naked, and no one would notice. Or care. So, no, no one knows anything about the top three. And if they do, they won't admit to it.

"For whatever it's worth, Charles, I think Abner Tookus is one of the top three. PIP is a female. That much I know for sure, so that lets her out. Tookus is either TRIPLEM or RCHood. RCHood has been on the scene longer than Tookus, so that's why I think he's TRIPLEM. Meaning RCHood is the top gun."

"Any suggestions on how we can get in touch with all three of them?" Charles asked. Out of the corner of his eye, he could see Fergus holding out a bowl of emerald-green peas. The first of the season. He motioned to a copper pot and mouthed the words, "Steam for two minutes. That's it."

"Just so you know, Charles, this is not going to be a nickel-and-dime operation. These guys command at least five figures. Sometimes high five or low six figures. Tell me if I'm authorized to pay out that kind of money."

"Just for information?" Charles said, his eyebrows shooting up to his hairline.

"Yes, and it still might not help us reach any of the three. It's a gamble, but I do have to say these people have their own code of ethics, so whatever information they divulge will be as accurate as they want it to be. They won't defraud us. After all, they have their reputations to consider. Like I said, they have their own code of ethics."

"Whatever it takes," Charles said.

"All right, then, have a good night. The next time you hear from me, I'll be in Vegas, setting up shop. Give some thought to Tookus being TRIPLEM and one of us getting in touch with him. How's that going to play out?"

Charles sighed. "I don't have the faintest idea. Have a safe trip, Avery."

Charles ended the call, threw his hands in the air, and looked at Fergus. "You heard it all on the speakerphone. What do you think?"

"What I think is we're going to have to have a come-to-Jesus meeting with Abner, and the sooner the better."

"My thoughts exactly," Charles said as he dumped the rest of the chicken into a pressure cooker, along with several cups of rice and some vegetables, for the dogs.

"How about a glass of wine, Charles? I think we could both use one about now." As he poured the wine, Fergus stared out the kitchen window at the driving rain. "I hope we're wrong about Abner, because I like him. I'm glad Isabelle isn't here. Actually, I'm glad all the women are gone. I don't mean that the way it sounds. You know what I mean, Charles," Fergus said as he handed him a glass of wine.

"Yes, I do, and I was thinking the same thing a little while ago. We've done all we can at the moment. For the moment, I think we're in good hands." He held his wineglass toward Fergus, clinked it, and said, "Here's to Las Vegas!"

Fergus laughed out loud, not as if he found it funny, as he echoed Charles's toast.

Fergus flopped down on one of the kitchen chairs and stretched out his long legs. "Seriously, mate, what do you think our chances are of finding out the identities of any one of the three hackers?"

"Zip. It's not going to happen unless someone volunteers the information, and I do not see that happening. Our best hope, I think, lies with Abner and where his true loyalty lies. All we can do is wait and see."

Fergus scrunched his face into a tight grimace. "And if he—"

Charles didn't let Fergus finish what he was going to say. "Then we do whatever we have to do. One of ours, one of theirs . . . We do what we have to do. We can't let emotions take over."

"Isabelle?"

Charles sighed again, a long, lonely sound.

"Yes, then there is Isabelle." He finished his wine, checked on his chicken Marsala, and said that dinner would be ready in ten minutes.

"Sounds good to me. I'll set the table."

"Busy work, Fergus."

"Uh-huh."

Chapter 4

It was ten minutes past the witching hour when Abner Tookus pulled into a Hampton Inn off the interstate. He wasn't tired yet, but he was feeling both anxious and frustrated. He'd been driving for over twelve hours, and his body was warning him to pay attention to what he was doing. Besides, he wanted to check his texts and e-mails. Even though he'd sent out that e-mail blast to all his contacts, urging them to call, he wasn't surprised by the fact that no one had. Hackers did not like talking on the phone; they preferred texting and e-mails so they could then erase it all, leaving no trace of contact. He understood their concerns to a point. But only to a point.

The night clerk, a college-aged kid, looked as frazzled as Abner felt. He looked up at

Abner and asked, "How do you want to pay for this, sir?"

The words were out of Abner's mouth before he could think about it. "Cash." He peeled off five twenty-dollar bills from a money clip in his pocket and handed them over. The kid didn't blink an eye. The motel wasn't one of those rent-by-the-hour places, so Abner was surprised that paying in cash did not lead to at least a raised eyebrow.

Abner pocketed the receipt and listened to directions on how to get to his room. Before Abner was out the door, the kid had his nose back in the textbook he'd been studying when Abner first arrived.

Following the kid's directions, Abner went around the corner and up one flight. His room, 302, was the second one on the left. It looked just like all hotel rooms. Neat and clean, with a brown, yellow, and orange bedspread and drapes. The bathroom was done in black-and-white tile and had plenty of towels. Small bottles of everything women liked: shampoo, conditioner, hand lotion, Q-tips, cotton balls, designer liquid soap that smelled like lilacs, a packet containing a needle and thread, and a shower cap. Everything was in sanitized plastic wrap. Thirty-six-inch TV, minibar. Wi-Fi hookup. Home away from home.

Abner tossed his duffel bag on a stool and stripped down as he headed for the shower. He lathered up and washed his hair as he stood under the pounding hot spray. When he rinsed off, only fifteen minutes had passed. There being no thick, thirsty robes at this motel, he wrapped himself in the extra-large bath sheets provided.

Back in the bedroom, he unzipped his duffel and pulled out a pair of well-worn sleep boxers and an equally worn oversize T-shirt. He yawned. Maybe he really was tired but too stupid to know it. He hooked up his computer, opened the mini-fridge, and popped a Heineken, which was not ice cold. He opened a bag of chips and a bag of peanuts and munched and swigged away as he scanned his e-mails. Nothing from RCHood. *Strange. Very strange.* He almost felt relieved. Next, he checked his texts. Forty-four in all. None from RCHood. *He's playing with me,* Abner thought to himself. *He's going to make me go to him, because he's my mentor. He knows something's up. He just doesn't know what it is yet.*

Abner wondered how many of the hackers had heard from RC today. He quickly sent out three e-mails and two texts to hackers he stayed in daily contact with to ask that very question. All five responded within minutes, saying RC had checked in around two that very afternoon, asking what was going on and if any of them knew where TRIPLEM was going. All five had told RC they knew nothing. They asked Abner where he was, in fact, going. To which Abner replied, **Jackson Hole, Wyoming,** without missing a beat. He hated lying, but given the circumstances, at the moment he saw no alternative. There was no way that he was going to reveal to his hacker friends that he was off to Las Vegas, given what was going down at the casinos there. He itched to call Jack or Harry . . . *someone.* He really needed to do that, but he also knew he wasn't going to do any such thing until he hit Vegas. The people who had raised him did not raise a fool.

The red numerals on the bedside clock said it was 2:10 a.m. when he disposed of his trash, brushed his teeth, and climbed into the bed, which he found surprisingly comfortable. His last conscious thought before drifting off to sleep was the words *Screw me over, and I will wipe out your entire bloodline.* He clutched the special gold shield in his fist, knowing he had backup in the form of Countess Anna de Silva, the sisters, and the brothers. No sir, his foster mama didn't raise a fool.

Abner slept for two hours and was back on the road by five in the morning, in his hand a cup of the lobby coffee, which was so rancid, he tossed it out the window after one sip. He'd stop at the first fast-food joint he saw. He settled back and let his mind race. Travel time from D.C. to Las Vegas by car was thirty-seven hours and two minutes. If his calculations were correct, and he drove straight through, with minimal stopping, he could reach Vegas by midnight. Possibly sooner if the troopers didn't catch him for speeding. He wondered if there would be a welcoming committee waiting to greet him. There was welcoming, and then

there was *welcoming*. He removed his hand from
the steering wheel just long enough to stick it
in his pocket to feel the comforting special
gold shield.

A new day! He turned on the Rover's stereo
and listened to Bon Jovi. He cranked up the
volume and sang along. Anything to keep his
dark thoughts at bay.

As Abner was hitting the interstate, Jack and
Cyrus were climbing in the F-150 and heading
to the farm, where Jack showered, shaved, and
changed his clothes. Cyrus romped in the yard,
chasing two squirrels, who, since they knew he
was not allowed to catch them, taunted him
mercilessly.

After he made an enormous breakfast for
the two of them, which they both devoured
like hungry wolves, he called everyone to say
he was on his way back to the BOLO Building.
All the members confirmed they were also on
the way.

Jack picked up the oversize duffel that he
had packed before going to bed, knowing he
wouldn't be coming back to the farm today. If
he had anything to say about it, they would be
ready to fly out as soon as Dennis alerted the
pilot for his Gulfstream. All he had to do was
convince the others that going in incognito
wasn't going to work. His gut was clicking away
on all cylinders, and he never ignored his gut
warnings.

By 10:15 a.m., everyone had arrived, and the Bunn coffeemaker was working overtime as Jack took to the floor.

"Look, we can vote on this, but I don't see the point. I say we go in as ourselves. We're on vacation because our wives are away. It's that simple. That way, we don't have to worry about tripping up on our legends or give Kelly a moment's worry. I'm going to call Bert and apprise him of our plan, if you all agree. Dennis, if we're in agreement, alert the pilot that we're ready to go. Let's hear it!"

Every hand in the room shot upward, including Dennis's right hand, since he was pressing in numbers with his left.

There was a slightly sour note to Charles's tone when he said, "Fergus and I came to the same conclusion last evening. As you can see by the door, we brought our bags with us. Our dog sitter arrived at six this morning, so we're good."

The others all had their own stories, but basically, they were all the same. There was luggage piled everywhere. Harry, like Maggie, traveled with only a backpack, and both of them were wearing one.

"Okay, we're all on the same page, then. For starters, I don't think any of us can even venture a guess as to how long we'll be in Vegas, so we just leave it as undetermined for the moment. I'm going to call Bert now. If you have any questions, have them ready."

Dennis raised his hand to speak. "Wheels up

in ninety minutes. We'll be on the ground mid-afternoon Vegas time."

Maggie poured coffee as Jack placed the call to Macau, China. Bert answered on the first ring. He quickly brought Bert up to date.

"It would help if you could arrange our stay—good rooms, concierge floor, that kind of thing. Don't forget about Cyrus. Snowden and his men are on the way. Actually, they took a red-eye flight, so they're already there, though we haven't heard from him as yet.

"Knowing Abner the way I do, I expect he'll arrive around midnight tonight. He'll drive straight through today. I don't know this for a fact, but I would guess he stayed on the road yesterday a good twelve hours. He'll be the last to arrive, so be sure to book his room, too. Do you have anything else we need to know?"

"No. Thanks for doing this, guys. You, too, Maggie. I hope I'm not sending you all on a wild-goose chase. I don't think so, but in this business, you never really know. You realize you can reach me any hour of the day or night on these special phones. Always use them, since they cannot be hacked. Hell, they haven't even been manufactured yet, just the prototypes we have. Snowden deserves a medal for getting them for us. He must know some pretty influential people."

"He does," Charles said, a smile in his voice.

"In that case, I think you all should communicate with each other only using these phones once you get to Vegas. And, of course, when you call me. Can't be too careful where all this is concerned. We're talking tons of money blowing out the doors of the casinos. I have to be honest with all of you. I can't believe I'm the only one who tumbled onto this. Those guys at Wynn and MGM are like sharks. If anyone should have tumbled onto it, it's them."

"Maybe they'll give you a finder's fee if we pull this off," Dennis chirped.

"That would be nice, now wouldn't it? I'd donate it all to the Wounded Warrior Project. Stay in touch. If you need me to run interference with Kelly, just let me know. Sometimes, he can be a real pain in the ass and full of himself. Step on him, and I'll set him straight."

The connection was broken.

"Sounds like we're good to go," Ted said.

Maggie unplugged the coffeemaker and rinsed the carafe out. "Now we're good to go."

Cyrus was already waiting at the back door, Dragon and Goldie clutched between his teeth. He was patient, knowing that Jack had to set the timers for the lights and key in the security code before they could go.

It was an hour past noon when Dixson Kelly made his way to the registration desk to make sure Bert Navarro's instructions were followed to the letter. He felt on shaky ground because he'd never heard that tone in his boss's voice before. Never mind the actual words, which had made the hair on the back of his neck stand on end.

"Don't give me any shit on this, Dix. Just do what I tell you, and do it as soon as we end this call. There's no reason for you to question me. I'm giving you a goddamned order, so obey it, okay? Whatever it takes, make it happen, and then get back to me."

He'd called down to the main desk, issued the order, and been told it was impossible. He was now on his way to make the impossible possible, bang some heads or worse, as he wondered what the hell was going on and who these people were that Bert had said deserved such VIP treatment at a moment's notice. He was supposed to be in charge—he even had a contract that said that was the case—and here was his boss, who was half a world away, telling him what he should do. "This damn well sucks," he muttered under his breath.

His face like a thundercloud, Kelly opened the gate that would allow him to step behind the counter. The senior floor supervisor immediately headed to his private office in the back, followed by Kelly. His name was Neal Sanders. He was a fussy little man with a full head of hair that wasn't real, contacts a shade of blue that wasn't on any color chart, and lifts in his shoes. Sanders took the initiative the moment he closed the door behind him.

"I'm sorry, Mr. Kelly, but I cannot accommodate you. Where do you think I can come up with fifteen rooms, with nine on the concierge level, at a moment's notice? Everything is booked, has been booked for months." To prove his point, the little man whipped out a room chart, turned on his computer, and started talking at warp speed, repeating the word *impossible* as many times as he could fit it into the conversation.

Dixson Kelly clenched and unclenched his teeth as he struggled to remain calm, professional, and authoritative. "I guess you didn't hear the words 'whatever it takes.' What that means to you is you have roughly two hours to clear out those rooms, give the guests whatever they want. If necessary, send them to Wynn. We have the same agreement with Wynn about our overflow as they have with us. Two hours, Sanders, not a moment more. And I want flowers and champagne in every room. Have housekeeping make sure to put in new robes and the big bath sheets. Go heavy on the amenities."

The little man started to run his hands through his hair, then thought better of what he was doing. "This . . . this is outrageous! What will the guests think? No one likes having someone else touch their things, much less pack them up. They will not understand. This can't be happening," he wailed. "Two hours! That is not nearly enough time."

Kelly leaned in closer, his eyes narrow slits that matched the grim slit of his lips. "Make it enough time. Help out your staff. My instructions are to tell you that if there is even one glitch, just one, you will be on the unemployment line tomorrow morning. I'd get cracking if I were you."

Kelly turned on his heel and left the office. He felt like a heel for reaming out the guy who, more than anyone else, really did care about their guests' comfort. But he was following Bert's orders to the letter, because he knew Bert would send him to the same unemployment line as Sanders if he didn't do as he was told.

Kelly walked the main casino floor, his eyes everywhere, his thoughts jumbled and confused. He headed for the Tiki Bar and ordered a cup of coffee. He carried it to his favorite dark corner and sat down. He could feel a monster headache coming, one that would turn into a full migraine, as he tried to make sense of Bert's order. Friends of Bert were checking in. That had to mean in some way that they were also friends or associates of Countess Anna de Silva, the woman with the diamond tiara who happened to be the owner of Babylon. As everyone in the casino knew, she was one lady you did not mess around with.

Kelly's head started to pound full force when he thought about relocating all the high rollers already in residence. A few of them would give him a pile of shit; he knew it as sure as he needed to draw another breath to keep on living. He thought of the bad press this was going to bring down around his ears. He gulped down the coffee, which was growing cold. He picked up his cup, walked back to the bar, and told the bartender to add two fingers of good whiskey. A first for him. He'd never in his life drunk on the job. Well, there was a first time for everything, and this was one of those times.

Back in his chair in the corner, Kelly pulled the sheet of paper out of his pocket where he'd scribbled the names of the arriving guests. Other than Harry Wong, the world's number one martial arts expert, who had been in Las Vegas for demonstrations many times, he recognized the name of only one person: Jackson Porter Sparrow, the director of the FBI. *Well, shit, shit, shit, shit!* He rubbed at his temples, his eyes closed. When he opened them, his vision was slightly blurry. Standing in front of him was the biggest man he'd ever seen in his life, one Philonias Needlemeyer, owner of not one, but two penthouse apartments here at Babylon. Bert had introduced him to the giant a few years back, but this was the first time he'd seen him since.

He tried to smile but knew he failed. He stood and held out his hand. "Dixson Kelly, Mr. Needlemeyer. Bert Navarro introduced us right after I came to work here."

Philonias held out one massive hand. "I remember that. You look like you might need some aspirin, Mr. Kelly," Philonias said, setting down a tempting-looking salad on the bar table.

"Oncoming migraine, sorry to say. Anything I can help you with?"

"No, but thank you for asking. I'm good." Philonias saw Kelly's eyes go to the spindly bar stool. He laughed, a great booming sound. "Not to worry. I'm not going to sit on it. I'll stand up and eat, the way I always do. I've heard that two Aleve will knock out a migraine within minutes. I don't know if that's true or not. Just thought I would mention it. Well, it was nice meeting you again, Mr. Kelly. Good luck with that migraine." That ended Philonias's end of the conversation. He turned his massive body toward the table and attacked his salad.

For no reason that he could fathom, Kelly felt like the big man chowing down on the healthy-looking salad in front of him had just issued a threat to him. He shook his head once, then again, to clear his thoughts. He never could think straight when he had a migraine. Either that, or he was losing it entirely.

Kelly felt like his head was on an anvil that was being pounded with a very heavy mallet. He walked as fast as he could out to the main floor, then to a boutique at the end of the hall, where he bought a bottle of Aleve and swallowed two of them dry. Then he headed for the elevator that would take him to his apartment. He needed to think. Really think.

What the hell, he wondered, had just happened in the Tiki Bar?

Chapter 5

Kelly pressed the digits on his in-house cell that would connect him with his assistant, Pete Justice.

"Pete, I need you to take over for me for the next two hours. I have something I need to attend to."

Assured that his orders would be followed, Kelly yanked at his tie with the perfect Windsor knot as he simultaneously tried to shrug out of his jacket. He tossed both on a chair as he kicked off his shoes, then flopped down on the couch, which was more comfortable than his bed. He took a second to set his internal clock for a ninety-minute nap, which hopefully would take the edge off his migraine. He'd promised Bert he would be on hand to greet his guests when they arrived. Knowing Bert, his ass would be grass if he didn't follow through on that promise.

Dixson Kelly woke precisely eighty-eight minutes later and realized that his headache was gone. Maybe it wasn't a migraine, after all, just a stress headache brought on by Bert Navarro's orders. Nonetheless, he got up gingerly, just to be on the safe side. Yep. Gone.

Within minutes, he had shed his clothes and was standing under a steaming-hot shower. He almost swooned at how good the hot water felt as it rolled off his shoulders. Then he danced under a freezing, needle-sharp spray, followed by another round of steaming-hot water.

Fifteen minutes later, he was shaved, scented, and dressed in one of his favorite Hugo Boss suits and ties. He checked himself out in the mirror over the dresser as he fastened his watch on his wrist. His gaze dropped to the top of the dresser, where nine burner phones were lined up like soldiers. Nine small spiral notebooks were next to each of the burner phones. On the back of each phone was a name under a strip of Scotch tape, and these represented all the women who were currently in his life and whom he juggled with an expertise that amazed even him at times. He knew there were messages on each and every one of the phones, but right now, he didn't have time to listen to them. He shrugged as he headed for the elevator that would take him to the main floor of the casino so he could relieve Pete Justice. His thoughts raced from one thing to another as he moved along.

As he walked around the floor, his gaze moving at the speed of light, he talked into his cell, relieving Pete Justice, then moved on to Sanders to see how he was doing with his housekeeping duties. He listened to the surly voice telling him about the complaints, the threats from the guests, and simply said, "I don't want to hear it. Deal with it, Sanders. That's what we pay you for. If you have a problem, Sanders, I'll be happy to give you Bert's number, and you can tell him what it is."

Kelly blinked when he realized he was talking to dead air. *Bastard.* He blinked again when he realized he was already outside the Tiki Bar. It was busy now in the mid-afternoon, with guests seeking a little refreshment after a morning of some serious gambling. He looked around to see if the same bartender was on duty. He was. He waited until there was a lull, then motioned for Adam, the bartender, to come closer.

Adam took the initiative and said, "Your headache gone, Mr. Kelly? You were looking a little ragged when you were in here before."

"Yeah, it's better. Listen, that big guy who was in here when I was here, what do you know about him?"

"Mr. Needlemeyer? I know *of* him, but other than what I hear, nothing. Why? Is he a problem or something?"

"Does he come in here often?" Kelly asked.

Adam laughed. "Are you kidding, Mr. Kelly?

I've been working the Tiki Bar for the last fifteen years, and today was the first time I've ever seen the man in the flesh. I heard he was big, but, man, he is *big*. I do know that he calls down sometimes in the middle of the night for our spring rolls to be taken up. Guess he doesn't sleep much. He tips really well, they say, and gives generously at Christmas. He leaves cards with crisp hundred-dollar bills in them around the tenth of December every year. You know he's one of the richest men in the country, right?"

"So today was the first time you have ever seen him personally? Do me a favor. Ask the other two bartenders if he comes in when they're on duty."

Adam moved down the bar and spoke quietly to the two bartenders there. He was back in a few seconds, shaking his head. "No, they've never seen him. What's going on, Mr. Kelly?"

"I don't know, Adam. Probably nothing. Call the guys who work the night shift. Do it now, please. And, listen, keep this to yourself, okay?"

Adam laughed. "Shame on you, Mr. Kelly. Don't you know the bartenders' number one rule? We're like priests. We never divulge what we hear. Stay here. I have to go to the office to get their numbers."

Kelly wondered whether he was being paranoid or if it was his CIA clandestine operations training kicking in. *Probably a little bit of both*, he decided. He just couldn't shake the feeling that the big guy had sought him out for some reason. Even with the raging headache, it hadn't felt right at the time. He remembered how the hair on the back of his neck had moved. He had learned from his training always to pay attention to the little things. Paranoid or not, he was paying attention. Because . . . because a gaggle of people was due to arrive shortly. And then it hit him right between the eyes, the little thing that was bothering him that he couldn't give a name to. The thought hit him just as Adam snapped his fingers under his nose.

"I called all three, Lionel, Connor, and Lala. None of them have ever seen Mr. Needlemeyer here in the Tiki Bar. Lionel has been here for thirteen years, Connor seven years, and Lala has been here close to twenty years. She has seniority. She said she saw Mr. Needlemeyer once in the parking garage, and someone pointed him out to her. Otherwise, she never would have known who he was. That's it, Mr. Kelly. Anything else? The crowd out there is getting restless. Gotta go."

Kelly handed over a folded twenty-dollar bill and winked at the bartender. "I'm good. Thanks, Adam."

Back on the main floor, Kelly looked around. He couldn't see any problems—things were running smoothly. That little thing. He needed to think about that. He looked at his watch as he headed to the registration desk so he would be on hand in person to welcome Bert's personal guests. He moved to the side and pulled out his in-house mobile and pressed the digits for Bert's number.

"Everything's under control," he said before Bert could identify himself. "Is there anything I need to be aware of, Bert?"

The silence on the other end of the phone bothered Kelly more than the words coming out of Bert's mouth. "Why do you ask?"

Kelly wanted to stomp his feet in frustration. "Did you forget who I used to work for? This crap you're shoveling my way has all the earmarks of an ongoing op about to go bad. Plus, my bullshit antenna is moving at warp speed. What? Did you think I wasn't going to recognize one of the names on the list? I'm starting to think you don't have a very high opinion of me, Bert."

There was that silence again. "I think highly of you, Dix. Hell, why do you think I put you in charge? Because I like the way you part your hair or the way you smell? Get real here. I pay you three times what the other guys on the street make, and I'm not jerking your chain when I say you're worth every penny. The bottom line is I trust you."

Kelly let Bert's declaration hang in the air for a full half minute before he responded. "Why is the director of the FBI among that gaggle of people who are due to arrive momentarily? Did you really think I wasn't going to recognize the name Jackson Porter Sparrow? Don't give me that NTK shit, either."

"They're all friends of mine. You do remember that before I came to Babylon, I was the director of the FBI, don't you? And Sparrow is both a personal friend of mine and a real favorite of Annie de Silva. The gang is on vacation. It's that simple. Even a director of the FBI gets to take a vacation once a year. I did when I was director. I want them to have a good time. You did close off the concierge floor from the other guests, right? I don't want my friends bothered. You need to get over that CIA-FBI rivalry. Fast."

Kelly clenched his teeth. "All taken care of. One more thing, Bert. Unless this is also NTK. What's up with that big guy from the penthouse, the one who is supposed to be richer than God? What the hell was he doing spying on me in the Tiki Bar? Telling me to take Aleve for my migraine. I can smell a setup a mile away. You want me to help you out here, and you tie my goddamned hands by telling me everything is goddamn need to know. Well?"

"What the hell are you talking about, Dix?"

"That guy Needlemeyer. What? You think I'm not on top of things?"

"Look, I don't have a clue what you're talking about in regard to that guy. Other than the time I introduced you to him, I've met him once officially. I've actually seen him twice, once in front of the casino and once by the elevator. Again, other than introducing you, I've spoken to the man only once since I took over Babylon. He's off-limits is what I was told. I never questioned Annie's orders. The guy is rich, like you said, owns two penthouses, and is a recluse. That is the sum total of what I know about him. Now, let me get this straight. You saw him, obviously talked to him, and he told

you to take Aleve for your headache, and you
see . . . what? A conspiracy with my friends arriving, along with the director of the FBI?"

Kelly chomped down on his lower lip. "When
you say it like that, it does sound weird, but
there's something there. I just know it."

"Well, when you figure it out, call me first.
Gotta go. Time is money. Take care of my
friends, Dix. I owe you for this."

"Yeah, right," Kelly mumbled under his
breath. Even a rookie CIA agent would have
picked up on this, he thought to himself as he
looked around. He knew that Bert was jerking
his chain, but there wasn't a damn thing he
could do about it. At least for now. For the
time being, he had to put a smile on his face
and be a welcoming committee of one for his
boss's friends.

Kelly felt a frown building on his brow as he
played and replayed Bert's end of the conversation concerning the penthouse owner's appearance in the Tiki Bar. He'd sounded
genuinely perplexed that he, Kelly, was reading something into the man's appearance
that wasn't there to begin with. "Yeah, well,
we'll just see about that," Kelly muttered under
his breath. He took a deep breath when he saw
a crowd of people who appeared to be all together enter the casino.

Bert's friends. With a quick glance, Kelly decided they looked normal enough, with the exception of Jackson Sparrow, the only person
he recognized. In fact, the group looked just
like the majority of the people in the casino.

Sparrow, though, was doing what he would have been doing if he were walking in his shoes, practicing his tradecraft: his eyes were everywhere, as if he was looking for something not quite right, off in some sense, something that didn't quite compute to his trained eye. Just the way Kelly had done when he'd met the rich recluse in the Tiki Bar.

Kelly extended his hand, identified himself to a tall man with a British accent; that was followed by an introduction to an equally tall man with a deep Scottish brogue. When the introductions were complete, he homed in on the director of the FBI and spoke just a tad too snidely, knowing full well that Bert was going to hand him his head on a platter when he found out. But he really didn't care—the moment was here, and he seized it.

"Ah, yes, Mr. Director, you're the man who let Hank Jellicoe get away. At the time, I was the senior field agent working for the CIA. We worked on that case for two solid years, and if I recall correctly, the Vigilantes duct taped him to the front door of the Hoover Building, and some ten-year-old kid on a skateboard cut him loose. And then you guys gave out that story that he was in a federal prison, safe and sound. No hard feelings, though. All in the spirit of agency cooperation and transparency. Two years' work shot to hell on our part, and some ten-year-old kid blows it for you. I'm just saying . . ."

Sparrow sucked on his tongue, wanting to

put his fist through Kelly's face, but he fought the urge and pasted a smile on his face. "Get your facts straight, Mr. Kelly. That happened before my time and not on my watch. You know what they say. You win some. You lose some."

Ted hissed in Maggie's ear, "This looks like it might turn ugly. Do something."

Maggie stepped forward, her hands up, palms toward Kelly. "This might be a good time for you and me to agree to how we're going to do our interview. Bert said you would be at our disposal, on orders from Countess de Silva. How about first thing tomorrow morning we start trailing you around? Will that work for you, Mr. Kelly?" Her tone of voice clearly stated that it better be all right.

Kelly suddenly felt like an ass. That round went to the Fibbies. "That will work for me, Miss Spritzer. I usually hit the main floor around ten o'clock. Meet me by the cashier's cage." He turned to the group as a whole and said, "Follow me, people, and I'll show you to your rooms. Bert requested the entire concierge floor, and that's what you're getting. Food and beverages twenty-four/seven. Your own personal chef and bartender. Suites, not rooms, so I think you'll enjoy your stay here at Babylon. I count only nine. Bert said there would be fifteen of you. Or am I wrong?"

The guy with the British accent informed him the others would be arriving shortly, with the last guest due in later that night.

Something didn't feel right to Kelly. He'd learned a long time ago that when something didn't feel right, it probably wasn't. Fifteen years out in the field, with no one to depend on but himself for his survival, was sending a message to his tired brain. He decided to play a hunch, hoping he wouldn't regret it. "Would you like me to notify Mr. Needlemeyer that you've arrived?" He didn't see the reaction he had hoped for. Okay, false alarm on his part. Maybe. Then again, maybe not.

"I don't recognize the name, Mr. Kelly. Who is Mr. Needlemeyer?" Charles Martin said in his best British accent.

"One of the penthouse owners. No problem, Mr. Martin. I think I have my guests mixed up. Enjoy your stay. I left my card in each suite. If you need anything, call. We're here to serve you. Enjoy your stay, folks."

Kelly couldn't get out of there fast enough. In the elevator, he kept taking deep breaths and letting them out with a loud *swoosh*. Damn it, something was off. Something, he knew, was wrong. He'd bet every one of those burner phones on his dresser top that he was not imagining things. Who the hell were these people he'd just left on the concierge floor? Friends of Bert? *My ass*, he thought to himself. Well, he might not have the answer right now, but he would find it; he always did.

On their own, with the connecting doors to Charles's and Fergus's suites closed, the group sat down in the luxurious sitting room.

"Someone call Avery and tell him to come straight on up here. I'm sure he and his people are on the floor, taking stock of the casino," Charles ordered.

Jack quickly tapped out a text to Snowden.

"Why are you pacing like that, Sparrow?" Harry asked.

"Because I'm getting a real bad feeling about that guy Kelly, that's why," Sparrow snapped.

"Does that real bad feeling have anything to do with Kelly's gibe about the FBI and the Vigilantes?" Ted asked.

"Yes and no," Sparrow responded honestly. "That did not happen on my watch. If it had, I wouldn't have tried to cover it up. You all need to understand something. Once an agent, always an agent. Your instincts that you honed to survive never leave you. You develop a seventh sense, for want of a better explanation. You, Charles, and you, too, Fergus, should recognize that. Bert and I both came up through the ranks. Bert at one time was the director of the FBI, the position I now hold. Neither of us would be here today, nor you, Charles and Fergus, if we hadn't relied on our instincts. And my instinct is shouting loud and clear to keep an eye on Kelly.

"And I can guarantee you that he is right now, this minute, thinking the same thing. Did you get that bit about a Mr. Needlemeyer? He didn't just throw that name out there, and guys like Dixson Kelly do not make mistakes. There, I've said what I think, so the rest is up to you. I do not know exactly what it is, and if Bert is right, what we're here to investigate probably has nothing to do with Kelly, since he has been here such a relatively short time. Still, something besides what we're here to investigate is way, way off here."

Dennis was so excited, he could barely contain himself. He inched closer to Ted and whispered, "This is going to get hairy, isn't it?"

"Count on it," Ted whispered back.

"We'll be able to keep an eye on him for the next few days and report anything strange or out of the ordinary," Maggie said.

A soft knock on the door sounded. Espinosa opened it to admit Avery Snowden and four of his operatives, two men and two women. Introductions were made, and card readers were turned over to their various suites.

"All present and accounted for except for Abner, whom I just sent a text. He just responded and said he's four hours out and is making good time," Jack said.

"All right then, we're right on schedule," Charles said. "I'm going to call Bert now and ask him how he wants us to proceed, now that we're all settled in. Get your questions ready, if you have any. This call is going through on the special phones, so we have no fear of anyone listening in. But before I do that, Jack, which phone did you use to contact Abner?"

Jack held up the special encrypted phone Snowden had gotten for all of them.

Charles locked his gaze on Snowden and said, "Is there even a remote chance that Mr.

Kelly, with his CIA background, and who, I am sure, still has some friends in high places, could somehow . . ."

Snowden grimaced. "The answer is no. These phones are prototypes. We're using them as a test. I'm saying no, but we all know about leaks and how things like this, it seems, sometimes just fall out of the sky. I'm sticking with no for the time being."

Charles nodded as he pressed in the digits to Bert Navarro's secure phone. Bert answered on the second ring. There was no small talk, no amenities.

"Bert, tell us how you want us to proceed. We're all here except for Abner, who is four hours out. Right now, we're pretty much like ducks out of water. But before we get to that, the director wants to talk to you."

"Put him on," Bert said.

"Your man Kelly, you vouch for him a hundred percent?"

"One hundred and ten percent, Sparrow. Why are you asking?"

Instead of answering the question, Sparrow asked another one. "Who is Mr. Needlemeyer?"

"Oh, crap! Look, that's just Dix being paranoid, which is sometimes a good thing." He went on to explain about Dixson Kelly's migraine and the casual meeting with Philonias Needlemeyer in the Tiki Bar. "Google the guy, Sparrow. He's right up there with Mother Teresa. Look, they don't come any better than Dixson Kelly.

"He'd still be the CIA's number one, but his

cover got blown, and it was either take a job pushing paper, be an instructor at Langley, or get out. Dix elected to get out, but he is still on, if you know what I mean. Just like you and me. Cut him some slack, but if you run into a problem, let me know. I need to warn you about one thing where he's concerned. Dix loves the ladies, and they love him right back. Just so you know."

"So where do you want us to start, Bert?" Charles asked.

"What I think you all should do is hit the casino floor as soon as we end this call. Gamble. Eat. Drink. Take in a show. You're on vacation, so act like you are. You really can't do anything until Abner arrives and we talk again. Maggie has a bead on it with starting out early tomorrow. While her and the guys are busy with Dix, the rest of you can call, and we'll work out a plan. Now, I've got to head out for a meeting. Call me after Abner arrives."

The call ended as everyone looked at each other.

"You heard the man," Ted said. "We need to act like we're on vacation." He rubbed his hands together in wild anticipation of making a big score, as if that were going to happen in a Vegas casino, even if it was the one owned by a member of the Vigilantes.

"I suggest we split up so we don't look so obvious," Fergus said. "We should make a plan to meet up somewhere around, let's say, eight o'clock, and we can have dinner together to discuss our wins or losses. That bar Bert mentioned, the Tiki Bar, sounds like a good meeting place. Are we all agreed?"

Ted, Espinosa, and Dennis were out the door before Fergus finished talking. The others followed, with Snowden bringing up the rear.

Chapter 6

The four hours leading up to the meet at eight o'clock in the Tiki Bar rushed by in a blur for the gang. Charles and Fergus hit the poker table and won eighteen hundred dollars in the four hours. Fergus said it wasn't a bad return for sitting on their bums and getting something for nothing.

Jack, Harry, and Sparrow hit the blackjack table with gusto. Their total winnings for the same four hours were twenty-nine hundred dollars.

Maggie, Ted, Espinosa, and Dennis took over a bank of slot machines and went at it full bore, with total winnings of $11,315.

Snowden and his people worked the floor, their eyes everywhere. From time to time, they would sit down at a slot machine, press the but-

ton, then walk away. Their total winnings for
the four hours were $8.50.

Chits in hand at the meet in the Tiki Bar,
they agreed that they would donate the money
to the Sunshine Foundation. It was Maggie's
honor to walk the donation to the front of the
casino floor, where an elderly, white-haired
lady cried at the sizable donations.

"We are dining at the Knife and Fork, on the
sixth floor," Charles said. "After dinner, we will
head for the concierge floor to wait for Abner."

The restaurant was just crowded enough
that no one paid attention to the lively group
as they waited for tables to be put together to
accommodate all of them.

Drinks were on the way and dinner had
been ordered when Jack held up his hand for
silence. "Okay, anyone notice anything while
we were gambling?"

Everyone started talking at once. The bottom line was they all felt like they were being
watched. All eyes turned to Sparrow, the pro in
the group.

"We're on Kelly's radar, that's for sure,"
Sparrow told them. "I really don't think that
Bert told him what's going on, and he is definitely miffed that whatever it is, he's not included. The guy is good. Bert told me all about
him a while back. Whatever you do, do not under-
estimate him.

"Right now, he's checking each one of us
out as he tries to figure out what the play is.
Hell, he probably did that the minute he left

us earlier. He could definitely be an asset to us, but we can't use him, since Bert, while he didn't say it out loud, thinks, despite the time differences, that he might be involved. Right or wrong, for now the man is tainted."

The group nodded as one.

"Avery, you and your people were cruising the floor. What, if anything, did you come up with?" Charles asked.

"I feel confident in saying Kelly assigned a tail to each one of us. I'm proud of all of you. You acted like everyone else on the floor. As far as I could tell, the tails went back to Kelly with their tails between their legs, no pun intended. In other words, they had nothing of substance to report. We're all doing just what everyone else is doing.

"Before you all go up to your rooms after dinner, I'm going to pass on dessert, leave a little early, and check to make sure the rooms are clean. By that I mean free of listening devices. Like Sparrow said, once an agent, always an agent."

The others nodded in agreement.

None of them failed to notice the impeccable service they were getting when their dinners arrived all at the same exact time. The Kobe beef and jumbo prawns that Babylon was known for were served piping hot, and no one had a complaint. Water glasses were constantly filled, as were the wineglasses. Waiters in crisp black and white stood to the side in anticipation of a request from one of the diners.

Maggie Spritzer, long known for her out-of-whack metabolism and ferocious appetite, mumbled something that sounded like "I could get used to this kind of dining real quick."

The others heartily agreed.

As dessert was being served, a double chocolate mousse cake, Jack's cell phone pinged. Abner had just sent him a text. He looked up at the others. "Abner just pulled into the parking garage. He wants to know what he should do."

"I'll go down to meet him and take him up to the room," Harry said. Other than Snowden, he was the only one at the table who had passed on dessert. "We'll wait for you."

Dennis looked at his dessert and frowned. Harry had told him more than once that sugar was a killer, and he had lost *all* that weight. "I'll come with you," he said, getting up from the table. Maggie's hand moved quicker than a magician's as she scooped up her multimillionaire junior reporter's dessert plate.

"I know you're all anxious to get up to your rooms, so go ahead. Fergus and I will settle the bill," Charles said.

All the guys were on their feet in a second, except for Maggie, who was stuffing the mousse cake into her face as fast as she could.

Charles raised his hand to indicate he was ready for the bill.

The head waiter smiled and said, "Sir, Mr. Navarro left instructions that you and your party are our prime guests, and as such, dinner is compliments of the house. We hope you enjoyed your dinners, and we look forward to seeing you again during your stay. By the way, we offer a varied menu for in-room dining, if you feel that is something you might like. The kitchen is open twenty-four hours."

Charles beamed his pleasure as he peeled off three one-hundred-dollar bills for the tip. "One way or another," he said to Fergus, "you pay. The life of a waiter or waitress is not easy." He turned to Maggie. "Come along, missy, and let's see what Abner has in store for us."

Well out of sight, Dixson Kelly listened to the voice at the other end of the phone he was holding to his ear, telling him that the last guest on Navarro's list had just arrived and was parking in the garage. The voice, which belonged to Pete Justice, further informed him that the last guest had just placed a phone call or sent a text. From his vantage point, he couldn't be sure which it was, not that it mattered all that much.

Dixson Kelly clenched his teeth together so hard, he thought his jaw would crack. All present and accounted for. At least for now. "Pete, what did you come up with on the background checks for this crew?"

"Done and on your desk, boss. Anything else?"

"Anything interesting?"

Justice laughed. "I'll let you be the judge of that, boss. It did make for some interesting reading, I will say that. A word of advice. Tread carefully around that guy Harry Wong. Just so

you know, on our best day, I and my entire
Delta team couldn't take him out. Even in our
prime. That guy Emery, even though he's some
kind of lawyer, is no slouch, either. Then there's
this young kid, a reporter who is Wong's protégé. In other words, when it comes to mixing
it up down and dirty, the three of them are a
force to be reckoned with."

Kelly made an ugly sound in the back of his
throat. "I knew about Harry Wong, since he's
been in Vegas a number of times, but you're
making it sound like Armageddon is right
around the corner. I'll keep it in mind, Pete."

Kelly took the elevator to his office, where
he poured himself a cup of coffee from the pot
that was freshened hourly, and settled down to
read the background reports on Bert Navarro's
guests. He perched a pair of reading glasses on
his nose and started to read.

When he was finished, thirty minutes later,
he snorted in disgust.

Four reporters here to do a week in the life
of a Vegas honcho. One lawyer who used to be
a district attorney. The number one martial
arts expert in the world. A Scottish gent by the
name of Fergus Duffy, who used to head up Interpol. A British chap who worked both sides
of the pond, was Elizabeth's childhood play-
mate, and was still on a first-name basis with
the queen of England. *Serious firepower there*, he
thought glumly.

Absolutely nothing on the guy Snowden and
the four people who were with him. His back-

ground was a pure blank, as were those of the four others. Aliases. Not against the law. He was going to have to dig into that.

Jackson Porter Sparrow. Framed by his own agents back in the day and spent a hitch in the federal pen, until Bert and a bunch of women proved he'd been framed. The president had pardoned him, and now he headed up the FBI, following the guy who had succeeded Bert, who had succeeded Elias Cummings.

Good guy. Salt of the earth. Usually went by the rule book until the book didn't work anymore, then, like Frank Sinatra said, did it his way. The moment he took over the Bureau, he cleaned house, set up new rules, and he was now actually the envy of the CIA. Yep, good man. The question was, what the hell was he doing here with this particular bunch of people?

Which left Mr. Abner Tookus, whose report had three times as many pages as the reports on the others. *Wealthy* was the first word on the report, followed by his marital status, followed by his friendship with Maggie Spritzer, currently the star reporter and formerly the editor in chief of the *Washington Post*, which just happened to be owned by Babylon's owner, Countess Anna de Silva. So that web of connections would account for Tookus being here and belonging to this particular group of people.

Kelly continued to read. Tookus did not have a nine-to-five job. He worked on his own as a freelancer, doing stints for every government agency in the nation's capital. Even the

FBI. He was a computer genius. He wrote code, did designer security, set up Web sites that could not be hacked, ones with impenetrable fire-walls.

Kelly snorted. There was no such thing, in his opinion, as an impenetrable firewall. Tookus's latest gig, as of six months ago, was installing a system for Homeland Security, for which he was paid a cool two million dollars. He snorted again when he read the words *the United States government's number one computer expert.* In paren-theses was the word *GENIUS,* in capital letters.

Well, woo-hoo, boo-hoo, and all that jazz, Kelly thought. *And here the number one computer genius in the country is suddenly, along with the number one martial arts expert in the country, right here, under my very nose. Not to mention the rest of the crew. Like I am really supposed to believe this whole gig is just a little gambling junket for fun and games. It has to mean something. But what?*

One thing he knew for certain was that these people were not here for a vacation or for shits and giggles. They were here for something else. Now all he had to do was figure out what that *something* was.

Kelly spread all the reports across his desk and looked at them. *Eeny, meeny, miny, moe, catch a monkey by the toe...* Where to start? What should he dig into first? He took a mighty breath and let it out slowly. The computer guy, of course, this Abner Tookus. But first he had to make some phone calls. To old pals still in the business. Old pals who knew their way around the different government agencies, who knew who had whose ear and what was going to go down before it went down. One way or another, he was going to find out what was going on.

An hour after his arrival, allowing time for Abner to shower, put on fresh clothes, and eat, the gang gathered in Charles's suite to talk.

Jack thought Abner looked and acted like a cat on a hot griddle. Harry agreed. He decided to spare the computer expert the dance he was getting ready to orchestrate and get to the bare bones of whatever it was that was bothering him.

"Okay, Abner, spit it out. I know . . . we *all* know something is bothering you big-time. We saw it back in the BOLO Building. Thank God you don't play poker, because if you did, your face would give you away. You know something. What is it?"

Abner cleared his throat. "You're right. I *think* I know something. The operative word here is *think*. I didn't say anything then, because I wasn't sure. I'm still not one hundred percent sure, but I'm going to tell you, anyway, and you can all judge for yourselves if I'm right or wrong. I know where my loyalties lie. With all of you. That's a given. But . . . I have another loyalty I have . . . had to consider. I'm able to do what I do because of my mentor of old. I owe him everything. He's never asked anything of me in return. He's like a beloved cyber grandfather. You probably don't understand that, but I had to weigh that against all of you. At the same time, I didn't want to bring the wrath of God down on him if I was wrong. I am having a real hard time with this, in case you haven't noticed.

"Think about all I've been able to do for all of you over the years. I don't know where we'd all be if I hadn't been able to help out. Able to help out because of the person who took me under his wing and worked with me, taught me everything I know. He was there for me all the way. What I am trying to say here is that there is only one person in this whole world who I think could do what Bert thinks was done. RCHood. That's his cyber name. I have no idea what his real name is. RCHood stands for 'Robin Cool Hood.' He robs the rich to help the poor. That's the bottom line.

"There is nothing he cannot hack into. I mean *nothing*. The man is a legend in his own time. You would have to live in my world to understand the fear the man generates. Fear and respect. I don't know. . . . Maybe you have to see the words in black and white to understand what I mean. RCHood is most famous among people like myself for saying, 'You screw me over, cross me, babble about me, or try to find me, and I will wipe out your entire bloodline.' Is it true? Would he do that? Does he have the capabilities? I don't know, and neither does anyone else, and none of us have ever, at least to my knowledge, tried to find out. Best to let sleeping dogs lie, as they say."

Avery Snowden wagged his finger in the air to indicate he had something to say. "What

Abner is telling you is the absolute truth. I've had my ear to the ground, as well as the ears of a lot of people in the field, and RCHood is the name that comes up time and time again. It is virtually the only name that came up. No one talks about him. I'm not guessing here when I say you could stick lighted matches under those hackers' toenails, and they still wouldn't talk.

"The thing is, they really don't know anything about the person himself. No one knows who he is in real life, and no one has met him, or if they have, they do not know that they have. It could be a woman, for all I or any of my sources know. But whoever RCHood is, he or she is the best of the best."

"Well, where the hell does that leave us?" Ted exploded.

"I met him. Once. I was sixteen at the time," Abner said.

The silence in the room was suddenly deafening.

"Maybe you should tell us about that meeting," Charles said quietly, his voice gentle, as if he were talking a child to sleep.

"I did meet him, but even if you put those matches under my toenails, I couldn't tell you what he looks like. I was sixteen, young, dumb, stupid. I heard there was this underground hackers' convention in New Jersey. To the dismay of my foster parents, I hitchhiked to the conference to meet what I thought were my idols. I was good. I knew that. I just needed guidance. There was this roundtable discussion where everyone got to say who they were, what their goals were, stuff like that. This one guy at the table kept watching me and later singled me out, and we talked. It was RCHood. We've been cyber friends ever since. I can't tell you how many times he's helped me out. He helps everyone out, asks for nothing but our loyalty."

"What's he look like?" Snowden asked.

Abner ran his hands through his hair. "Just a guy. Hey, I was only sixteen. He looked just as grungy as the rest of us. Dark hair. Tall. I think. Big hands. Really big hands. That's what I was really looking at, because those hands, the fingers, literally danced on the computer keys. I wanted that capability. That's the only thing that really registered with me. Also, remember at that time, he wasn't the legend he is today in the hacker world."

"How much did he weigh? How tall was he?" Jack asked.

Abner shrugged. "He was sitting down, so he was a lot taller than me, and I was sitting next to him. He had some meat on him. The only reason I even noticed was that the rest of us were pretty skinny, and that goes for the girls that were there. 'Average big guy' would have to be my answer."

"Eyes . . . what color? What color was his hair?" Dennis asked.

"I have no clue as to eye color, but his hair was dark."

"Any markings? Tattoos, pimples, boils, scars?" Espinosa queried.

"None that I remember. It was a long time ago. I was full of myself back then. I'd defied my foster parents where I was raised, hitch-hiked up to Jersey, and was on my own for the first time in my life and was hell-bent on enjoying every minute of it. On my way here, I even thought about hypnosis, wondering if it would help. The bottom line is I didn't pay attention to the person, just his hands, what they could do with a keyboard and a computer and the words that came out of his mouth. Now, if you showed me a picture of his hands, his nails, I'm sure I would have total recall, because that's where my focus was. As I recall, he had a nice voice, kind of comforting. Soothing, actually, now that I think of it. At the same time he was trying, I think, to figure out which one of us was worthy of his time and effort. He chose me and a girl whose cyber name is PIP. Stands for 'Pretty in Pink.'

"He even gave me my cyber name. TRIP-LEM. Means 'Triple Mister Magic Money,' or Triple M, as he put it, because at that age, all I thought about was money and being rich. The two of us have to use the cyber names he christened us with when we communicate with him. That's all I use it for."

"Any clue where he actually lives?" Harry asked.

"No. And don't think I didn't try to find out. He sent me a warning to cease and desist, and I obeyed. PIP did the same thing and got the same warning."

"So what you are saying is the man knows

everything there is to know about you, but you know *nothing* about him. Is that right?" Fergus asked.

"That's it in a nutshell," Abner said.

"Did you ever go to any other of those conventions? Did you ever see him again in person?" Sparrow asked.

"I've been to hundreds. All over the country over the years. And before you can ask, I think that PIP and I are the only two people who come slightly close to what he can do. I doubt we'll ever reach his status, but that's okay. Once you're at the top, there is no one else to look up to.

"But to answer your question, no, I never saw him again. Once I asked him if he had ever gone to any of the conferences, and he said he had not and did not plan on attending in the future. I took him at his word. I did ask him why, and he said the new generation of hackers coming up were pussies, afraid they'd get caught, afraid to believe in themselves. That's all I can tell you. You can grill me for hours, and I can't tell you any more than that. I know it is not very helpful, but that is all I know about RCHood."

"When was the last time you were in contact?" Sparrow asked.

"A month ago. But . . . here's the thing. He sent me an e-mail early yesterday morning, five o'clock in the morning, to be precise. Just a chatty note asking what I was doing, that kind of thing. I think the reason he sent it was that I sent out an e-blast telling everyone I was taking a road trip and to call instead of e-mailing for the next few days. I think the guy monitors my e-mails and my texts, too. Don't look at me like that, you guys. I'm not dumb enough to put anything important in an e-mail or text. I always use Snowden's phone when I'm in contact with you. RCHood cannot crack that."

"So that means he knows you're here?" Jack said.

"No, I don't think he does, Jack. I told the people who asked that I was going to Jackson Hole, Wyoming," Abner drawled. His shoulders sagged now that he'd unloaded his secret. It was such a relief, he thought he was going to black out.

Chapter 7

Philonias Needlemeyer looked down at his idle hands. What he saw was a first for him. To the best of his recollection, he'd never experienced a moment like this. A brief flurry of panic invaded his being. Another emotion he'd never experienced before. He, Philonias Needlemeyer, had made a mistake. And he *never* made mistakes. Not ever. He revised his crippling thought. Not really a mistake. No, he'd made an error in judgment. Everyone did that at one time or another. Didn't they? And calling what had happened an error in judgment certainly sounded better than saying he'd made a mistake. Nonetheless, his massive shoulders started to shake. He didn't know if he could handle having made a mistake. If he had made a mistake, he would have to admit to there being a blight on his perfect record.

But he had to face it, an error in judgment was, all things considered, the same thing as a mistake, and only a fool would think otherwise, and whatever else they had done, his parents had not raised a fool. So he needed to own the mistake, correct it as best he could, and move on.

What in the world had possessed him to go down to the Tiki Bar? He never went out in public. That was the mistake, the error in judgment, that he'd made. And an error he had compounded by not keeping quiet. By saying something to, of all people, Dixson Kelly. If only. In and of itself, going to the bar for lunch was not really a mistake. Not even an error in judgment. But opening his mouth, speaking to Dixson Kelly—that was a big mistake.

Earlier in the day, he'd hacked into Bert Navarro's and Dixson Kelly's cell phones and listened to their conversation, something he did every day so he could stay on top of things. The truth was, he did it more to amuse himself than anything else, because he knew neither Navarro nor Kelly would ever figure out what he was doing. Referring, of course, to the daily withdrawals, where he helped himself to a portion of the deposits from the casino.

That was when he'd put two and two together, when he'd learned that TRIPLEM's sudden road trip was here, to Vegas, and not to Jackson Hole, Wyoming, as TRIPLEM had told his informants. He recalled how he'd almost collapsed when he realized that not only was

TRIPLEM a personal friend of Bert Navarro's, but he was also on his way here, to Babylon. Along with the current director of the FBI. His gut had started to churn at the thought of what it could all possibly mean, and he didn't like where his thoughts were taking him.

Philonias looked down at his hands. He could see and feel the tremor in them. He grew light-headed at what he was experiencing. Then a second paralyzing thought hit him. He'd made another error in judgment by contacting TRIPLEM. Abner Tookus was no one's fool. By now he'd probably finished working on the same math problem and realized two plus two equaled four. Two mistakes. *Two!* How was he going to live with that?

Philonias felt a sourness start to build in his stomach. Maybe he needed fresh air. He needed to do something to clear his head. He made his way from the computer room, across the vast living room, to the French doors that led to a long, narrow terrace filled with colorful spring plants. He gripped the handrails and struggled to take deep breaths. He did it ten times, then another ten times, until he felt reasonably calm.

His thoughts all over the map, Philonias wondered if his errors in judgment could be corrected. You could always rectify a mistake. At least, that was what he'd been led to believe. But since this was a first for him, he had no way of knowing for certain. He'd read somewhere, many times, in fact, chapter and verse about people who made mistakes and were not only forgiven but also given the chance to correct their mistakes.

But how in the name of all that was holy was he to do that and not bring attention to the error in judgment? He needed to decompress. What he needed to do was think outside the box.

Lighter fare. He needed to do something amusing. Something that had nothing to do with Navarro, Kelly, or TRIPLEM. Impossible. Right now, those three names consumed his entire being. Well, that wasn't quite true. He could tap in to Dixson Kelly's nine burner phones, which Kelly thought no one knew about. It was always amusing to read the various texts his women sent him.

Genius that he was, it still boggled his mind how the security chief managed to walk a tightrope while simultaneously carrying on affairs with nine women and make it work for him, with none of the women being aware of each other. Speaking strictly for himself, Philonias had had a hard time keeping all of Kelly's machinations straight, even when he made a chart to follow the progress of the lothario's romantic endeavors.

Another set of ten deep breaths convinced Philonias that he was good to go, so he headed back inside. He made his way to his inner sanctum and sat down. He looked at his hands. Steady as a rock. A sigh of relief escaped his lips as he concentrated on Dixson Kelly's nine burner phones.

From time to time, he found himself smiling; twice, he even laughed out loud at the sexy messages. That is, until he switched gears and hacked into a phone registered to a showgirl named Kitty Passion, who appeared to be Kelly's most recent conquest. Well, almost a conquest. He hadn't scored as yet, but he was working hard at it. He scrolled down through the list of texts she'd sent to two of her friends. That was when the fine hairs on the back of his neck started to move. Kitty danced and tended bar at Luxor. What set the fine hairs on his neck moving was one of her outgoing texts, which read, **To all Dixson Kelly alumnae! Listen up, girls! I have news. We need to talk. Let's meet at the Cat & Cradle on Friday. Noon. My treat. I think we got good old Dix right where we want him, and no, he doesn't suspect a thing. And before you can ask, the answer is a resounding no. He's throwing everything he has at me to get me to take off my clothes, but I'm making him work for it, just like you all instructed.**

"Well, well, well! What have we here?" Philonias muttered to himself. He moved the chair he was sitting on across the room and placed a big *X* on Friday's date. Normally, he didn't eat lunch out on Fridays or any other day, but two days from now, he would make absolutely sure that he was dining at the Cat & Cradle downtown. Because, as everyone knew, information was power, and Philonias Needlemeyer was all about information and power. Information and power were his two best friends in the entire world.

* * *

"We need a plan," Jack said. He looked over at Charles, their in-residence plan maker, as Cyrus scoured every inch of the suite for all the strange scents he was picking up.

Charles picked up the ball. "Abner, on a scale of one to ten, how sure are you that your friend RC is the one helping himself to the casino money? Based, of course, on what little we know at this point in time."

"As sure as I know I need to keep breathing to stay alive," was the snappy reply.

"Then we need to up our game and set a trap for Mr. RCHood. What are the chances that you could enlist the aid of your fellow hacker, PIP? How could you go about that without RCHood knowing what you're doing?"

"Almost impossible. Short of a face-to-face with her, I wouldn't know where to start. Even if we made that happen, there's no guarantee she would help us. Like all the others, she's afraid of RC."

"Then how did your pal RC ferret out your own background? How did he do it? Is there a program? I'm not up on this hacker stuff, but if he did it, then as his almost equal, you should be able to do it," Ted said.

"Yeah, you would think so, but I tried. These people use encryption, double passwords, and sometimes they change them hourly. Their servers are all over the world. I know for a fact that RC can and does use satellites to aid him. I told you, the man has no equal. Everyone is fearful of him, including yours truly. His reach is limitless."

"No one is that good," Dennis snorted. One look from Abner made him clench his teeth.

"I have an idea," Snowden said out of the blue. "Do you think you could describe PIP? Espinosa is a good sketch artist. If he could get a good sketch, we could run it off some face-recognition software and see what we come up with. Maybe we could track her down that way."

"Yeah, sure. It's been a few years since I've seen her, but I don't think she would have changed that much. But I have to ask, to what end? How do you think she could help us?"

"At this moment I don't know," Snowden said, "but checking it out is better than doing nothing. She might have paid more attention to RC than you did. As you well know, women have a different mind-set than men. You focused on RC's hands. Maybe she focused on his smile, his eyes, or his nose. I think it's worth a shot, since we have so little else to go on."

Espinosa pulled a small sketch pad from his duffel bag and moved back into the main part of the suite, with Abner in tow. Snowden moved off to Charles's computers and sat down to check out his software. Thirty minutes later, he was satisfied with what he had done, just as Espinosa waved a picture under his nose.

"It's the best I could do, Mr. Snowden. It's been a few years since I've seen her, but what you're looking at is as good as it's going to get,"

Abner said as he stared at a plain-looking woman he thought of as PIP.

"Let's see what we come up with. It might take a few hours, or it might take a few minutes, or somewhere in the middle," Snowden said, his eyes glued to the screen.

Twenty-three minutes later, Snowden's fist shot high in the air. "Got it! Abner, is this your friend PIP?"

Abner peered over the top of his reading glasses. "Yep, that's her. A younger her, but it is PIP. Younger, I'd say, by ten years. Where does she live?"

"Gilbert, Arizona. Not that far from here, as the crow flies." Snowden looked over at his people and nodded. They left the room immediately.

"Where are they going?" Dennis asked.

"Probably out to heist a vehicle so they can drive to Arizona. That's what I would do if I were them," Jack said.

"Why not just rent a car or truck?" Dennis asked.

"Paper trail, kid," Ted said. "Don't worry, Mr. Dudley Do-Right. They'll leave money on the seat when they return it. They're just borrowing it for now."

"What if the owner calls the police?" Dennis persisted.

"What? You think this is those guys' first rodeo? They know what to do and how to do it. They'll go into the garage, look for a car with dust on it, one that looks like it hasn't been driven for a while, and hot-wire it. When they return it, no one will ever know. Does that make you happy, kid?"

Dennis didn't know if it did or not, so he clamped his lips together and crossed his arms over his chest, disapproval written all over his features.

Harry moved next to him. "Get over it, Dennis. Like now. Do not ever question what we do again. Are we clear on that?"

Dennis swallowed hard. "It's crystal, Harry. Really, really crystal. I'm over it. I am so over it, you wouldn't believe me if I told you." He eyeballed Harry and was rewarded with a smile that sent better men than him running for cover. "See, see, I'm loose as a goose. You want fast and loose, I'll give you fast and loose." Harry walked away, to Dennis's relief. His knees started to buckle, but Ted caught him just in time.

"Okay, people, here is PIP's profile, thanks to Google. She's thirty-nine years old. This proves she does have a personal life aside from her . . . ah . . . other life. Her name is Mary Alice Farmer. She sells organic plant seeds online. And she makes a living at it. Has a small specialty shop in Gilbert. She owns her own house, no mortgage. She drives a vintage Ford Bronco. According to her credit-card history, she travels five or six times a year by plane. Odd places, so I assume those trips are to attend hacker conventions. She doesn't charge a lot on her credit cards—gas, drugstore purchases, Home

Depot stuff. Single, never married. No pets. Dates maybe once a year. However, she has a very robust brokerage account at Wells Fargo. High, high seven figures. She must sell a lot of organic seeds to account for her bottom line. Even a fool could look at this and realize she has an outside income. Hard to tell from this report. Mode of dress is sneakers, jeans, T-shirts. No fashion plate. Abner, does this sound like the PIP you know?"

Abner shrugged. "I don't know anything about her personal life. I'm hearing this all for the first time, just the way you are."

"Okay, okay. I get all that, but based on the picture here on the screen and what I've just told you, do you think this is PIP?"

"Yeah, yeah, I do."

"Okay, that's good enough for me. Hold down the fort, people. When you see me next, I will have Ms. Mary Alice Farmer in tow. We won't be coming back here, however. We'll take her to The Venetian. Someone call and reserve a room in the name of Zack Hammer. Here's a credit card to charge the room to. Not to worry about returning it. I have a duplicate card for when I check in."

"They're going to kidnap her, aren't they?" Dennis squeaked.

"Yes, Dennis, they are," Charles said.

"Well then," the young, intrepid reporter said, knowing that all eyes were on him, "that is *exciting*. You know, being part of a kidnap escapade, with no worries of federal intervention."

"I like the way you think, young man," Sparrow said as he eyeballed Dennis.

Dennis managed a sickly grin as he imagined himself in a federal penitentiary, sporting an orange jumpsuit.

"Now what?" Maggie asked as she sent off a text to Snowden, who had already left. She gave him the room number and the amount of the charge.

"Now I think we should all call it a night and get some sleep," Charles said. "We'll meet up on the concierge floor for breakfast at, let's say, seven thirty."

No one argued as they left Charles's suite and headed for their own rooms. It had been a long, stressful day. Tomorrow was another day, and they were three hours behind, with jet lag kicking in.

No one seemed to notice that Sparrow lagged behind and closed the door. He looked over at Charles. "We need to talk."

"I think I know what you want to discuss. Dixson Kelly, right?"

Sparrow nodded. "I'd like to take a look inside his room. I think someone said Kelly is staying in Bert's apartment, and Kelly keeps a room here for his late nights. A perk. He also has an apartment or condo in town. We need to find out where and visit it, too. There's something about that guy that isn't sitting right with me, and no, it's not that jab he took at the FBI. For obvious reasons, I can't do the breaking and entering. But as soon as Snowden gets back here, I say we put him on it. He's the pro here. Your thoughts, Charles."

Charles stroked his chin as he stared first at Sparrow, then Fergus. "I agree with you that there is something *off* about Kelly. I'm just not sure it has anything to do with why we're here. For some reason, I think the man is ticked off that Bert called us all here and hasn't really told Kelly why. He sees us as invading his turf and taking over. Bert swears by him, and that's good enough for me."

Sparrow's head bobbed up and down. "I hear you. He might have a gig going on, something that has nothing to do with any of this, which he'd just like to keep to himself. First thought off the top of my head is his life with the ladies. Right there I am seeing a dozen red flags going up. Just wanted to mention it, Charles. We can't do anything until tomorrow, when Snowden gets back. I'll say good night now."

Charles walked the FBI director to the door and locked it once he closed it. He turned to Fergus. "He's right, Fergus. Something isn't right here in regard to Dixson Kelly. Thankfully, Maggie and the boys will be on him twenty-four/seven starting in the morning. They will keep him so busy, he won't have time to worry about us."

Fergus threw his hands in the air. Another way of saying, "What will be will be."

Charles laughed. *Yes, indeedy, what will be will be.*

* * *

Avery Snowden steered the stolen SUV into the parking lot of a twenty-four-hour supermarket on the outskirts of Gilbert, Arizona. Next to the fancy-looking supermarket was a mom-and-pop café that said it served breakfast and lunch.

"Here's the plan. We have breakfast first, because it's just seven thirty. We hit the supermarket, buy some flowers and balloons, then head to Mary Alice Farmer's house on Primrose Drive. That should be around a quarter to nine or so, if we don't mess around. I'll sign the card 'TRIPLEM,' and with any luck, that will get us into her house. From that point on, we wing it."

Everyone agreed.

"What if she doesn't open the door, or worse, what if she isn't home?" one of the operatives asked.

"Then we're screwed. Once she looks out her window, sees an SUV and me with a bunch of flowers and balloons, she won't be able to resist opening the door if she's home. If she isn't home, we break in. Women are like that," Snowden said flatly.

The operatives looked at Snowden skeptically but decided it didn't pay to argue with the boss. The group headed for the café, sat at a table for five, and ordered breakfast, which they gobbled down, and they were back outside and headed for the supermarket within forty-five minutes. The selection was easy: the flowers were already wrapped in green florist wrap and stuck in a clear vase that called for water. Snowden grabbed two bunches of roses mixed with multicolored tulips, then moved over to the clusters of balloons that were tied to a stick with sparkly sandbags at the end to weigh them down. He picked three bunches and handed them to one of his female operatives. He tapped his foot impatiently as he waited for the classy-looking lady ahead of him to pay for a bunch of ferns wrapped in green tissue paper.

He sighed when the cashier said, "It's nice to see you again, Claudeen. Bet you're having a dinner party tonight, and the ferns are for your flower arrangement."

Claudeen laughed, waved good-bye without giving Snowden so much as a glance, her thoughts obviously on the dinner party she was planning.

Snowden stepped forward. He handed over a fifty-dollar bill and pocketed the sixteen cents in change the cashier handed him.

At seven minutes past nine, Avery Snowden walked up the path to Mary Alice Farmer's house and rang the bell. The others watched from the SUV as they all waited to see if the front door would open. It did after Snowden hit the doorbell a second time.

Tookus was right. Mary Alice Farmer was on the plain side, but she had a spark in her eyes and a lopsided grin. She looked at Snowden and said, "I think you are probably at the wrong house. No one ever sends me flowers and balloons. I'm thinking you might want the house two doors down. A young airline stewardess lives there, and she gets a lot of flower-and-balloon deliveries." She made a move to shut the door.

"Is your name Mary Alice Farmer? That's who this delivery is for. From someone named TRIPLEM. Does that ring a bell?"

"Ah . . . I . . . Let me see that card." Snowden tilted his head to the bouquet and the small white card nestled among the flowers. He was pleased to see the instant recognition as the woman stepped aside for him to enter.

"Where do you want these? The balloons are tied to bags of sand. The vase needs to be filled with water."

"In the kitchen, I guess. If you wait just a minute, I'll tip you."

"No tips are allowed. Are you upset, ma'am? You sound . . . *upset.*"

"Yes. No. I . . . just wasn't expecting . . . I don't under . . ." *Oh, God, how did TRIPLEM find me. How?*

A chime could be heard coming from the front of the house, an indication that Mary Alice Farmer had a security system that alerted her when the door opened.

"Oh, my God, someone just came in my house!"

"It's okay. They're with me," Snowden said.

"What do you mean, they're with you? Who

are you?" Fear was written all over Mary Alice's features as she hugged her arms to her chest.

"Names aren't important right now. I apologize for my trickery, but we weren't sure if you would open the door to a stranger based on . . . your . . . uh, profession."

"Selling organic seeds?" Mary Alice shrilled.

"No. Your hacking. Look, let's cut to the chase here. TRIPLEM sent us. He's in some trouble, and he wants us to take you to him. He thinks you can help him. Now, think about it, young lady. How would I know your pal TRIPLEM if he didn't send me? You need to pack a bag and come with us."

"Well . . . I . . . I don't think so. I can't leave here. Tell . . . tell TRIPLEM to text or e-mail me. No. I'm not going."

"Trip did tell us that you would say that. He said to tell you that RCHood is onto you and him. He said you would understand what that meant. Do you?"

Snowden didn't think the young woman's face could get any whiter. She swallowed and nodded.

"Good. One of these ladies will help you pack a bag. Be quick about it. Now, as to all those computers I saw on the way to the kitchen . . . I am assuming you might want to take the hard drives with you?" It was a question.

"Who . . . who are you?"

Snowden didn't bother replying as he and the other three operatives set about removing the hard drives from Mary Alice Farmer's computers.

Sixteen minutes later, they were settled in the SUV and headed for Vegas.

Six hours later, Snowden drove into the underground garage at The Venetian.

"We made good time. Those three hundred twenty miles really zipped by," Snowden said, just to hear himself talk. "You guys go on up to the room. I need to . . . uh . . . return our wheels and let the others know we're back. Don't do anything but watch TV until I knock on the door."

"You're spooks, aren't you?" Mary Alice said. They were the first words she'd spoken since being abducted.

"That depends on your definition of the word *spook*. Make sure you all have everything and are not leaving anything behind."

Snowden waited in the SUV until he saw the elevator door open. He watched as his people formed a cordon around their charge. The moment the elevator door closed, Snowden turned on the ignition.

Snowden parked the SUV exactly where it had been parked previously. He checked again to make sure nothing was left behind, then wiped the vehicle down with Clorox wipes from his backpack to make sure no fingerprints remained inside or out. Satisfied that all was well, he peeled off five hundred-dollar bills and placed them in the glove box. He'd filled the tank right beforc pulling into The Venetian. The only thing he couldn't fix was the 650 or so miles he'd put on the SUV. His best hope was that eighty-five–year-old John Masters, the owner of the SUV, wouldn't notice the change in mileage.

Phone in hand, Snowden sent off a text to Charles, reporting that he was on his way up to the concierge floor. The words *MISSION ACCOMPLISHED* were typed in capital letters.

Chapter 8

Jack was so antsy, he thought he'd explode as he paced the confines of the sitting room between Charles's and Fergus's suites. Cyrus had given up trailing him and sat by the door, waiting to see if his master's furious pacing would lead to a walk with some food at the end. "I have to get out of here. I have cabin fever. I'm getting tired of asking what the plan is. Bert has sent six texts asking what we're doing. We need to come up with something and fast."

"Look, Jack," Snowden said, "tell Bert to hang on to his britches. There's a right way and a wrong way of doing things, and simply because he has his knickers in a knot at the moment doesn't mean we can or should move any faster—and, might I say, safer—than we are. We have PIP in a secure location. We can head on over there and start to grill her, but that means we have to pull Espinosa off the *Post* detail with Maggie. That might, I say might, raise a red flag with Kelly.

"We need Espinosa to do a sketch if PIP can remember what RCHood looks like. Abner said she has a pixel-sharp photographic memory, so right now Espinosa is our best bet," Snowden explained, his eyes on Charles to see if he agreed with his assessment of the situation.

Charles nodded.

"What did you think of PIP?" Abner asked Snowden.

"You mean Mary Alice. There wasn't a peep out of her on the ride here. She was quiet, stubbornly so, for the whole six hours. She put up a token resistance at the beginning, nothing we couldn't handle. She's fearful. You were right, Abner, when you said she has a fill-in-the-blanks personality. You're her peer. I'm sure she'll open up to you. Make no mistake. We cannot let her go until this mess is over and done with. We can't have her out there, floundering around and getting in touch with your head guru. You're good with that, her being a friend and all, right?"

Abner sucked on his lower lip and nodded. "I'm good with everything. Mary Alice is the one you have to worry about. She's active, and I'm on the sidelines. Make no mistake. Her loyalty is to RC. I just keep my hand in the pot so I can keep up with the latest . . . um . . . you know, tricks."

Fergus held up his special phone, on which a text was showing. "Espinosa will meet us at

The Venetian. Since he is the photographer, he said he left something behind back home for his camera and has to head out to a camera shop to buy a new part. Once he gets to The Venetian, if Miss PIP cooperates, he can get us a workable sketch in less than half an hour. My advice is to scatter, and we'll meet up there as we get there. Go in pairs, since that should mean less scrutiny."

Jack, Harry, and Cyrus were out the door in a nanosecond. The others followed at ten-minute intervals.

Sparrow and Abner were the last to leave the suite, talking as they walked.

"Something is bothering you, Sparrow. I can see it on your face. Want to talk about it or . . ."

"I can't put my finger on it, Tookus. Something's off. I'd like to get inside Kelly's apartment for a look around. Even I know I can't do that, but Snowden should be able to pull it off. When the hair on the back of my neck moves, I know something isn't right. I have good instincts. All those years in the field, when the only thing I could depend on was my instincts, and they never once failed me, are at work. I don't expect you to understand that."

"Oh, but I do. My left eye twitches when something's wrong or trouble is brewing. I understand fully. You have any ideas?"

"I really think Kelly is a straight arrow. Otherwise, Bert wouldn't have hired him in the first place. Annie likes him. She's a shrewd judge of character. If he is involved in whatever is going down, I do not think he is aware of it, at least not yet. I think he's like us, trying to figure it out and wondering why Bert hasn't included him in the loop. Is that your take on things, Tookus?"

"It is. I think Jack and Harry agree. When we get to The Venetian, we can share your concerns with Snowden and have him do a little B and E. I heard Jack say—I think it was yesterday—that Kelly had a condo in town. He just moved into Bert's apartment at Babylon when Bert left for China. He works long hours and is on call around the clock, so it makes sense for him to be on the premises. He also keeps a room here, which is off-limits to everyone. The guy has it going on. That's for sure. So our bottom line here is we think he's clean and is just like us, trying to figure out what's going on."

"That's my take. Okay, we're here. How do you want to do this? We splinter off? You go your way, I go mine, and we meet up in room four-twelve?" Sparrow asked.

Abner nodded and headed left, to a bank of slot machines that were ringing so loud, his ears hurt. He didn't look over his shoulder to see where Sparrow was going. Looking over one's shoulders was for the real spooks, like Sparrow, Jack, Harry, and the others. He was just a geeky nerd who could hack his heart out. No one ever paid attention to people like him. *Big mistake,* he thought grimly as he shoved a twenty-dollar bill into a slot machine and pressed the red button. He almost jumped out of his shoes when a dazzling bright light started to spin over his machine. And then the bells and whistles started shrieking. So much for being an anonymous geek.

Other players gathered around his stool to see what he'd won. He was curious himself, as an attendant with a false smile slapped a form in front of him to sign for the IRS. "What did I win?" Abner asked as he scrawled his name on the form after showing the man his driver's license and a credit card. The attendant in the crimson jacket compared the signatures and handed them back.

"Eleven grand, mister. It's my job to tell you to gamble wisely. There, I told you. You can cash out at the cage to your right."

Abner trotted over to the cage, presented his chit, and watched the elderly woman count out hundred-dollar bills and then stuff them in an envelope. She handed it over with a flourish and a warning. "That's a lot of money to be carrying around, son, so be careful."

Abner nodded. He wished there was a way to contact Isabelle so he could tell her that he'd won eleven grand. She'd laugh and say she needed a new pair of Jimmy Choo shoes or a new Chanel bag, or else she'd say something silly, like "Let's put it in the bank for a rainy day."

Before he knew it, he was standing in front of room 412. He knocked loudly. Snowden opened the door and locked it immediately once it closed behind Abner.

"Abner! That's your real name! Well, I'm going to make you wish you were never born, *Abner*! Just as soon as I finish with these people! What do you have to say for yourself, Abner Tookus?" Mary Alice, aka PIP, screeched at the top of her lungs.

Cyrus reared up and growled deep in his throat, a menacing sound that PIP ignored. No damn hairy dog was going to intimidate her. Cyrus growled again to let her know he wasn't intimidated by her, either.

Abner threw his hands in the air. "Whoa! Whoa! I'm sorry. *No*! Actually, damn it, I am not sorry at all. Listen, PIP, don't go all nuclear on me. You need to help these people. And stop being such a hard-ass. I know you're afraid of RC and worried you're going to end up behind bars. Just listen, okay? We're your safe port in this storm."

"What?" Mary Alice screeched again. "Did you forget what he said he'd do if we ever tried to put a face to him? Well, I didn't forget. I have a bloodline, a long bloodline. And I want to keep that bloodline alive and well. Do you hear me?" Her voice was so shrill that Abner had to cover his ears.

Cyrus decided to take matters into his own hands. His ears went flat against his head as he tucked his tail between his legs. He bared his teeth as he advanced toward the screaming woman. This time, PIP took a good look at the snarling dog and clamped her lips tight as she sat down. Cyrus squatted right in front of her.

Harry reached over and tweaked his ear. She went quiet, her eyes suddenly glassy. Cyrus moved off after he nudged Harry's leg and was rewarded with a hard tickle behind his ears.

"You need to lower your voice, young woman. We do not want to disturb the other guests in the hotel. Now, in case you are thinking about telling my colleague and our resident sketch artist something other than the truth in regard to Mr. RC, don't. If you do, I will permanently relocate your nose to right under your left eye. Can you visualize how you would look if that were to happen?" Harry asked quietly. "Good, good. I see you are following me here. Please be accurate in your description."

Mary Alice's head bobbed up and down. "Who . . . who are you? All of you, who are you?" she asked in a hushed whisper.

"No one you want to take home to meet your mother," Jack said so quietly, PIP had to strain to hear the words. "We're counting on that pixel-sharp photographic memory that Abner said you had. I know you don't want to disappoint us." Jack turned his back on her and winked at Abner. Women were so predictable. He gave Cyrus a thumbs-up. Cyrus woofed softly.

"Are you sure about those ears? They look too big," Espinosa muttered as he stared at the picture he was sketching.

"I'm sure. I told you RC is a very large man. That means his head is big, and so are his ears. Everything matches up to his size. I know what I saw and what I remember. Show it to that Benedict Arnold over there," PIP said, tilting her head to where Abner was standing, "to see if that's how he remembers him."

Espinosa waved the picture under Abner's

nose. Other than having a little more detail, Mary Alice's memory of RC was almost a duplicate of the sketch Espinosa had made based on Abner's recollection.

Charles intervened. "Had you ever seen the man before that particular convention?"

"No. I've never seen him since, either. All of our contact is via e-mails and texts. He's never gone to another convention, to my knowledge, and I did ask around. I was just as curious as your pal over there. RC doesn't have to go to those things. He's the head guru."

"You did a remarkable job of describing the man to my colleague here. Is there anything else you remember about his person? I know it's a lot to ask, but it is vitally important. Please think. What, if anything, do you remember?" Charles said in his most complimentary voice.

"He was like a giant. Think *Jack and the Bean-stalk*. Not just big. *Really* big. He dwarfed the room. Took it over. He was the eight-hundred-pound gorilla that day, and we were all so in awe of him. I was very jealous when he singled out Tookus over there, because he was just a green kid. I think he would have to special order his clothes. That's how big he was.

"For such a big man, he was very soft spoken. He was also kind. He managed to take a few minutes with everyone in the room. He spent the most time with me and Tookus there. I was flattered that he took me under his wing and worked with me all these years, and now you want me to betray him. I don't think so!

Unless you plan on killing me, you had better let me go right now!"

One look at Harry and Cyrus, and she backed down immediately. "Please let me go. I won't tell anyone about this. I swear I won't."

Charles stood up. "Unfortunately, Miss Farmer, we can't do that right now. I do want to assure you that you are safe with us. No harm will come to you. We have a very serious situation here that we are investigating. At the moment, unfortunately, I am not at liberty to disclose any details to you. That may change as we go along, but for now, you will have to be content to enjoy your . . . Let's call it a mini-vacation. You can order anything you want from room service, as much as you want from the four five-star restaurants in this fine establishment. You can catch up on the latest movies. What you are *not* free to do is leave this room, unless one of our people escorts you. And make no mistake. You will be on an invisible leash. When this is over, we will compensate you for any income you might have lost because of your . . . um . . . vacation. It goes without saying that you will have no access to a computer or cell phone."

Mary Alice looked around the room at the faces staring at her. Her gaze lingered on Harry and Cyrus longer than on the others. "That damn well sucks!" she exploded. "How long am I going to be here? I know that guy!" she said, pointing to Harry. "He's some kind of martial arts guy!"

Harry smiled and offered up a deep bow.

Her eyes on Abner Tookus, Mary Alice directed her question to Harry. "You were kidding about moving my nose to under my eye, right? You can't really do that. Can you?"

"Yes, I can, and no, I wasn't kidding," Harry said quietly.

Cyrus let loose with his one bark of agreement.

"Oh, shit! Okay, okay. Since I don't have any other choice, I'll do what you say. I want it on the record that this is kidnapping. You kidnapped me! When this is over, I am going to put the word out on you, Tookus. Count on it!"

Abner hated the look on her face. No one had ever talked to him like that before. "When this is over, I hope you feel differently. If not, I guess I'll have to live with it."

"Damn straight you'll have to live with it," Mary Alice said belligerently.

As one, the group moved off to the sitting area of the room and conversed in low tones. It was finally agreed that two of Snowden's people, one male, one female, would stay behind to watch over their guest while the others headed back to Babylon.

Snowden sent off a text on the ride down in the elevator. "I sent out a call for three more operatives. They'll be on the next flight out. What's the plan?"

The plan they decided on within thirty minutes of returning to Babylon was to check out Dixson Kelly's digs. First, Charles sent an e-mail to Maggie to warn her that under no circumstances was she to let Kelly out of her sight. Jack then sent off a text to Bert, asking what they needed to be aware of in regard to other security. Bert called back within seconds on the secure phone.

Bert bristled a bit when Jack outlined their plan, but he finally agreed to call a one-hour closed-circuit meeting in conference room three with Pete Justice, Kelly's second in command, along with the rest of Babylon's security team.

He bristled again when Sparrow said very matter-of-factly that something was off in regard to Kelly. "I'm hoping we come up dry. If not, we'll do what we have to do. That's the way it works. You know that. Look, buddy, you called us, not the other way around. You want to call this off, say the word, and we're outta here."

"No, no. We need to know what's going on. Let's just hope it's a false alarm where Dix is concerned. Call me back the minute you leave his apartment. Are you planning on checking his condo in town and the room he keeps at Babylon?"

"That's a really stupid question coming from a former director of the FBI," Sparrow said.

"You're right. Old habits die hard. Call me when you're out of the apartment."

Sparrow promised to do that very thing and ended the call.

"Abner, you need to . . . uh . . . short-circuit the feed to the floor cameras. You can do that, right?" Fergus asked.

Abner nodded.

"Do every other floor or every third floor, so they think it's just a glitch. Ten minutes on, ten minutes off, that kind of thing. Remember, these people take security more seriously than they do at the White House. We'll keep an open channel for Sparrow so they can enter on the ten minutes off and exit the same way."

Abner was busy clicking away as Snowden, Jack, Harry, Cyrus, and Sparrow left the suite to take the stairs down to the seventeenth floor. Snowden's two operatives left for the eighth floor, where Kelly kept a room. Sparrow would stay in the stairwell to stand guard. They all agreed that the condo in town would be searched later.

Snowden cracked the fire door and looked out into the long, luxurious hallway, which was decorated with fresh flowers—lilacs—the scent heady and intoxicating. He looked over at Sparrow, who had his phone to his ear. He nodded. Sparrow nodded, then said "Go!"

He watched as the three men sprinted halfway down the hall to room 1709. The card reader went in and out; then they were in the room, the door locked behind them. Sparrow let loose with a long sigh just as the elevator door opened and three giddy women ran down the opposite hallway, laughing and joking about their three-hundred-dollar win on the penny slots. He wished he were in the room with the guys, but he knew if there was anything to find, they'd find it.

Inside the room, the three men split up. It took only a few minutes to discover that Dixson Kelly liked fine things. He had a closet full of designer suits and shoes. The dresser drawers revealed top-of-the-line monogrammed shirts. Another drawer held pricey cashmere sweaters and outdoor wear. The top drawer held men's jewelry: several Rolex watches, a dive watch, a West Point ring, gold chains, three different pinkie rings, diamond cuff links, and a stick pin.

Snowden turned to the guys and said, "These things must be gifts from women. Wonder how he keeps them straight. Must keep a black book somewhere. Imagine showing up wearing some other chick's gift?" Snowden cackled at his own wit.

Jack and Harry just rolled their eyes. Cyrus patrolled the apartment by sniffing everything and anything but came up dry and went to sit by the door.

The second closet held ski equipment and other sports items: a tennis racket, duffel bags, two bowling balls, a set of weights. Other sports equipment had been pushed into the back of the closet. There was no way of knowing if the equipment belonged to Bert or Dixson Kelly.

"Kitchen and living room are clear. Looks like he's a mystery reader. That's about it. The books look like they've been read, unless they belong to Bert," Jack said.

"Nothing in the fridge but bottled water, wine, and beer," Harry said.

Snowden laughed. "Boys, the mother lode is right here in front of us, on this dresser. Take a look." He cackled. "Nine burner phones. With a name alongside each one in a little black book. I gotta say, this guy has it going on. Okay, quick now," he said, glancing at his watch. "Check the messages and the dates they were left. Be careful not to delete them. Upload them to your phones and send them off to Charles. Then we gotta get out of here. What's Sparrow saying?"

"He just sent a text saying we need to move our asses. Lots of traffic in the hall. Said security is running around like headless chickens. They're due to hit this floor anytime now," Jack said.

"Tell him to cause a diversion!" Snowden barked.

"Like what?" Sparrow barked in return over the open channel.

"If it looks like they're heading this way, go down a couple of floors and pull the fire alarm. Then meet us up on our floor."

"Stupid is as stupid does," Sparrow mumbled under his breath as he made his way down the stairs to the next floor, the phone tight against his ear. Even in the stairwell, which was solid concrete, he could hear the running feet and the shouts outside the fire door. Snowden was right; these people did take their security seriously.

"Almost done," Jack said. "My hat is off to this guy."

"He should be dead by now, if what all these women are saying is true," Harry growled.

"I wonder when he sleeps," Jack said as he finished the last upload to Charles. "Okay, done!"

"Me, too!" Harry said.

"Make sure the phone numbers match up to the names they're assigned to," Snowden said.

"We're good. C'mon. We need to get out of here," Jack hissed.

"Everything put back in place?" Snowden asked.

"We didn't touch anything but the phones, so yeah, everything is okay. Let's go!"

"Are we ten on or off? I lost track," Harry said.

"We're coming up to off. A minute to go, according to Sparrow, and security is on the fifteenth floor and working their way up here. Come on, come on. Move!" Jack cracked the door to look out into the hallway in time to hear the elevator swish shut.

They raced to the end of the hall, with Cyrus in the lead. They barreled through the door and galloped up the steps, taking them two at a time. They exited on the concierge floor and flopped down on the buttery leather chairs in the hospitality area. Jack popped up a moment later and grabbed three beers from the refrigerator under the counter and a bottle of water, which he poured into a bowl for Cyrus, who lapped up the whole thing. Jack pulled out a fourth longneck when he saw Sparrow walk through the door.

Their breathing had just returned to normal and they were sipping on the longneck Buds and discussing their winnings when the door flew open and six men rushed into the hospitality area.

"Hey! Hey! What's going on?" Snowden

said, brandishing his longneck. "No one is supposed to be on this floor but us. What's going on?" he repeated.

Cyrus was on his feet in a second, snarling and growling. The security team stepped back.

Jack thought they looked like Special Forces guys, even though they were wearing suits and ties. "Yeah, what's going on? Easy, Cyrus. They're friendlies."

Sparrow remained quiet, hoping against hope that the men didn't look at him too closely.

"Camera feed went out. Sorry for the intrusion, gentlemen. Everything is okay here on the floor?"

"Other than the beer isn't ice-cold, we haven't had any complaints. Feel free to pass on my comment," Harry said coolly.

The spokesman for the group stepped forward. "And you would be . . . ?"

Harry stuck out his hand. "Harry Wong. I'm a personal friend of Bert Navarro, as are these other gentlemen, as well as the dog. Actually, Bert is the dog's godfather."

"I know . . . you're the . . . okay, okay, sorry for disturbing you folks. Just doing our job."

"And I'm sure you do it very well. We'll pass that on to Bert the next time we talk to him, won't we, guys?" Harry smiled his special evil smile.

"You bet," Jack said.

"Absolutely," Snowden said.

"Yes, we will," Sparrow mumbled as he turned to look at something over his shoulder.

Cyrus barked three times.

The moment the door closed behind the six men, Jack had Abner on the phone. "Wrap it up, Abner. We're good here. We'll be coming down the hall to the room any minute now, so have the door open."

Snowden rubbed his hands together. "I think that went rather well, all things considered. Now we can concentrate on the messages on those nine phones. *Nine* phones! This has to be a first!"

Chapter 9

Even though the windows were tinted on the concierge floor, the gang could see that it was going to be a beautiful day. They had assembled, per Charles's orders, to discuss strategy and eat the breakfast that had been set out for them.

With the sun doing its best to invade the large, spacious area where they were all gathered, Charles assessed the group. He wasn't happy at what he was seeing. Maggie looked like an angry wet cat, her eyes spewing sparks; Ted was sullen and nontalkative. Espinosa simply looked out of it, while Dennis chowed down on fluffy golden scrambled eggs, which the others were just picking at.

Charles let his gaze go to Abner, who looked like he hadn't slept a wink. His hair was stand-

ing on end, he was unshaven, and his eyes were
red and bloodshot. He was drinking tomato
juice and nibbling on toast. His gaze moved to
Jack and Harry, who simply looked . . . He
searched for the word he was looking for and
came up with *expectant.* From there, his gaze
moved to Avery Snowden, who looked ready,
in his opinion, to pounce on someone or
something.

Cyrus was the only one who looked happy
and content. He'd had his early morning out-
ing, followed by a monster breakfast, and was
now waiting for tidbits from the dawdlers.

"Who wants to go first?" Charles asked.

Maggie raised her hand. Then she waved
her arms about as she grappled with what she
wanted to say. "I've been in this business for a
long time, and the guys agree with me. Kelly is
on to us. Oh, he's cooperating, saying all the
things he thinks we want to hear, but he is
bored out of his mind. His cell phone is glued
to his ear, and he was on it, talking or texting,
the whole time we were with him. Every so
often I'd catch a sly grin, like he knew he was
yanking our chain. Then, when he found out
that Bert had called a special meeting in conference room three, with that guy Pete Justice
running the show, he about exploded. I heard
him arguing with Bert that he should be in
there with the security staff and asking what
the hell was going on. He was not happy. Right
guys?"

The guys agreed.

"Today is going to be more of the same, and he's just about ready to send us packing. I feel it coming," said Maggie.

"I know we signed on for this, but damn, that guy is a piece of work," Ted grumbled.

"He doesn't like to get his picture taken, either. I'm wondering if that might have something to do with those nine burner phones you all were talking about last night. You know, with the ladies and all," Maggie said.

Dennis decided it was time to voice an opinion. "That makes sense. If he has a . . . *harem*, like you guys said, and he's trying to keep his conquests a secret from the others, he doesn't want his picture plastered all over. I gotta say, the guy is photogenic, and he dresses like a male model. It's just my opinion, for whatever it's worth, that he is more worried about the women than about what's going on here at Babylon.

"You guys did catch that moment when he wanted Pete Justice to stand in for him, right? Maggie chopped him off at the knees and told him this article was about him, not Pete Justice. I don't think it would hurt to get some stuff on Justice and a couple of good shots. The guy is a good-looking dude, and he was in Special Forces. The public eats up that kind of stuff. In other words, when the public reads this article, as well as the casino owners, they are going to feel really safe and secure knowing these two guys are protecting them and safeguarding their interests. Like I said, that's my opinion."

"And a sterling onc it is, kid," Snowden said.

Harry clapped Dennis on the back in a show of approval. Dennis turned various shades of pink at the compliment.

"Okay, we'll work that angle today," Maggie said. "But just for the record, I'd rather be trailing around with you guys. What else do we have? Anything I can play into our article?"

All eyes turned to Abner, who was yawning.

"What do you have, sport?" Snowden asked.

"Do you want the short version, or do you want to know what I did? If I told you this is all about unbreakable encryption, diversified cipher keys with rights that afford different degrees of access, would you know what I was talking about? Meaning access is top level, midlevel, low level. Double, triple passwords that are changed hourly sometimes. These casinos use a very sophisticated encryption program. Ever hear about ten-twenty-four-bit polymorphic encryption? Or twenty-forty-eight, forty-ninety-six, or eighty-one-ninety-two?" Abner looked around and said, "That kind of stuff is top level, Pentagon, White House, all top government agencies, and yeah, even the FBI. We're talking rocket-science smarts here."

"So does that mean you can't find out who's helping themselves to the casino's money?" Charles asked.

"I didn't say that. I was just explaining what I am dealing with. And I'm just one person. I hate to bring this up, much less even suggest it, but how about if you bring PIP on board, and the two of us work on it? You want quick. That's the only way I can give you quick, and even then, no matter how much I would like to, I cannot guarantee anything."

"You still think it's that guy RCHood?" Fergus asked.

"More so now than ever. Then you guys had me stop and go to work on those burner phones. I was up all night doing that. I'm going to blow your socks off with what I found."

"What?" they chorused as one.

Cyrus was up and stood at attention. He'd heard the excitement in Abner's voice. Excitement always turned into action, and he did love action. He barked to show he was listening.

Snowden moved forward. He'd finally found something to pounce on.

Abner rubbed at his gritty eyes. "I only had time to run off one copy of all of this, so you can share what I got until you can make more copies. These women, ladies, girls, whatever you want to call the people the phones are allocated to, are past as well as some current relationships Kelly has had and is still involved in. The messages from all of the nine phones are there, separated for easy reading and identification. You may find yourself squirming or getting uncomfortable, because all of them are pretty explicit. I myself got light-headed a couple of times. All indications are that these nine are more or less recent and just the tip of the iceberg. Let me just say, this guy is a legend in his own time.

"Except for burner phone number nine,

which is allocated to one Miss Kitty Passion. She does a lot of purring on the phone, and she also does a lot of 'meowing.' She is not yet a conquest, but Kelly is working on it with all deliberate speed. In other words, they have not as yet slept together. She seems to be playing hard to get, but Kelly is not taking no for an answer. As you will see when you read through all that is in front of you, the man has sent Miss Passion some very provocative messages.

"I listened and was going to finish up, but somehow, for some reason, I just knew that I had to hack into Miss Passion's phone. And let me tell you, I almost fell off my chair when I heard some of the conversations she had with her friends, who are collectively referred to as the Dixson Kelly Alumnae Club."

"I'll *knock* you off that chair if you don't spit it out, Tookus," Harry said.

Abner yawned again before he smacked his hands together to show he was about to get into it. "Okay, okay. Miss Meow is a shill. You all know what a shill is, right? Of course you do. You're in the spook business. These women— and there are a lot of them, thirty or so— they're all showgirls here in Vegas. All of them have had a relationship with Dixson Kelly. Except Miss Kitty Passion, also known as Meow. She's new to Vegas, has only been here for a little over two years. One of the girls at MGM recruited her, and she's all for it.

"As I said, these women refer to themselves as the Dixson Kelly Alumnae. They are banding together to do . . . something to him. What, I don't know. I went back and hacked into all their phones, but while they talked around it, up and down it, they never came outright and said what nefarious deed it is that they're going to try to pull off.

"One of the women—Kitty, I think—arranged a meeting in town, at a place called the Cat & Cradle, for Friday at noon. That was their original plan, but two of the women called and said they couldn't get off their day jobs, so the meeting was moved up to *today* at noon. You all might want to think about attending." Abner yawned again, barely able to keep his eyes open.

"Did you get any sense of what this dastardly deed is that the women are planning?" Jack asked.

"Yes and no," Abner said, his eyes drooping. "Whatever it is, they said he would go to prison, and when and if he got out of prison, his dick would be the size of . . . I can't remember the word they used, but it made me laugh out loud. These women are vicious. Can I go to bed now? Everything is there for your reading pleasure." He tapped the tabletop to make his point before he stumbled out of the room.

As one, those in the group looked at each other. Clearly, none of what Abner had told them was anything any of them had expected.

"This might be the thread that does link Mr. Kelly to what Bert is worried about. Obviously, some of us need to attend this particular luncheon. I suggest Harry and Jack. But Cyrus has to stay behind on this one. Avery, I want you to put your two operatives on this," Charles said, pointing to Abner's report on the nine burner phones. "Sift through those messages and texts. Something might jump out at you. There might be something that Abner was too tired to pick up on. But only when you get back from the Cat & Cradle. You three need to be Harry and Jack's backup at the restaurant."

Maggie jumped to her feet. "Charles, did you just say what I think you said? You're sending men to do this, without a woman in tow! I can't believe you would do that! What are you thinking? We either need to give Kelly the day off or just have the guys babysit him. I need to go to the Cat & Cradle. I can come up with a story and maybe get invited to join up since I already know the backstory. If they're determined to burn Kelly, I might be able to add some fuel to the fire. By now, you all should know it pays to have someone on the inside, and I am obviously that someone."

"Sounds good to me," Jack said. "Harry, what do you think?"

Always a man of few words, Harry simply nodded and said, "Yeah."

"Then I guess that settles that," Charles said. He looked at Maggie and smiled. "I don't know what I was thinking, my dear. Forgive me. You are absolutely right. Now, is there anything else we need to discuss?"

Sparrow spoke for the first time. "Abner mentioned that it might help if we could convince PIP to join the cause. While I am not a computer wizard, I do understand what he is talking about. Two sets of fingers tapping and hacking are better than one set. How about if I meander over to The Venetian and escort PIP back here, along with Mr. Snowden's two operatives? I think we can smuggle her in."

Charles tapped the spook on the arm. "Are you in agreement, Avery?"

Without taking his eyes off his reading material, Snowden nodded.

"All right, then, let's sit here and plan Miss PIP's extraction," Fergus said.

"Hold on. Hold on. Should we inform Bert? We don't know for sure that this little side venture has anything to do with why we're here. He might not want us wasting our time on a gaggle of women wanting revenge on the man because they were scorned," Jack said.

"Let's not tell him till after the luncheon. If it's nothing of concern, all we've done is waste an hour or so," Maggie said. "But if it will make you feel better, we can vote on it. Raise your hand if you're in favor of holding off on informing Bert." Every hand in the room went in the air. "Well, I guess that settles that!"

Maggie was so gleeful, Jack cringed. Maggie could be the proverbial bull in a china shop. He relaxed almost immediately when he thought about the reporter's uncanny ability to ferret out what needed to be ferreted out and make it seem natural.

The group scattered to get ready for whatever the rest of the day held in store for them.

* * *

Philonias Needlemeyer stepped out onto his skinny terrace, coffee cup in hand, to view the new day. He loved spring. Hated summer because he sweated like a Trojan. He could take or leave winter. With nothing on his agenda, he might throw caution to the winds and take a walk, go to a park, feed pigeons, contemplate his navel, and think about the luncheon that he planned to attend tomorrow at the Cat & Cradle.

Philonias finished his coffee, looked around at the new day from his lofty penthouse perch, then entered his apartment. He never bothered to lock his French doors. The only way anyone could enter the penthouse was by dropping from the sky. The thought always amused him.

He looked down at his watch. Ten thirty. He'd slept in this morning, something he never did, unless he had a cold or the flu. But he hadn't gone to bed until six o'clock, because he'd been up all night hacking into Bert's, Kelly's, and Pete Justice's text messages. In the end, there had been nothing to alert him to anything of concern.

It was eleven thirty when Philonias, showered, shaved, and coiffed, took his seat in his computer room. Half the day was already gone. He hated that. Now his whole day was ruined; his routine shattered. He might as well chalk it up to a wasted day and sit down and read a good book. But something perverse in him made him take his computer out of sleep mode and do *something*. He recalled his parents telling him as a child that one had to do *something*, no matter what it was, each and every day, or the day would hold no meaning. He still, to this day, subscribed to that old adage.

Very little had happened in the early hours of the morning. If something had happened here at Babylon, a warning alert would have shown up the moment he brought his computer out of its sleep mode. That had not happened. Those four hours of sleep from six to ten had been an uneventful time. So, what should he do? He finally decided to check on Miss Kitty Passion to see if any other showgirls were going to attend the luncheon tomorrow besides the ones she had personally called herself. The Dixson Kelly Alumnae Club. He chuckled at the thought. If Kelly only knew.

Philonias tapped the keys, then stared at what he was seeing. *No!* He blinked and then blinked again. "Damn it to hell! They changed the date!" The words exploded out of his mouth like gunshots. He forced himself to look at his watch. Eleven fifty. There was no way in hell he could make it to town, even if he sprouted wings. Traffic in Vegas was horrendous no matter the hour of the day. In order to be on time for anything, especially in town, you had to allow for an extra hour traveling. Plain and simple, he was not going to the meeting of the Dixson Kelly Alumnae Club at the Cat & Cradle. Not tomorrow, not today, not ever.

Fluent in five languages, Philonias cursed in all of them as he stomped his feet in frustration. He spent all of ten seconds wondering if there was some way he could still make it, even if he got there late. Lunches where women were concerned usually ran to ninety minutes, ditto for businessmen. He wasn't stupid. Even if by some miracle he managed to get to town, he would have to enter the café and have everyone in the room stare at him, which then meant they would remember the big man. Not an option. He cursed again, this time more loudly.

He was beaten, and he knew it.

Angry and frustrated, he marched to the kitchen for another cup of coffee. While he heated it in the microwave, he munched on an apple. His day was truly ruined.

All he could do was check his own phone texts, his e-mails, and when he was done with that, read some sappy novel that never should have been published in the first place. He had no idea what had happened to the publishing industry in the years since he came of age, but it seemed as if the bulk of what was published these days was either about vampires running around in fancy cars or heroines from the Regency period hooking up with some duke or earl who was either penniless or worth more than the queen of England.

Maybe one of these days, he'd write a book. A book that would send people scurrying for cover for their blatant stupidity. Someday.

Cup in hand, Philonias made his way back to his computer room. He took a gulp of coffee and yelped at his burned tongue. "Son of a bitch!" He plopped the cup down on the desk with such force, the hot coffee spilled and trickled down his pant leg. He cursed again.

He knew in every pore in his body that things were closing in on him. He could feel it, and he could smell his own fear. The urge to cry was so great, he squeezed his eyes shut to ward off the burning feeling. When he finally opened them, he took deep breaths to calm himself down. Clicking the keyboard was hypnotic for him. Always was, always would be. Other people needed Xanax. All he needed was a computer keyboard to bring his world into focus and calm down.

He tapped now to check his e-mails. He had hundreds, most of them meaningless. He would get to them eventually; he always did. What he didn't see were any e-mails from TRIPLEM or PIP. He'd sent out two to each of them, and neither had been answered. In the past, he'd always gotten an instant response from his two star pupils. Philonias could feel his heartbeat escalate. He hacked into their phones. Dormant. No calls out in over twenty-four hours on either phone. PIP had a few incoming calls and texts. He read them. Nothing to send up a red flag. PIP's calls concerned her organic seed business, she had a few personal texts about taking in a movie with a girlfriend, and the post office had called to say she had a package to pick up. Nothing there. He went on to TRIPLEM, only to see absolutely nothing.

Nothing was worse than something. Alarm

bells started ringing in his head. And then Philonias started to shake.

Philonias looked around his lair. He'd lived here a long time. It was home. He loved it. The thought of possibly losing it brought tears to his eyes.

He needed to get out of here, even if it was just for ten minutes. He remembered the promise he'd made to himself earlier, that he'd go for a walk to the park to feed the pigeons.

And that was exactly what he was going to do. Right now, right this minute.

Chapter 10

Jack opened the door to the Cat & Cradle at precisely ten minutes to eleven, with Harry and Maggie behind him. He sniffed appreciatively. The smell of cheese and garlic permeated the air in the cozy old restaurant, which was a Las Vegas fixture. At least that was what the brochure at the hotel attested to.

The Cat & Cradle was owned by a fourth-generation Italian couple: Stella and Tony Cordello. The place was nestled between two ricky-ticky casinos that were just as old as the Cat & Cradle itself. Over the years, the Cordellos, along with the owners of the two ricky-ticky casinos, had been offered millions for their little slices of real estate. Much to the chagrin of those making the offers, and renewing the offers at least once a year, the owners always turned them down. The response to the offers was always an impeccably polite "No thank you. We are quite happy with the way things are." And despite attempts to get the city of Las Vegas to exercise its right of eminent domain and sell the property to those making the offers, the restaurant had such strong support in the city that no politician would go anywhere by taking it away from the Cordellos. Which protected the two casinos, as well.

The eatery was overseen by the elder Cordellos, but they did little more than *schmooze* with the customers. The day-to-day operation was handled by two sons, two daughters, and assorted grandchildren, who milled about, filling water glasses, handing out extra napkins, helping with the to-go bags, which every customer left with. As the elder Cordellos said, the youngsters were learning to handle the practical side of the operation, which would one day be their own.

When they first opened the place, the original owners, the first generation of Cordellos to own and operate a restaurant, had decided to serve only breakfast and lunch. Lunch would run to four o'clock, and then the place would be shut down and cleaned from one end to the other. The great-great-grandfather of the clan had said that money was more easily made by selling eggs, pancakes, and waffles than by serving a steak at night. His family had followed his tradition, and they all went home to their families at night, because that was where families belonged—at home. The kids, too, because they had to be up at four in the morning to start serving breakfast at six o'clock to the long line of customers waiting outside the doors.

The decor was simple, comfortable, and homey, so much so, in fact, that the diners had to be prodded to leave once the bill was paid, so the others in line could take their place. Black-and-white-checkered curtains hung on the windows and were washed and starched once a week. The windows were also washed once a week and sparkled in the spring sunlight. The tables were round, solid oak, old, and scarred, full of character, with red-and-white place mats, which matched the cushions on the comfortable captain's chairs that graced every table.

The main dining area had eighteen tables, and off to the side was a special room for extra-large parties, called the Reservation Room. Off to the left and down a short hallway was the ladies' room, and to the right and down an identical short hallway was the men's room.

Maggie took it all in at a glance, and she knew exactly where she wanted to be seated once she noticed that the long table in the Reservation Room, which could easily seat at least twenty people, was already set up. She immediately knew the table had been set up for the Dixson Kelly Alumnae Club.

She locked eyeballs with a young, rosy-cheeked woman with merry eyes and a fat, curly ponytail running down her back. The girl smiled and asked how many were in their party.

"Just three. We'd like to sit over there," Maggie

said, pointing to the table closest to the Reservation Room.

The young woman, whose name tag said she was Emily, smiled and led the way to the table. Maggie looked at her watch. Eleven fifteen. Forty-five minutes to settle in and wait for the club members to arrive. She looked around and saw that the main dining room was already filled to capacity, so that meant they wouldn't be booted out too quickly. She was allowing a full ninety minutes before the pert little hostess would show them the door.

"What's the plan?" Jack asked, looking around.

"I'll let you know when I figure it out. Truthfully, guys, I don't think there is going to be a plan. I think I'll just wing it. Don't look at me like that, Harry. I'm pretty darn good at flying by the seat of my pants. I've found over the years that an opportunity invariably presents itself if you're patient. You just have to be ready to seize the moment—you know, carpe diem— when you see it. A suggestion here . . . When our waitress comes to take our orders, say you need more time because everything looks so good, and you can't decide. That will give us at least an extra ten minutes, not a minute more."

A little boy around seven or so carried one glass of water at a time, using both hands so he wouldn't spill it, to their table. He grinned, showing his missing front teeth. He lisped when he spoke to welcome them to the Cat & Cradle.

"I think this is going to work," Maggie said.

"As you can see, they're really busy. They haven't taken our drink order yet. When they come to do that, they usually ask if you're ready to order. That's when you say no and pretend to study the menu to gain time. If my calculations are right, we should be placing our food order just about the time that the members of the so-called club start to arrive. I think this place is the kind of place where, if you are not on time, they give your table to those who are waiting in line. I can see a long line outside from here."

"You look nervous, Maggie. You need to kick back here, or you're going to blow it," Jack warned, not liking how tense she looked.

"I know. I know. I guess because my gut is telling me this is really important and has to do with what Bert is worried about. It's my gut, so that could or could not mean *something.*"

"I think so, too," Harry said, surprising both Jack and Maggie that he had even been paying attention. Sometimes, Harry Wong was a mystery.

"Here comes the girl to take our drink order. Play it up, boys."

All three ordered iced tea and begged for a few minutes. Maggie did her best to engage the young waitress in conversation by asking what the specials were and what the Cat & Cradle was best known for. The girl, who looked a bit frazzled, said everything on the menu was delicious and cooked from scratch, even the bread. She said she would be back in a few minutes. And that was the end of that.

The time was 11:51.

Out of the corner of her eye, Maggie noticed five tall, attractive, casually dressed women weaving their way through the tables to the Reservation Room and then to the head of the largest table in the room.

"Game on," Jack whispered as he buried his nose in the oversize menu.

At five minutes past the hour, the threesome placed their orders. Maggie and Jack opted for the spaghetti and meatballs because they figured they would gain a few minutes until the pasta was cooked. Harry ordered a garden salad after the waitress promised the greens were from the owners' very own garden. He asked for the soy dressing on the side, then asked if they could double the amount of edamame beans in the salad. The waitress assured him that could be done.

Thanks to Maggie's wise choice of tables, she and Jack had a clear view of the women at the long table. Harry had only a partial view, but that didn't prevent him from offering up a comment.

"It's hard to believe all those women are showgirls. They look more like soccer moms or suburbanites. Look at how they're dressed." With Harry, it was hard to tell if he was voicing approval or disapproval.

"Incognito to a point," Maggie said as she eyeballed the women's attire. Some wore jeans with holes in the knees, sneakers, capris with flip-flops, slacks and tees. None of them appeared to be wearing makeup or jewelry, and yet they still managed to look beautiful and drew plenty of male attention from the diners, and even from a couple of the waitstaff. Two of the women wore baseball caps and had long ponytails hanging down their backs. All of the women carried whopping carry bags or backpacks.

"Obviously, this is their day off, and they don't want to wear all that theatrical makeup, which is so hard on your complexion, and dress to the nines. This is a girls' luncheon with *an agenda*. La natural. In other words, guys, they do not want to call attention to themselves and really do not care how they look."

The threesome continued to watch as the women greeted one another, laughed and joked as they poked each other on the arm. For all intents and purposes, a fun luncheon with a large group of friends. Carafes of white wine were placed on the table. The little boy who had delivered the water to their table had been replaced with a gangly young boy who carried a tray of water glasses and set them on the table for the women to help themselves.

"They're just socializing right now. They won't get to the main event until they've finished the first glass of wine. So, relax, guys. I know how this works," Maggie said, her voice ringing with authority. Since this was really Maggie's show, there was really nothing for Jack or Harry to do but go with the flow.

"Hold that thought, guys. A text is coming through from Sparrow," Jack said.

While Jack's fingers worked the keys, Maggie looked around to see if she could spot Snowden and the two operatives he'd brought with him. She finally spotted one of the females in the little hallway by the women's restroom. She smiled to herself, because she knew that the button on the operative's blouse was a mini-camera and that she had positioned herself to film the women she could see at the long table. Maggie's gaze traveled to the opposite hallway in time to see the male operative doing the exact same thing. That was good. They had photographed everyone on both sides of the table. At least now they would know who they were dealing with. They no longer had just a burner phone with a name. They had real flesh and blood to complete the ID.

What happened next made Maggie's eyebrows shoot up to her hairline. She kicked Jack under the table and rolled her eyes. Snowden's two operatives converged at the same moment from the restrooms and collided at the end of the long table. Both laughed and apologized profusely to the women, who just stared at them, mesmerized by their clipped British accents. Maggie wondered if anyone but she and Jack saw the clever sleight of hand with which a listening device was planted under the table just as Snowden himself showed up, presumably to enter the restroom. He deftly sidestepped the two operatives, and a second device was planted behind one of the women's chairs.

"Slick," Harry said as he speared a chunk of lettuce onto his fork.

"Yeah. That's why he gets paid the big bucks," Maggie said.

Maggie's cell phone vibrated in her pocket. Charles. She looked down at the text, then over at Jack. "Do we stay or go?" she hissed.

"Time to go," the two Snowden operatives on babysitting duty said at the same time.

Mary Alice looked at them with defiance, wondering what, if anything, would happen if she dug in her heels and refused to leave now that the Chinese guy and the killer dog were gone. Then, her eyes narrowed into slits, she looked over at Sparrow, who was watching her carefully.

"I know what you're thinking," he said. "I know what you *think* you can do once we get you outside. You *think* you'll be able to alert someone by screaming or somehow calling attention to yourself. Right now, right this very second, I want you to rid yourself of such foolish, negative thoughts, because it isn't going to happen. Do you want to know why that isn't going to happen, Miss PIP?"

"Why? Because you're going to kill me! You goddamn well kidnapped me, and that is against the law. In broad daylight," PIP shrilled. "I know who you are, too! So there! I've seen your pictures in the paper. You head up the FBI. Wait till I get out of here! You just wait! I'm going to sell my story to every damn tabloid there is. Picture this, you bastard! Director of FBI kidnaps woman and takes her across state lines to hack into a gambling casino! Can you picture that! Huh? Well, can you, huh?" she screeched.

"No. Because that is not going to happen. I want you to picture *this*. It's a felony to lie to an FBI agent. We can hold you for seventy-two hours without benefit of counsel. People other than myself, those more . . . shall we say . . . attuned to dealing with people like you, might take it into their heads to secure or extract whatever they think might be in your head. Waterboarding is not off the table. Sodium Pentothal is another possibility. Now, if you ever want to send out another packet of your organic seeds to your customers, straighten up and fly right." Sparrow threw his hands in the air and said to the two operatives, "Do it. She's not going to cooperate."

"Do what? What are you . . . listen . . . okay, okay," Mary Alice screeched.

"What did I just tell you about your decibel level? As my mother always used to tell me, 'Indoor voice. Indoor voice.' Or do you have some sort of hearing problem? No, you're lying. I can see it in your eyes," Sparrow said. He turned to Snowden's two operatives. "Just do it so we can leave," he said to the two operatives.

Before she could move, blink, or draw a deep breath, PIP felt something go around her neck and clamp shut. She tried to grab for it, but someone yanked at her arm and held it steady. Snowden's operative then clamped a bracelet onto her wrist that was attached by a fancy, gem-studded chain to an identical bracelet, which she clipped onto her own wrist.

"What you're now wearing, Miss PIP, is something that is more or less like a dog collar that pet owners use to train their dogs. This collar, while pretty and sparkly, will choke you if you so much as make a whimper. All that pretty lady has to do is move that jewel-studded tether, and you're toast. Nod if you understand what I just said. Remember what I said would happen to you if you so much as whimper."

Mary Alice's eyes filled with tears as her head frantically bobbed up and down so fast, the air moved around her head to create a breeze.

"I thought you'd see it my way," Sparrow said happily. "I'll meet you all at the elevator. I want to go through this suite one more time, just to be on the safe side."

Ten minutes later, the foursome climbed into a rental SUV with tinted windows. Sparrow sat in the passenger seat up front, while PIP and the female operative sat in the back.

Traffic was a bear, as the operative put it. Traveling from The Venetian to Babylon should have taken less than ten minutes, but with all the traffic, it took a full thirty to get them to a parking spot in the first-floor parking garage. Earlier, Sparrow had been the one who rooted around in the maintenance room until he found four bright orange road cones and who then positioned them in the parking space so it would be available to them on their return.

He climbed out, stacked the cones, and carried them back to the maintenance room.

Sparrow practiced his tradecraft the way he always did when he found himself in strange surroundings. He was instantly aware of everything around him. He saw two cars move, one parking, one backing out. He heard and half saw the stairwell door open, saw a figure walk through the opening and continue down the side of the garage just as the doors of the SUV opened to allow PIP and the operatives to climb out. Nothing bothered him or put him on alert until he saw PIP jerk and point, and he knew she was about to try to scream or shout.

Sparrow ran across the garage, expertly avoiding the car backing out of its spot and straightening out. He watched as PIP frantically pawed at the jeweled collar around her throat, her eyes wild and yet pleading, as her arms and hands jabbed forward.

"Take it off!" Sparrow ordered. The operative did as she was told.

Mary Alice gasped again and again as she struggled to draw air into her lungs. "That was RC! I just saw him. When the door to the stairs opened, he walked right out into the garage and went that way!" she croaked hoarsely as she pointed to her left.

Sparrow didn't stop to think or to wonder if the woman was lying. He reacted to the moment and his long years of training. He ran, shouting over his shoulders for the operatives to reconnect the collar and take PIP to the concierge floor.

Sparrow was glad at the moment for all the early morning hours he had spent in the gym. He wasn't even breathing hard, much less breaking a sweat, as he tore outside, brought up his hand to his forehead to ward off the sun, and searched to see if PIP was telling the truth. There was no sign of the big man whom she and Tookus had described. He squinted to let his mind race. The frantic young woman had seen someone who was on her radar. Like he had half seen someone exiting the garage door. He looked right and left and saw a young man in a brown uniform patrolling the perimeter of the casino.

"Hey, did you happen to see a really big guy out here in the past few minutes?" Sparrow asked.

"Yeah, and he was clipping along. That's for sure. He went that way," the man in the brown uniform said, pointing a finger to the left of the driveway. "There's a side street over there, and sometimes cabs line up there. I think he hailed a cab. Can't be sure, because I really wasn't paying attention. He was big, though."

Sparrow took a deep breath. "Describe big!" He fished around in his pocket and withdrew a twenty-dollar bill and held it out as an incentive.

"Well now, let me think. You look to be around six-two, right?"

Sparrow nodded.

"Okay, that guy had twelve inches on you. You know that Asian guy who played basketball? Yao Ming, I think. He was that tall. Weight-wise . . .

close to three hundred pounds, but even so, he moved easily. He didn't, you know, lumber the way some fat guys do. This guy was not fat. He was just big. Does that help?"

"Have you ever seen him before around the casino?"

"Nah. I'd remember someone that big. Check and see if there's a line of cabs over on the side street. Talk to them. I really think he took a cab, so I must have seen something out of the corner of my eye."

After handing over the twenty, Sparrow took off at a fast sprint. There were four cabs parked in a line. He walked up to the first one in line and posed his question. The driver just stared at him until Sparrow handed over a fifty-dollar bill, because that was all he had in his pocket.

"Yeah, a great big guy did come this way. Couldn't make up his mind if he was going to take a cab or not. Then someone else came along and climbed in. He left, went down this street, and the only thing in that direction is a crummy park with a little pond that's all scummy. Sorry I can't be more help."

"What about the other drivers? Do you know them?"

"In a manner of speaking. The two behind me speak little to no English. The last guy I don't know at all. They all just sit there and read their papers while they wait for a fare. The last guy in line is a foreigner, too. He might speak English, but I'm not sure."

Since he was out of cash, Sparrow also figured he was out of options, so he ignored the last cab in line and ran down the street, toward what the first cabdriver had described as a crummy park with a scummy pond. He was right on both counts. An overweight teenager was throwing a Frisbee to a yellow Lab, who jumped in the air to catch it. Sparrow chuckled to himself as he toyed with the idea of telling the kid to have the dog toss the Frisbee so he could run to catch it.

Instead he said, "Hey, kid. Did you see a big guy come through here a few minutes ago?"

"Yeah. Why?"

"Did you see where he went?"

"Nope." He tossed the Frisbee high in the air.

"You sure?" Sparrow asked skeptically, his gaze sweeping the area for clues.

"Dude, I am so sure. You want me to swear on a Bible or something?"

"No. Nice dog. What's his name?"

"It's a her, not a him, and her name is Nellie. Why do you care what her name is? What? You writing a book or something?" the kid asked belligerently.

"Are all you kids so fresh, or is it just you?" Sparrow demanded. He shook his head as he walked away, wondering what had ever happened to courtesy and manners. His shoulders sagged as he walked back the way he'd just come. He'd been *that* close.

When Sparrow was out of sight, the chunky young boy said, "You can come out now, mister. He's gone."

Philonias Needlemeyer stepped out from behind a thick, twelve-foot-high, overgrown privet hedge, which had concealed him from sight. He handed some folded-up bills to the boy and tweaked Nellie's ears before he strode off. His heart pounding in his chest, Philonias exited the crummy park and flagged down a taxi. Two bad ideas in one day. Three mistakes. Things were not looking good.

All he knew was that they were somehow onto him, and he wasn't sure how he should or *could* get rid of them. Whoever the *them* were. He wished now that he had paid more attention to the little skirmish he'd seen out of the corner of his eye as he raced around the corner of the garage. That little to-do had to be something the guy chasing him was involved with. Who were they? How did they get onto him?

Chapter 11

Maggie looked down at her cell phone, then at Jack, just as their waitress appeared to refill their water glasses. Her eyes were full of questions, the main one being: "Leave or not leave?" She shook her head. The spaghetti and meatballs were just waiting to be devoured, and besides, she hadn't had a chance to put her plan into action. Whatever was going to go down back at Babylon could wait. With Charles, Fergus, and Sparrow in charge, she didn't see the need to hustle back. She did love spaghetti and meatballs, and the sauce was just the way she liked it. She sucked on a long strand of spaghetti, the way she'd done when she was a kid. Jack laughed and did the same thing. Harry grimaced, his eyes on the long table in the Reservation Room.

Maggie was well on her way to finishing her

third meatball when one of the women got up
from the table, walked around the end, and
headed for the ladies' room. Maggie was on
her feet in a second and headed in the same
direction. All Harry and Jack could do was
stare at her retreating back.

"What the . . . ," Harry said.

Jack sucked up another long strand of
spaghetti. He looked over at Harry. "I think
that's her plan. Whatever it might be. I'm
thinking we should probably finish up here,
ask for the check, and be ready to leave. Something tells me when she comes out of that
room, she's going to head straight for the
front door. Or . . . she is going to join those
women at the table. If I were a betting man, I'd
go with she's going to be joining the ladies."

Harry popped a thick slice of cucumber
into his mouth. "And you know this . . . how?"
He crunched down, his eyes never leaving the
table where the women were seated.

"Pure gut instinct," Jack said, waving for the
waitress to compute their bill.

Inside the restroom, Maggie headed straight
for the sink, crying and sobbing, as though her
heart were breaking. All she had to do to make
herself cry at any given moment was to remember the day her beloved dog Daisy died. Even
though it had been years since the little dog
passed over the Rainbow Bridge, the memory
was still painful.

The fourth stall at the end of the room
opened, and a young woman with a long
auburn ponytail rushed up to her. "What's

wrong, honey? Are you okay? Are you sick? Do you want me to call someone? Let me help you."

Maggie raised her head and stared into bright blue eyes. She continued to sob. "Do you know how to fix a broken heart?"

"No, no, sweetie, I don't. I wish I did. Been there, though. I'll tell you what all my friends told me. No man is worth your tears. You know what else? Your heart isn't broken. You can't break a heart, because a heart is a muscle. Your heart is just bruised. That means it will heal, even if you don't think so right now. You aren't buying this, are you?" the woman said with a wry grin.

Maggie shook her head. "He promised me the world. He said I was his soul mate. That he wanted to grow old with me. I was supposed to be the mother of our children. He said he wanted four kids, all girls, and for them to look like me. I believed him. I came all the way from Washington because I hadn't heard from him for over three weeks. *Three weeks.* That's an eternity! I met him eight months ago, when I came here to visit my brother. He said we could make a long-distance relationship work, and I believed him. It was all a lie! Oh, God!" Maggie wailed again.

"I've called and called and sent dozens of texts. He never responded, so that's why I came here. Then my brother, who warned me about him when I first started dating him, said he saw him with a beautiful showgirl. I refused to believe him. That's another reason why I came here. I wanted to confront him in person, but I can't reach him. He said we would get engaged next month. He promised me a three-carat emerald-cut diamond. I didn't care about a ring. It could be a zircon, for all I cared. He has money, because he really wined and dined me. He promised a fall wedding, because I love autumn, and he said he did, too." Maggie sobbed harder.

"My brother lives and works here, and he warned me that Dix was a playboy, a love-'em-and-leave-'em kind of guy, but did I listen? Hell, no! Would you listen to your brother or to the man who professed undying love? Oh, God! Oh, God! What am I going to do? I love him so much. Maybe he's sick or in the hospital. I need to check that." Maggie reached for a wad of paper towels and blew her nose. More hard sobs followed as she remembered how she'd wrapped Daisy in a soft, fluffy pink towel. She started to shake then for real, the memory was so strong. "I don't think I can live without him. I don't want to live without him. Oh, God, what am I going to do?"

The young woman, who said her name was Hana, wrapped Maggie in her arms and mouthed soothing words. Maggie had no idea what she was saying.

"I'm sorry. I didn't mean to . . . You've been very kind to someone you don't even know. I need to clean up here and go back to . . . to my brother. He's outside. He and a friend of his brought me here to cheer me up. My brother works at the casino where I'm staying. It's free for me. It's where . . . *he* works, too."

"Did I hear you call him Dix?" Hana asked.

"Did I? I can barely say it out loud, but yes, that's his name. He's some big shot at the casino. At least my brother said he was. Jack— that's my brother—wanted to punch out his lights, but then he'd lose his job, and he needs the job. His friend Harry is a big martial arts guru, and he said he could cripple him or something. Oh, God, I don't want him hurt. I love him. I don't know what to do! Tell me what to do before I lose my mind." Maggie started to wail again, a high keening sound of pure misery, as she recalled how she'd handed the fluffy pink bundle over to the vet.

"You just wait right here, honey. Wash your face and stop crying. I'll be right back."

Outside, Jack handed his credit card to the waitress and stood up to follow her to the cashier. "Move it, Harry."

"What about Maggie?"

"If I'm not mistaken, Maggie is going to be joining that party of women any minute now. See those three women heading for the restroom? That's Maggie's plan. If you can't beat them, join up. In her mind, I guess she thinks it will work. I gotta say, I didn't see that coming. She's got guts. I'll give her that," Jack said.

Outside and fast approaching their rental van, Jack and Harry stepped aside to avoid running into Snowden and his two operatives. After Harry and Jack were ensconced in the

van, Snowden joined them, while his operatives remained on the sidewalk. As far as Jack
could tell, no one was paying any attention to
any of them.

"Nice sleight of hand, Snowden. That was so
slick, I almost missed it," Jack said.

Snowden inclined his head to show he also
marveled at his own sleight of hand. Snowden
did have an ego. "What's taking Maggie so long?
You guys know it's never good to stay in one
place more than a few minutes. Especially out
in the open like this."

Jack filled in Snowden on what he thought
Maggie was doing. "Look, I could be wrong,
but knowing Maggie, it's the only thing that
makes sense. Think about it. I actually believe
she can make it work."

"It's too pat. There is no way she can pull
something like that off. That bunch of women
reeks of savvy to me," Snowden growled, displeased that Maggie had taken matters into
her own hands without his approval.

Like lightning, Harry swiveled around and
put out his hand, the palm a hair from Snowden's face. "You do not know Maggie." His
tone was low and menacing.

Snowden didn't bat an eye, and he didn't
back down. "I may not know what makes Maggie Spritzer tick, but I do know women! And
there is no way in hell that bunch of women is
going to welcome her, a total stranger, into
whatever they're planning."

Jack and Harry both burst out laughing.

"First of all, Snowden, the man hasn't been

born that knows what women are all about," Jack said. "If you think you do, then you're a fool. Since we're in the gambling mecca of our country, I'm willing to make a wager, and Harry, too. We're putting our money on Maggie, ten big ones. What do you say, Snowden? Put up or shut up."

"You're on, hotshot! I concede that I might not know *everything* about women, but I do know a lot. So the bet is Maggie is going to worm her way into the group, they're going to accept her and spill their guts to her, and she will, in turn, spill her guts to us. That's the bet. I just want to be sure."

"That's the bet," Harry said.

"What's the time frame?" Snowden barked, his eyes suddenly worried.

"Ninety minutes for lunch, ten minutes saying good-bye, another ten minutes arranging another meet, travel back to Babylon . . . two, two and a half hours. Three at the most. Make sure you have your money ready, and Harry and I do not take checks. Beat it now. We're heading back to the casino. I'm suddenly feeling lucky."

Snowden offered up his famous single-digit salute, but he did exit the van to return to the Cat & Cradle to keep his eye on what was going on.

"I never did like that guy," Harry said.

"Me, either, but Charles swears by him. It's a Brit thing, I guess."

"Jack, you okay with leaving Maggie here?"

"Yeah. Maggie is smart enough to know we'll

figure out what she's doing. She's a big girl. She can get back on her own. She's fast on her feet and quick on the draw. You know that. If there is a downside, it's that she isn't going to be able to trail around with Kelly and the boys anymore, and that alone will make her happy. One of those women might spot her, and her cover story, whatever it is, gets blown out of the water. She'll be fine, trust me."

"Okay, if you say so. Wonder what's going on right now."

What was going on was that the two women Hana had brought back to the restroom were consoling Maggie and inviting her to join them for lunch. She protested a little and wailed some more when they exited the restroom.

"Look. My brother and his friend left. I don't blame them. They're sick of hearing me cry and whine." She swabbed at her eyes again. She wondered how bad she looked, not that she cared.

"Don't you give it another thought, sweetie. We'll make sure you get back to your hotel safe and sound. We're all going to help you. All of us," Hana Frey said as she pointed to the twenty-five women sitting at the table and eyeing her curiously. "We're actually a club. Of sorts," she said vaguely. "That means we've all been in your shoes and know what you're going through. We help each other. We're going to help you, too, because that's what we women do. We're always there for each other. I just want you to know you can count on us."

Kitty Passion, the shill and the newest mem-

ber of the group by two years, held up her
hand. "I'm not sure this is the place to discuss
what needs to be discussed. I have an idea. How
about we just have lunch, split up, and meet
out at the ranch this evening and have a regular sleepover? We can grill some steaks, drink
some wine, and have a regular girl fest. And, of
course, figure out how we can help Maggie."

The ranch Kitty was referring to was a recent
inheritance and the reason she'd moved to Las
Vegas from Philadelphia. While she didn't have
as much tenure as the others, she'd stepped up
to the plate and become a regular within weeks
of moving to Las Vegas two years ago. The fact
that she was young and had been a showgirl in
Atlantic City had aced her acceptance into the
group. The women loved going out to the ranch
and just doing girl things on their days off. Once
Kitty became comfortable with the group, she'd
handed out keys and said, "*Mi casa, su casa.*"
She'd gone on to say they were welcome anytime, and there was no need to call ahead.
There was only one rule, and that was that no
men were to be brought to the ranch.

Kitty's initiation into the group was that she
had to meet Dixson Kelly, make him fall for
her, then keep him at arm's length. She was to
lead him on, then pull back, to give him a taste
of his own medicine. Kitty had gone at it full
bore and had ended up with Dixson calling
her at all hours of the day and night. Her last
report to the club members was that she had
him right where she wanted him, salivating and
begging her to go out with him. She, in turn,

had told him she was saving herself for marriage and was not some fast and loose chippie. Saving herself meant she was a virgin. She had giggled when she told the club that Dixson had done everything but howl at the moon.

Maggie finally stopped crying, did a few hiccups for good measure, and started to sip at her glass of wine. Charles would have been appalled at the way the women chattered and babbled as they ate their Caesar salads and swigged down wine. Within minutes, Maggie knew she was being interrogated, and it was so masterfully done, she was in awe. No one brought up Dixson Kelly's name; nor did Maggie mention it again. She stayed with her story as they asked in various ways the how, the when, and the what of her relationship with the Vegas honcho, as they called her lover. Between tears and a few sobs, she got her story out.

"I was out of my league. I think I even knew it, but I was in love. I mean, look at me, ladies. I'm a 'what you see is what you get' kind of girl. I'm not beautiful like you all are. Kitty said you're all showgirls. That's the kind of girl he should have been attracted to, not someone like me. I was so flattered. I couldn't believe he hit on me when he did. I guess I'm the stupid one, because when he said he was fed up with false eyelashes, war paint, contact lenses that were all colors of the rainbow, and hair that wasn't real, I believed him. He said he liked running his hands through my curly hair because it didn't come off in his hands.

"When he kissed me, I thought he was going

to suck out my tonsils. I'm going to miss that. He used to trace my freckles with his forefinger. He said my freckles were endearing. Then he said he was glad I didn't wear gobs of makeup, because he hated having to send his suits to the cleaners after a date, because sometimes the makeup didn't come out, and he'd have to toss the suit. He wore custom-made suits, too. But he said he didn't have to worry about that anymore, now that he'd met me."

Maggie squeezed out more tears and used the napkin by her plate to wipe at her face. She had a rapt, attentive audience. She decided to quit while she felt like she was ahead. Then she decided to throw one last tidbit into the ring. "I even picked out my wedding dress. A Vera Wang." She boo-hooed again and sat back in her chair, as though she were exhausted. She risked a glance at her watch, wishing there was a way to alert Jack and the others about what was going on.

She sniffled a few more times for effect and said, "I feel like this is my lucky day, meeting all of you, and you wanting to help me. I . . . I was never . . . you know . . . kicked to the curb before, so to speak. Why couldn't he just be man enough and say he wanted out? Why?" she cried in a tormented voice. She should have been an actress.

"Because he's a first-class louse," one of the women said.

"Wouldn't it be nice if we could turn the tables on guys like him so he could see how it felt?" suggested one of the women at the far end of the table.

Maggie swallowed hard at the words. She knew where this was going. "I sure would like to do that. I haven't been able to eat or sleep for weeks." Her words were so bitter-sounding, she realized she was a better actress than she had even thought.

"Well, we can talk about that tonight out at the ranch, when we get all comfortable and cozy," Kitty said. "I'm sure between all of us, we can come up with a plan so you get your wish. That's if you're really serious."

Maggie looked around the table at all the expectant faces waiting for her response. "I am very serious, but I want you all to know it's going to kill me to do it. I don't know how to turn off my feelings."

"See! See! That's the thing. The men who did us dirty don't stop to think about *our* feelings, so why should we worry about *theirs*? You need to get hopping mad and go for the jugular. Teach that skunk a lesson he'll never forget," Hana said. A rousing cheer went up around the table.

Maggie sniffed again and wiped at her eyes. "You're right! Okay, I'm in for whatever you all come up with. I want to look into his eyes and tell him what a low-life, bottom-feeding, lying, cheating scumbag hc is. That's what I want!" Maggie cried dramatically.

"And that's exactly what you are going to

get, my dear," Kitty said. Then she grinned and said, "*Meow.*"

The women all laughed, even Maggie. Man, she was so in like Flynn, it was scary.

The women decided to forgo the Jell-O dessert and asked for the bill. Everyone but Maggie scurried to come up with her share, and then they were outside. One of the women hailed a cab for Maggie. Kitty handed over a slip of paper with directions to her ranch.

"Your best bet is a cab," she told Maggie. "Bring enough stuff to spend the night. We'll give you a ride back to town in the morning."

The good-byes were long and loud. And then the cab was pulling away from the curb just as Avery Snowden hopped into the cab behind hers.

Maggie thought she was going to explode as she pulled out her phone and sent one text after another. Lordy, Lordy, she'd hit the mother lode.

Chapter 12

Everyone was sprawled on the furniture and the floor as they watched Abner and Mary Alice tapping away at their computers in the little room off the main suite. They all looked worried, especially Charles and Fergus. This was taking too long. The hackers had been at it for hours, with nothing to show for their efforts. Sparrow just kept shaking his head and chewing on his bottom lip.

The door to the suite opened to admit Jack and Harry. They quickly related in hushed voices, so as not to disturb Abner and PIP, what had gone down at the Cat & Cradle. The others digested the information.

Sparrow spoke first. "Why are we spending so much time on Kelly's love life? So he's a Romeo, a Casanova. Who the hell cares? I really don't see how that is of interest in terms of what we're here for. Will someone please enlighten me?"

"It's a thread. It might or might not tie into why we're here. While it may not seem important, we can't just ignore it, either. If it's nothing, then no problem. We put it behind us. If it turns into something, we play it out to the end," Charles said. He turned to Jack and demanded, "What's your gut feeling? Do you think one has anything to do with the other?"

"I don't know. Part of me says yes, and part of me says no. It's a crapshoot, Charles. Maybe when Maggie gets here and tells us whatever she's found out, if anything, we'll know more."

The room went quiet again so that they could hear Abner and PIP's disgruntled commentary. They heard mutterings about how the guy had to have software on his computers that erased the hard drive if someone hacked or tried to copy it or used the wrong password, in which case it would wipe the computer clean.

"Hey, maybe since we don't have access to the classified feeds, we could port in through a private virtual network," Abner said. "Wanna give it a shot, PIP?"

"I already tried that. You watched me. You're burned out, and so am I. I give up. We're never going to catch this guy. He's way too smart for us."

"That's it! I'm done!" The group looked up to see Abner getting up off his chair and throwing his hands in the air. "This is impossible! We can't do it! That guy has got to be an absolute genius.

"Listen to me and pay attention. This guy has malware that is so sophisticated, he could use it to dispense cash from ATMs without any physical contact with the machines themselves. Then he could have what the money guys call mules walk by, scoop it up, and that's the end of it. It's a new era in cyber crime. It's here whether you like it or not. I read about it, and so did PIP. It's called an APT attack, which stands for 'advanced persistent threat' attack. This is just like those Russians who hacked the one billion dollars from the banks. Hell, RC probably set up the malware for that caper. Wouldn't put it past him, either, and PIP agrees.

"We simply cannot hack in! No one except the guy that set it up can, and my money is on RC. I never thought I'd live to see this day. The guy has to have an army backing up what he's doing."

Mary Alice, her eyes red and gritty, looked like she was ready to cry. "Abner's right. No matter what we do, we hit an invisible firewall. The guy is good. Actually, better than good. He's without equal. This is a waste of time. You need to give this up and find another way to get to him."

"What would you suggest, Miss PIP?" Fergus said.

"Like I know! I thought you people knew what you were doing? Obviously, you don't, so how do you expect me to help you? Can I go home now?"

"Not yet," Sparrow said.

Cyrus barked his agreement just as Maggie blew into the room, her eyes sparkling.

Knowing what was coming, Jack winked at Abner as he escorted him and PIP to the room adjacent to Charles's sitting room. "Keep an eye on her. Not that she can get out of here with Cyrus standing guard. Just be careful and don't trust her."

"Like you know me well enough to make a statement like that," Mary Alice snarled. "For all you know, I could have Houdini qualities."

"I don't think I want to know you either," Jack snarled back as he closed the door.

"Okay, okay, what'ya got, Maggie? How did it all go down?"

Maggie was in her glory. She smacked her hands together and sat down before she said, "Gather round, kiddies, and listen up. The ladies invited me out to Kitty's ranch tonight for a sleepover. A girl thing. You know, steaks on the grill, lots of wine, girl talk. Guy bashing, that kind of thing. The one named Kitty inherited this chicken ranch out in the desert. It supplies all the eggs that are consumed here in Vegas. She's rich. I think. We didn't get into that. She's a showgirl from Atlantic City. She came here when her favorite aunt passed away and left her the ranch. She said she works it. She also said she's giving up the showgirl gig because it's too hard on the body. I'm going."

Charles's expression was one of alarm. "I don't know if that's wise, Maggie. I could see you going if you had backup, but going cold, that's another story altogether. We need to discuss this, young lady."

"I'll be fine, Charles. I can handle myself. Besides, they bought my tale of woe, and they're ready to step up for the kill. I can feel it, sense it in every bone in my body. I also know who the ringleader is." Maggie sat back and waited for comments, which came immediately.

"What? They announced themselves?"

"Are you guessing?"

"How do you know?"

"I know because I am a woman, and I pay attention. The ringleader is someone named Lena Adams. She's the oldest of the group. I'd put her at around thirty-five or so, way too old to be in a chorus line. She's been Botoxed into submission. The others have Botox, too, but not to the extent Lena has it. The other girls are midtwenties, with Kitty Passion being the youngest at twenty-three. She told me how old she was, so that's how I know. They asked me my age, and I said thirty-nine, and they looked at me like I had sprouted a second head. What that means to you is that Dixson Kelly only likes them young, and they couldn't figure out what he saw in *me*. And I am *not* showgirl material. No one mentioned Kelly's name except for me, and I pretended to let it slip in the restroom. When Hana went out to get the others, I'm sure she mentioned my slip of the tongue. The name never came up again, which I found very strange. I'm onto something. I feel it. I just don't know what it is."

"Do you think you'll find out tonight?" Sparrow asked.

"Oh, yeah," Maggie drawled. "Those women are out for blood. Look, they're all looking for love, as the song goes. Some want a sugar daddy. Others just want security. Dixson knows all that, and he played them all. But it's Lena who is leading the march here. That tells me she was hurt the most. That she truly did love him. Probably still does. But now she wants vengeance, and what better way than whatever it is they're planning? I do not have a clue what that is yet, but I know it will be the end of Kelly if they pull it off."

"And you have no clue what that something might be?" Jack said.

"At the moment, no. When I get back here tomorrow morning, I expect I will have the answer."

"Do you think that whatever it is, it has something to do with why we're here? Where's your gut or your reporter's instinct on that?" Sparrow asked.

"Right now, out in left field somewhere. If you absolutely need an answer right now, then I'd have to say yes and no."

"Tell us your observations on the women," Fergus said, pad and pen in hand so he could jot down notes.

"Like I said, Lena is Miss Botox herself. Also the oldest. Kitty, who likes to say meow a lot, is the youngest and, in my opinion, is awesomely beautiful. With the exception of Kitty, they are all surgically enhanced. Kitty is just plain perfect. A guy's wet dream, if I can be so crude."

At the guys' puzzled looks, she said, "They all have boob jobs. Showgirls need big boobs. And long legs. These women have it going on. Oh, one other thing. None of them work here at Babylon. Lena did back in the day, but she left and didn't say why. She works at MGM now. She's their lead dancer."

Maggie eyed the group and worried at their silence. "Okay, I had my say. So what did you guys learn while I was doing my gig?"

Charles grimaced. "Abner and Miss PIP have come up dry. Both of them are disgruntled, especially Miss PIP. They can't help us at the moment. Right now we are at a standstill. And mind me now, that fact alone is the only reason I am allowing you to go out to that ranch this evening. Just on the off chance that somehow, someway, you can tie the women into what Bert is worried about."

Maggie nodded. "Any word from Ted and Dennis? How's that all going?"

Charles grinned. "Not well. Mr. Kelly is tired of being photographed and making nice to the customers. Today he was supposed to explain how they transport the casino's money to the bank. Armored cars, of course, but they have a foolproof system in play here. The nightmare of every casino owner is a robbery like in *Ocean's Eleven*. Remember that movie? Young

Dennis was eagerly awaiting that particular part of the interview. Ted simply said he was goddamned tired of babysitting Dixson Kelly. End of story."

"I know the feeling. The guy is a total bore. Or else he is one damn fine actor. Okay, people, I am off to get ready for my next adventure. You'll see me when you see me."

"Maggie, wait. Are you presenting yourself as yourself, as Maggie Spritzer, star reporter for the *Post*? Or are you going in as someone else, you know, a fake name, a legend Charles created for you? What are you carrying with you, in case one of those women decides to go through your things?" Jack asked.

"I'm going as me. Easier that way, and I won't trip myself up. As Annie likes to say, this is not my first rodeo, guys. I'm not taking anything with me but my jammies and toothbrush. My ID, of course, but that's it. You're all suddenly looking like a bunch of mother hens. Relax. I know what I'm doing."

"What about the special gold shield and the encrypted phone? You are leaving those behind, right?" Sparrow queried. Maggie gave him such a disgusted look, Sparrow blanched. "Just asking. You can never be too careful. Sometimes you think you did something, and that's it. You just thought you did, when, in reality, you didn't do it at all."

Maggie showed the FBI director another disgusted look and left.

"Guess we know where that leaves you on Maggie's list," Harry guffawed.

The room went suddenly quiet when the door opened to admit Snowden, his two operatives, and the three new people he'd requested. All three of the new operatives were women. Introductions were made; then everyone took a seat.

"I passed Maggie in the hallway. I'm sure she updated you all. I waited till all the women had left before I removed the bugs." Snowden held out the little squares to Fergus.

Fergus then took them to the other room, where Abner and PIP were still snapping and snarling at one another. He handed them over. He wagged a finger under both their noses and said, "You two need to give this up already and work together. You're both acting like six-year-olds. Stop it right now!"

Cyrus barked his approval of the order as his ears went flat against his head, his eyes on PIP.

"He's right, Abner," Mary Alice said wearily. "I'm too tired to keep fighting with you. I just plain old give up. I don't care what you do. I really don't. At least we now know neither one of us will ever be as smart as RC. See, that's why I don't care anymore. It was always my goal to be better than him. It ain't gonna happen. I know that now. Not now, not ever." She swiped at her eyes with her shirtsleeve.

"That was your goal?" Abner said in stupefied amazement. "Really?"

"Really?" Mary Alice snapped. "Are you saying that wasn't *your* goal?"

"Hell no! My goal was and still is to never get caught."

"RC always said you and I were the best. If the two of us can't crack him, then no one can. That doesn't say much for you, Tookus, or me, either. I never wanted to find that out, and you people pushed my face in it. Now I have nothing to strive for. Nothing!" she cried pitifully.

In spite of himself, Abner laughed. "Hey, PIP, you still have all those organic seeds you sell online. And you earn a living at it and file taxes like the rest of the world. That has to mean something."

"Yeah, well, you tell me what it means, Tookus. It means squat to me now. Oh, I get it. My new goal should be trying to be better than you, right?" She laughed, an ugly sound that Cyrus did not like. He moved forward. Mary Alice leaned backward. "Listen, dog, I was just giving my opinion here. No harm, no foul. Be a good doggy and go back to sleep."

Cyrus threw his head back and let loose with a howl that made the hair on the back of Abner's neck stand on end. Everyone knew Cyrus did not like to be referred to as *doggy*. Abner explained this in great detail to PIP out of the corner of his mouth.

"Okay, okay, I get it. Listen, Cyrus, I didn't know. It was a slip of the tongue. I apologize."

Abner grinned as the big shepherd tilted his head to the side and stared at PIP, as though he was trying to decide if she was telling the truth. He made a snorting noise deep in his throat and went back on duty, sitting on his haunches as he eyeballed the female hacker.

"Abner, tell me the truth here. Why are we doing this? What did RC do that has the FBI onto him, as well as that martial arts expert? I mean, what the hell? We're hackers. You do it. I do it. We make money doing illegal hacking. Why aren't they after us? What makes RC so different from us? Come on. What did he do?"

"I can't tell you that, Mary Alice. I would if I could, because I respect you and your talent. I like to think you and me and the others are smart enough to know how far to go, how to cover our tracks and not cross that invisible line. That's how we've all survived so far. RC crossed it because he thought he was infallible. Personally speaking, I think he knows we're onto him. Either he's on the run, or he's getting ready to wipe out our entire bloodlines. Right this moment, I think it's the latter. These people I'm with . . . They're the best of the best. Believe me when I tell you that. For now, you're safe. Accept it, and you will have a life to go back to."

Mary Alice Farmer broke into tears as she tried to figure out where all this was going. Abner felt his own eyes beginning to burn and sting as he envisioned losing his opportunity to hack and having to live a life of leisure on the millions he had accumulated over the years. The vision was so depressing, he feared that he'd shoot himself in a week.

In his and Mary Alice's world, failure was never an option.

Upstairs in the penthouse, Philonias paced as he socked one big fist against the other. He muttered and mumbled as his pace picked up. He stopped in the middle of the dining room and looked around. He'd always thought of this space as his personal nest, which no one could invade. A fortress of sorts. He was comfortable and safe here. *Safe* being the operative word. He'd never felt anything his entire life other than safe and happy. Even as a child, he'd always felt safe. Perhaps his size had something to do with the feeling. He could understand, almost, how the kids, then the teenagers, and finally his college mates could be intimidated by his sheer size, and yet he'd never presented—at least he didn't think so—a threatening attitude to anyone.

He realized that he no longer felt safe. At least that was what he thought he was feeling. He was unsure, since he'd never felt emotions like what he was now experiencing.

Philonias started to pace again. So maybe they were onto him. So what? They couldn't prove a thing. Computer-wise, he was safe. There was no person walking the face of the earth who could pin anything on him. They *could* try. They *would* try. And while they were doing that, what would he be doing? Probably sitting in a cell that he could barely turn around in. Should he alert his lawyers? And tell them what? His worries, his suspicions? If he did that, it would make them, the attorneys, look at him with suspicion. Better to wait until they arrested him, if it came to that. But first they had to find him before they could arrest him, and that was not going to happen.

Philonias stopped pacing again. He was in his sunroom, which had wraparound windows that offered him a view of the town he loved. At night, with the lights on and the stars shining, it was like his own magic wonderland. If he had to leave here, he would wither away and die. He was too young to die. Way too young.

Maybe he was looking at this all wrong. Instead of hiding, instead of being such a recluse, maybe he needed to put himself out there more, actually become visible. But if he did that, wouldn't people start to wonder why, since that was not his MO?

Talk about being between a rock and a hard place.

Philonias found himself standing in the doorway to the state-of-the-art kitchen he'd designed himself. He loved all the push buttons. Not that he was too lazy to do certain things. More like he enjoyed simply pushing a button and watching things unfold.

Coffee sounded good, the flavored kind that he liked so much. Maybe the caffeine would create some kind of clarity and would help him decide what to do.

He started the coffeemaker and sat down on

an oversize bar stool, mesmerized as the water dripped ever so slowly into the pot. One plop at a time. Like his life to a certain extent. He needed to form a plan, a course of action. He needed to think outside the box and stop doing things the way he'd always done them.

He thought about TRIPLEM and PIP. He knew deep in his gut that they could both give an accurate description of what RCHood looked like. What one missed in a detail, the other would pick up on until they had a clear picture of what he looked like. Then they would go the facial recognition route. There was no doubt in his mind that PIP, who was actually Mary Alice Farmer, was already in their clutches. Not one iota of doubt. TRIPLEM, Abner Tookus, was already here in Vegas, at Babylon. If whoever was after him, meaning Navarro and his people caught up with TRIPLEM, the first thing they'd do if they had any brains was have a sketch artist do a rendering of him from the details the two hackers offered up. From there, they'd run it through facial recognition, and *bam*! But they hadn't done that. Yet. He knew because he'd hacked the program. But they had run PIP's picture and come up with her identity. Not so Abner Tookus. Of course not. He was right here, front and center and part of whatever was happening. Why hadn't they run his sketch? Sloppy work on their part. Or was it something else? If it was, he couldn't figure it out.

Philonias stared at the coffeepot. *Funny*, he thought, *how the last plop always sounds different, the alert that the coffee is ready to pour.* Man, he needed to get with the program here and stop thinking about plopping drops of water in a coffeepot.

He carried his coffee cup, which was as big as a quart pot, back to his computer room. This time he set it down carefully and waited for the coffee to cool. He looked at the computers that graced every wall in the room. He knew that if every computer expert in the entire world walked into this room and sat down at any one of the computers, they wouldn't be able to open a thing. An army of experts could disassemble each and every computer with the same results. He, of course, would be leaning up against the wall, laughing silently at what they were doing, knowing exactly what the outcome would be. Of course, the computers would all be ruined. Little did they know, and he certainly wasn't going to tell them, that he'd worked diligently for over six months to set up this exact room in one of his many rental properties.

Years ago, he'd bought a block of condos that were under construction. There were twelve in all. No one lived in any of them, because he didn't want anyone seeing him coming and going. He paid the taxes and utilities on time. Each unit had a name attached to the title. Mail, mostly junk, was put through a slot on the main doors. He even went so far as to park cars in the designated parking spots, and he moved them every so often. And the condos were far enough out in the desert so that he didn't have to worry about having neighbors wonder what was going on. He thought of it as a retreat of sorts.

If nothing else, Philonias Needlemeyer was a thorough, dedicated man, true to his profession and to his creed of never being caught doing what he did. "Always have a backup plan" was his mantra. Until this moment in time, he thought of the condo complex as a safe harbor, never believing for a minute that he would need to avail himself of its safety. "Which just goes to prove that nothing lasts forever," he muttered to himself.

Philonias stared at his computer as he waited for it to boot up. He had one thing to do, and now was as good a time as any. With a few quick taps to the keys, he brought up TRIPLEM's e-mail address. He started to type, his fingers as fast as his thoughts. Then he sent a duplicate text to Abner's phone.

> *Dear Abner,*
> *Yes, I know your real name. I know where you live, who your friends are, who you do work for. I know everything there is to know about you. And about PIP, as well. I also know that you are at Babylon and that Mary Alice Farmer is with you. I had hoped never to have to write what I am now writing. I say that because I trusted you both. I helped you both 24/7 and never asked for a thing in return except your loyalty. You both failed me. Betrayal is such an ugly word, and yet that is what you did. You betrayed my trust in you. This may*

sound dramatic to you, but they, whoever they are, could have threatened to burn me at the stake, and I would never have divulged your true identities. Never.

I miscalculated, misjudged you both, so I have to own it. You both have destroyed my trust. For what? What are you gaining from helping those people to find me? Money? I find that hard to believe since I made you both richer than you could ever have possibly imagined. I've asked myself a hundred times why you both would do this to me, your mentor. I can't even begin to conceive the answer.

This e-mail will be our last contact. Five minutes from now, RCHood ceases to exist. You and your people can try from now to the end of time to find RC, but all traces that he ever existed will be gone. A massive feat to handle, but I know that you both know I can do that. I am now dead to you and Mary Alice.

As Mary Alice is with you, please relay this message to her since she has no access to her own computer network at this moment in time.

Good-bye, TRIPLEM.

Good-bye, PIP.

Philonias sipped at his coffee, which was now almost cold. His eyes felt suspiciously moist, meaning tears were about to sting his eyes. His mother's childhood words rang in his ears. *Do not be a crybaby, Philonias. You are too big to cry, and it is not manly.* How could he have been manly at the age of six? He'd read somewhere that crying was cathartic. Since he couldn't remember ever crying, he didn't know if it was true or false.

Philonias straightened his shoulders and got up to carry his coffee cup to the sink, where he washed and dried it before replacing it in the cabinet over the stove. He cleaned the coffeepot and checked that everything was neat and tidy in the kitchen before he made his rounds of the penthouse. If and when anyone entered the apartment, it would look like he had gone for a walk and was planning on returning.

All he had to do now was walk out the door, go to the sixth floor, and drive his custom-built Bentley out to the desert and take up residence at his condo, with the hope deep in his heart that one day he would be able to return to his beloved penthouse.

And yet, for some reason, he couldn't make his feet take him to the door. Instead, he turned around and walked through the ten-thousand-square-foot penthouse one last time. So he was a romantic, a nester. So what? As he walked around, he touched a memento from his parents, a childhood treasure, a favorite book on the table by his favorite chair, a bowl of peanut M&M'S, which he liked to snack on while he was reading.

Ten minutes later, he realized he was just postponing the inevitable. He looked at his watch. He'd spent ten minutes walking around, and now he felt worse than he had before. "I'll be back," he whispered. "I don't know when, but I will be back."

"And life goes on," he mumbled to himself as he took his personal elevator to the sixth floor. "And life goes on." Philonias bent down to pick up a small duffel that contained cell phones, passports, a wallet, and a box of flash drives.

Chapter 13

Abner felt his cell phone vibrate in his pocket. He hated that his hands were shaking as he struggled to pull it out. When he saw the sender's name, he grew light-headed. He struggled to take a deep, mighty breath as he squeezed his eyes shut. When he finally expelled all the air in his lungs, he opened his eyes and read the text. He bit down so hard on his lower lip, he felt the skin split. *No, this isn't happening. No!* But he knew it was happening, because he was seeing the text with his own eyes in real time. In the background, he could hear the others talking as they discussed the day's events. Out of the corner of his eye, he could see Maggie gathering up her backpack and leaving the suite.

Abner felt Mary Alice's eyes on him. Then

he felt her touch his arm, her way of questioning him about what was in the text. He handed her the phone and watched her eyes start to flood as she sagged deep into the chair she was sitting on. Somehow, she managed to whisper a tormented "What are we going to do, Abner?" Her hands were shaking so badly, she needed both of them to hold the cell phone so she could hand it back to Abner.

Abner licked at his bottom lip. White-hot, scorching anger ripped through his body as his eyes narrowed, then focused on Charles and the others, who were babbling away, albeit quietly. Then he looked at Mary Alice, who looked like a beaten dog as she whimpered into the arm she was holding against her face. He reached for her arm, tugged it away, and whispered, "Come with me. We're outta here."

Jack sensed something was not right at the far end of the suite. He blinked at what he was seeing, then nudged Harry to follow his gaze.

"Abner! Wait up! Where are you going?" Jack demanded.

"All of a sudden you care about where I'm going! Don't give me any more of your goddamned bullshit, Jack. I'm leaving, and Mary Alice is going with me. We're done here! I am so damn done with you all, I want nothing more than to vomit. Now, get the hell out of my way before I knock you silly."

"What the hell is going on?" Sparrow bellowed.

"Yeah, what the hell!" Abner parroted. He tossed his cell phone so hard across the room that Jack had to leap in the air to catch it. "That's what's going on!"

Jack read the text lightning fast, then tossed the cell to Charles. "Listen, Abner, I know you're upset! Will you listen to me, please!"

"See, Jack, that's the problem. I *did* listen to you. I did everything you asked, because I'm a good team player. PIP, even though you kidnapped her and brought her here, tried to help, too. We both told you RC would figure it out. You're holding the proof. And the guy is right. We, PIP and I, betrayed him. Me willingly, PIP not so much.

"I still don't understand why you are all so hell-bent on catching the guy. He just does what I do and Pip does. What makes him so different from us? I've worked and hacked for you guys for years. *Years*, Jack. He taught me and PIP everything we know. If he hadn't done that, I would never have been able to help you. Everything I've done for you and the sisters is thanks to RC. When it benefited you, it was okay what I did, and you didn't care how I had learned to do it. A wink, a nod, look the other way.

"Why couldn't you do that this time with RC? I can guarantee he did not keep any of the money, if he did indeed steal it. He would have given it all away. I don't know how I know this, but I know that RC is so filthy rich that he does not need to steal to feed his bank account. Any more than I ever needed to keep any of the money I turned over to you and the sisters, admittedly, for a nice fee in the beginning, before I no longer worked for them but became a member of the gang. You need to think about all that and own it.

"It makes no difference what he did or how long he has been doing it. And I would bet that the money that he has liberated was put to much better uses than if he had left it where it belonged. You're never going to catch him. Never! And if there's a way for me to help him, I will, and so will PIP. You've ruined our lives, you sons of bitches! I hope you're happy now. I will never again admit that I know any of you."

Mary Alice felt like she was at a tennis match as she switched her gaze from Abner to the others, then back to Abner, as she tried to figure out what was going on. It sounded like Abner was now on her side. She felt herself being pulled toward the doorway of the suite, but at the last second, Abner turned and shouted, "Just because Bert is half a world away—by his choice, I might remind you, because Kathryn gave him his walking papers—and he has time on his hands, so he can dig into the financials because he has nothing better to do, then he can demand that we all come here and do his dirty work. Well, have at it, boys. I'm done and done. One last thing. I *do* know how to get in touch with Isabelle, who, if you're smart enough, will figure out she's in touch with the others. You think this is bad. Just wait!"

Abner slammed the door so hard, Jack could hear his teeth rattle.

"Like you said before, Jack, I sure as hell never saw that coming," Sparrow barked.

"I did," Jack said.

"Yeah," Harry said.

"Oh, dear, this is a problem," Charles said.

Fergus agreed.

Cyrus pranced around the room, not knowing whom he should side with. He growled when no one paid any attention to him. Then he threw back his head and barked, the sound so loud and shrill, they all covered their ears. The shepherd was relentless with his barking.

Finally, Jack patted his leg and said, "It's okay. A minor disagreement. We'll work on it, Cyrus."

The door opened to admit a disgruntled Ted, Dennis, and Espinosa. All three looked like dark thunderclouds.

"What's going on? I just saw Abner and his friend at the elevator, and he wouldn't even look at me. He looked . . . mad. I don't think I have ever seen Abner mad. Come on. Someone tell us what's going on," Ted said.

Charles explained the situation. Ted digested the information.

"How could you guys let that happen?" he asked. "We need Abner. How many times has he ridden in to rescue us with his . . . *abilities*. You were wrong to put him in that spot. Dead wrong."

Espinosa's head bobbed up and down in agreement.

"You're right, Ted," Jack said wearily as he rubbed at the bridge of his nose. "It's done now, and we can't unring the bell. If any of you have any bright ideas on how to handle this, now would be a good time to voice them."

The room went totally silent.

"That's what I thought," Jack said wearily. "We need to fall back and regroup."

"To what end?" Ted asked. "This whole gig is turning into a big bust. Kelly flat out sent us packing. Said he didn't care if Bert fired him or not. He was not doing one more stupid interview, and he sure as hell wasn't having his picture taken again. And he told me to shove this article you know where. That's why we're here so early. He's done, and he means it."

"The guy was fed up. That's for sure. Can't say as how I blame him, either," Espinosa said. "Where's Maggie?" he asked.

Fergus explained Maggie's situation.

"And you let her go! With no backup! I don't believe this," Ted said, spinning on his heel, ready to leave the suite.

"Calm down, Ted. Did you ever try to talk Maggie out of anything? Ah, I see you have, and I know what the outcome was. Maggie has a mind of her own, and she is going to that . . . sleepover, female fest, whatever it is, and wild horses can't keep her here, so don't even try," Fergus said.

"If you interfere, Ted, Maggie will make you pay big-time. You know that. Better to let her do her thing and trust she knows what she's doing," Jack said. "Right now, we need to think about calling Bert to see how he wants to handle this latest development. I want to go on record here, right now, this very moment, as saying that if Abner says the guy is gone and won't ever be found, then I believe him. As much as I hate to admit it, we lost this round."

"It ain't over till the fat lady sings, Jack!" Espinosa said fiercely.

"You're wrong. It's over, and we lost. You wanna take a vote?" Jack said.

"Well, if that's true, why aren't we packing up to go back home?" Ted demanded. "Who cares about Dixson Kelly and the truckload of women he has on the string? Who cares?" he thundered to the room.

As one, they responded, "Maggie cares!"

Ted's shoulders sagged. He walked over to the minibar and yanked out two Buds. He opened both and held one out to Espinosa, who gulped it like a man who had been stuck in the desert for a week.

"She might find a thread, a link, something that will help us," Jack said. "I don't know about the rest of you, but I do not want to go home with my tail between my legs, knowing we failed. If there's even the remotest chance Maggie can come up with something, then we need to give her time to either prove it or disprove it.

"Here is something else for you all to think about. When the girls discover that we bombed out, we will never, as in never, never, *ever*, hear the end of it. And if Abner was telling the truth, that he can contact Isabelle . . . Do I need to say any more?"

"Since I wasn't here in the room for the fireworks, I have to ask. Was Abner just venting, or was he . . . you know, serious, and he is not coming back?" Ted asked.

Until now, Dennis had remained quiet, watching everything play out. "He's not coming back," he said quietly. "You broke his spirit. Abner is a sensitive guy. You might not think so, but he is. He's what you call true blue. He's thinking you used him, played him. Maybe at some point, he'll forgive you, but not for a very long time."

Harry stared at the young reporter through narrowed eyes. Then he put his arm around his shoulder. "You are absolutely right, Dennis. That's how I see it, too. Nice going, kid."

Jack felt sick to his stomach, and his heart ached. He picked up the phone to call Bert, Abner's words fresh in his mind.

Mary Alice was breathless as Abner dragged her to the end of the hall. He held the door to the stairwell open for her to enter.

"Where are we going, Abner? What just happened back there? Why are we taking the stairs? Talk to me, Abner. Where are we going?" she asked a second time, her tone verging on hysterical. "I'm not taking another step until I know what's going on."

"You were there. You heard everything. You're no dummy. What part of what just happened didn't you get?" Abner said, one foot on a step and one on the landing.

"The part about who the hell you all are. Do I need to remind you, you all kidnapped me?

Normal people do not kidnap people and take them across state lines. Are you mercenaries? What's the endgame here? I don't even have any money or ID on me. How am I supposed to get home? Where are we going? I'm not going to ask you again, Abner. If you don't answer me, I'm going to start screaming. I mean it!"

"Okay, okay. But let's talk as we make our way to the sixth floor, where my truck is parked. I'll explain everything once we're away from here. I'm going to drive you back to Arizona, because you have no ID to get on a plane. Snowden's people would just grab you again."

"What did RC do?"

"He helped himself to close to a billion dollars of the casino's money over a period of time. Bert figured it out. Bert, who years ago was the director of the FBI, runs security here at Babylon, and Babylon is owned by Countess Anna de Silva, one of the richest women in the world. Presently, owing to personal reasons, Bert is in Macau, China, overseeing the building of a new casino for the countess. He left Dixson Kelly, his right-hand man, in charge. Kelly doesn't appear to be in Bert's confidence. He's an ex-CIA spook. You getting all this?"

"I don't know if I am or not. This is like some bad novel or movie that you just shake your head over when you're done. I'm not getting it. I have nothing to do with you people. I'm no different from you."

"You and I are the only two people who ever sat down with RC and talked to him. Yeah, it was years ago. I lied to them. I tried telling them I was just a kid and didn't pay attention to how he looked. Hell, I remember everything about him, right down to the pimple he had by his left eyebrow. The reason I remember it is that it either bothered him or he was embarrassed that a grown man like himself had a pimple. How's that for remembering trivia? You lied, too, PIP. You told them he had blue eyes and sandy hair. He has big brown eyes and black hair."

"You still aren't telling me who these people are, Abner. I want to know. Avengers, vigilantes, crackpots? Who?" she gasped, her breathing ragged with the pell-mell run down the stairs.

"All of the above, okay? Look, we're at the sixth-floor parking garage. There are cameras everywhere, so keep your head down, not that it's going to do any good. But there is no sense in making it easy for them. I'm parked in the first row, next to some fancy cars. I drive a Range Rover, champagne colored, so just walk next to me and remember to keep your head down. We have to cross the whole length of the garage. Just so you know. Now, talk to me just like we are a couple and are having a conversation on the way to picking up our ride. You can do that, right?" Abner said, his gaze everywhere.

"Well, sure, Abner. I think I'll wash my hair tonight with some special avocado shampoo I've been dying to try. Supposed to make your hair thick and luxurious. That's after I send out eighteen hundred packets of my organic pumpkin seeds."

Mary Alice raised her head and looked

around defiantly. She spotted the champagne-colored Range Rover at the same moment she saw Philonias Needlemeyer standing next to a custom-made Bentley. "Oh, my God! Abner. Do you see what I see?" But Abner was already racing ahead of her, having seen the big man at the same time.

"Whoa there, big guy!" he almost shouted. "RC, it's me, TRIPLEM, and this is PIP with me. What are you doing here? They're after you. Get in the damn car already. There are cameras everywhere."

Philonias stood rooted to the concrete. Ten minutes. If he hadn't spent those last ten minutes being sentimental, he would have gotten away clean. *Son of a bitch!*

"Didn't you hear me, RC? I said, 'Get in the damn car!'" Abner growled.

Mary Alice tried to push the big man, but it was as though his feet were glued to the concrete. Then reason took over, and RC opened the car door and climbed in. Abner and Mary Alice scrambled in behind him.

"We can get out of here. I know we can. We just need a plan. Where were you going, RC?" Abner asked.

"They kidnapped me, RC," Mary Alice shrilled from the backseat. "They're either vigilantes, avengers, or crackpots. And they have this killer dog that wanted to rip out my throat. Abner says they're all of the above. Your text made me cry, RC. Abner, too, but he probably won't admit it. We didn't want to help them. Honest."

"But you did," Philonias said quietly.

"Yes. And I think I can explain if you give me a chance," Abner responded, just as quietly.

"Now what?" Philonias asked.

Abner let his hands flap in the air. "We want to help you. Just tell us what we can do. We split from the others. I couldn't do it anymore. I refused, so I dragged PIP out of there. My plan was to drive her back to Arizona in my Range Rover, because she has no ID and can't fly. We can go with you wherever you're going. If you'll have us, that is. Right, PIP?"

"Right," Mary Alice said.

"How do you know I'm not on my way to the post office or the supermarket? What makes you think I'm taking it on the lam?" Could he trust them? He thought so, but . . . There was always a *but*.

"The duffel bag. Just big enough to carry the essentials. Your text. A ten-year-old could figure that out. You actually live here, don't you?" asked Abner.

Philonias snorted. "What was your first clue? Took you long enough to figure it out. I have to say I am disappointed, TRIPLEM."

"I figured it out when Dixson Kelly said he met this really *big* guy in the Tiki Bar. For whatever it's worth, I didn't voice my thoughts to anyone. So where are you going? You got a hidey-hole somewhere?"

"Out to the desert. And the answer is yes. Are you serious about helping me? Can I trust you?"

"Yes," Abner and Mary Alice said in unison.

"All right then. It's not like I have options here. PIP, get down on the floor. Abner, follow me in your Rover. Give me a five-minute head start before you follow me. Just stay on my tail until we reach our destination. If we get separated in traffic or for some other reason, I'll send you a text so you can find your own way. No, I am not going to evade you, so you can get that thought right out of your head. Even I know right now I'm on a slippery slope. We good here?"

Abner, his head down, was already out of the Bentley and running toward the Rover. He was glad now that he'd had the foresight to fill the gas tank before he arrived at Babylon yesterday. Or was it the day before? For some reason, he'd lost track of time. Or maybe it was that suddenly time had no meaning.

Abner waited the requisite five minutes, then peeled out of his parking space, tires burning rubber. He wasn't sure, but he thought he took the ramp on two wheels.

The sun was about to set, but there was still a golden glow to the day as he kept his eyes on the silver Bentley up ahead. Abner's thoughts raced as he settled into the heavy traffic. He knew the others back at Babylon were still trying to figure out what he was all about. He also knew they were trying to contact him, because both phones in his pockets kept buzzing. "Screw you all," he muttered under his breath. Then he remembered Isabelle's cigarettes. He fished around in the middle console, where he had stashed the pack he found in the glove box, found the package, and fired one up. He coughed and sputtered but kept on puffing. He rolled down the window. If ever there was a time for a cigarette break, this was that time.

Abner had no trouble following the silver Bentley, because RC was a cautious driver and, for obvious reasons, did not want to get pulled over by some overanxious state trooper or local cop.

The drive took ninety minutes before RC turned on his right-turn signal and headed up a long, manicured drive to a security fence. Abner watched as he tapped in a code. The gate opened, and both cars sailed through.

Abner blinked at what he was seeing, a condo complex. It was hard to believe RC would live among a bunch of thirtysomethings. Then again, RC was proving to be a constant surprise.

Both vehicles parked, and everyone got out.

Mary Alice stretched her neck right, then left. "I'm thirsty," she announced.

Abner stomped his feet to get his circulation moving. "Which one is yours?"

Philonias waved his hands in the air. "All of them. No one lives here. I just come out here from time to time to sort through things. I guess in the back of my mind I thought someday I might need a . . . hidey-hole, as you called it."

Mary Alice looked around. "Who owns all these cars?"

"I do. I wanted to make it look real. I have bogus names on the deeds to all the condos. Even the one I use has a bogus name. No one comes here but the mailman. I pay all the bills, taxes, and insurance online and a year in advance through a secure server in Bucharest. Very little mail other than occupant stuff comes through here. Last year, for some reason, I changed the mail drop to the post office, so now not even a mailman comes out here. I think I must have had some kind of epiphany. All right, come along, and let's see what we can do about this current situation."

Mary Alice rolled her eyes at Abner, who rolled his eyes right back to her. In for a penny, in for a pound, or whatever that saying was that Charles was so fond of using. *Charles.* Abner clamped his teeth shut. This was no time to think about Charles or any regrets about what he had just done.

Philonias keyed in his code at the door, then opened it. The condo had a beautiful layout, but it smelled musty from being closed up. He quickly turned up the air-conditioning and looked around. "The room at the end of the hall is mine. Pick whichever ones you want. Each has its own bathroom. The room in the center is the computer room. While you're settling in, I'll head for the kitchen to see what I can rustle up for dinner. I have a freezer full of food and a pressure cooker. No problems with power out here, but if there is a blackout, I have a generator attached to each unit."

"Nice hidey-hole, RC," Abner said. "Do you think this place is safe?"

"I did up until I saw you in the garage. I

could have sworn I didn't screw up cyber wise. How did you find me?"

"By accident. We were leaving, and so were you. They have no clue you live at Babylon. Dixson Kelly *thinks* you are somehow involved in whatever he thinks is going down. No one believes him, so he's more or less whistling in the wind. Even Bert Navarro had to set him straight."

"There was an episode in the garage."

"My fault. I thought it was you but wasn't sure. I'm the one who sounded that alarm, and Sparrow, who is the director of the FBI, took it as spot on. Glad you managed to elude him," Mary Alice said.

"I'll start dinner and make us some coffee. Go along and do whatever you want to do— shower, freshen up—and then come back here to the kitchen."

"By any chance do you have a toothbrush, RC?" Abner asked.

"Everything you could need is in the bathrooms and closets. I keep sweat suits here, all sizes. Don't ask me why. Survival training or something I read along the way. Just another one of those instances of you never know what is going to happen or what you will need, so be prepared for any and everything. It took a long time to outfit this complex."

Both Mary Alice and Abner started down the hall, then splintered off to shower and change into whatever was available.

Thirty minutes later, they joined Philonias

in the kitchen. He had cups out, along with frozen cream he'd thawed in the microwave oven. A red light glowed on the stainless-steel pressure cooker. RC noticed them looking at the pressure cooker.

"I actually know how to cook, but today I just dumped a roast with a bunch of frozen vegetables into the pot. I mixed up some dough, and bread is baking in that other machine that has a glowing red dot. We won't starve, but I don't guarantee tastiness. Pour your coffee, and let's sit in the family room, where we can be comfortable and can *talk.*"

In the blink of an eye, the threesome was settled into soft, buttery leather chairs that were more comfortable than any bed. Abner took the initiative.

"We're here, RC, so that should tell you we're on your side. I say we give up on the cyber crap for now and just be three human beings talking to one another. We, PIP and I, know you know everything there is to know about us. We're actually okay with that, but it would be nice if you'd share a few facts about yourself. I give you my word that you can trust me. PIP?"

"Me, too, RC," Mary Alice agreed.

"So let's get started here. From here on in, I'm Abner and PIP is Mary Alice. You are Philonias Needlemeyer. What kind of name is that, anyway?"

Philonias nodded. "I was born Needlemeyer. My mother named me Philonias because she said no one else would ever have that name.

She wanted me to be different, special. I guess she didn't think my size qualified for different or special. I might ask you what kind of name Tookus is."

Emboldened by Philonias's easy acceptance, Abner said, "One of my many foster parents gave me that name, but I can't remember which one. I really don't know who I am or where I came from. I was dumped at an orphanage when I was born. So, moving right along, we're going to call you Phil. Growing up, didn't your friends call you Phil?"

"I didn't have any friends growing up, Abner."

"How about when you were a teenager or when you were in college? What did your peers call you?"

"Freak," Philonias said flatly.

"Well, Phil, Mary Alice and I are not them. We're flesh-and-blood people, and we are your friends. We live, we breathe, we laugh, and we cry. We can do that because we are real people. Right now, we are not hiding behind our cyber names and tapping our fingers to the bone. We are no longer invisible. Are we all on the same page here?"

Mary Alice nodded.

Phil took a little longer, but he also nodded. "But you both betrayed me. I would never have betrayed you. Never."

"Yes and no, Phil," Abner said. "You set up the rules early on. You need to own your part of all of this. Trust goes a long way. Had you not done that, we might not be sitting here having this conversation. And in your heart you know the why of it all. Do not pretend otherwise, or this new friendship is not going to work. We share a hundred percent. Tell me if you agree."

Phil wagged his index finger in the air. Mary Alice did the same thing.

Abner went on. "We, Mary Alice, myself, you, and all our brothers and sisters out there who belong to our . . . hacking family, are not leading normal, healthy lives. Actually, the truth is, we have no lives other than the obvious one. Take yourself, for example, Phil. You said you never had friends, still have no friends. That's not good. I stepped out of the box, got married. Mary Alice has her seed business, but she doesn't interact with people. Nor do you. I do. I want us all to be normal and help each other. In other words, mingle with the human race and stop hiding behind what we do.

"Having said all that, and I'm sure it didn't come out right, here's the bottom line. You have to give the money back, Phil. I know it's going to be a bitch of a job, but I think you kept records, so maybe it won't be that hard. If you don't, they *will* find you. Not because of Mary Alice or me, but because those people will do what they do. Just like you, Mary Alice, and I do what we do. So, what do you say, Phil?"

Phil didn't bother to argue. He had known all along that someday it might come to this. And he was prepared. What he hadn't prepared for was having two helpers.

"Okay. It's a lot of money, Abner."

"I know. They were saying almost a billion. That's with a *b*."

Phil laughed. "True."

"What did you do with it?" Mary Alice asked, her eyes sparkling with curiosity.

"I gave it all away. I didn't keep one penny. In my own defense, I made a lot of people happy. What makes me so different from you, Abner?"

"What? You're actually asking me a question like that! You're an outright thicf, Phil. You ripped off all these casinos. Why?"

"Why? Because I could. You and Mary Alice do the same thing. What makes me so different?"

"We're not the same. I'm going to speak only for myself, and you already know what I am going to say. I deal with bad guys. Bad guys who are doing bad things to good, kind, decent people. I keep a finder's fee, in case a job comes in where there is no money involved, just information. Evening the odds a bit. Justice is blind sometimes. We take off the blindfold and do the best we can. I have never gotten caught. Not even close, because I am aware of that invisible line I cannot cross. You stepped on it, then crossed over it, just because you could. Now you have to give it back. Mary Alice?"

"I couldn't have said it any better. Abner is right. I operate the same way."

Phil burst out laughing. "So what we have here is the teacher now becomes the pupil. Somehow I think this is very fitting. I don't know why. I knew when I picked the two of you, I was on the money.

"I guess it's okay to tell you this now. I almost didn't pick you, Mary Alice. It was a tie between you and LB-Nine. Cyber name Lady Bug Nine. She was your match in every way, but there was something in her eyes that didn't sit well with me. I can't explain it any better than that. Your eyes, Mary Alice, were full of wonder and excitement. I couldn't see anything in hers. Just so you know, I never regretted choosing you."

"What happened to her?" Abner asked.

Phil waved his arm. "She's about. I check on her from time to time," he said vaguely. "First thing tomorrow morning, we'll get to that. Tonight is for talking. Three friends talking, getting to know each other," Phil added.

Abner felt light-headed. This was way too easy. But at the same time, he wasn't picking up on anything negative. "You said you gave it all away and didn't keep a penny, right?"

"Right."

"Do you have enough money to pay it back?"

Phil laughed again. "Kids, I have so much money, I could repay that debt ten times over. Now that you're putting me on the straight and narrow, I think you could probably convince me to pay interest."

"You would do that?" Mary Alice asked, her eyes popping wide.

"If we're going to do it, then we need to do it right. How about a nice chilled glass of wine?"

"That would be . . . lovely," Mary Alice said.

"Yes, lovely," Abner said, echoing her words.

Five minutes later, Phil was pouring wine into exquisite cut-glass wine flutes. "What should we drink to?" he asked.

"I think we should drink to tomorrow," Abner said.

And that was what they did.

With gusto.

Chapter 14

Maggie nibbled on her thumbnail as she gazed out the window of the taxi that was taking her to Kitty Passion's ranch. She admitted to herself that she was a tad nervous. Why, she didn't know. She was a pro. She could handle herself in any situation and always managed to come out on top. This, though, was different. Here she was, working on a lie of her own making. Not that she couldn't carry off the lie . . . She could. It was the twenty-five or so women who supposedly had lived the truth of her lie.

As she continued to chew on her cuticle, she let her thoughts take her back to the lunch at the Cat & Cradle. She'd formed a snap opinion right out of the gate, which was unlike her. Why had she done that? Was it because she had felt inferior, given that the women were all beautiful showgirls and she was a dowdy plain Jane? Compared to them, she was a mutt at the Westminster Kennel Club Dog Show as she tried to compete. No, it was more than that.

On the surface, the women were all smiles, friendly, but . . . maybe that was it. It was a surface thing, a facade they were presenting to the world, when in reality they were anything but who they were pretending to be. That was it! It was all an act. She remembered a glimpse, a spark, a hastily spoken word they had hoped went unnoticed. They were a group of bitter, hateful women bent on destroying the man who had . . . what? Trifled with their affections? Lied to them? Broke promises? Led them down the primrose path, where they found nothing at the end? Certainly enough to make one angry, but not to the point of . . . whatever they were planning.

She wished she knew what it was that was going to go down that would put an end to Dixson Kelly. When something was over, you simply moved on. What was it about these women that had forced them to band together to wreak vengeance on Kelly? The sheer number of them that he'd trifled with? Anger at themselves for not being smart enough to see through his promises and lies? The loss of the fairy tale, at the end of which they all lived happily ever after?

Maggie made a snorting sound. If you truly wanted happily ever after, you got a dog or a cat who would love you unconditionally while you waited for Mr. Perfect to show up at your door. And if he was a no-show, at least you had the dog or cat to keep you company.

She leaned forward to speak to the taxi driver. "How much farther?"

"According to the GPS, two more miles. I've never had a fare out this way, so I can't be sure. Are you running late?"

Maggie didn't know if she was running late or not. She was simply showing up, and whatever happened, happened.

She leaned back against the seat. She hated events like this, where she was winging it, as opposed to going in with a plan. A plan was always good, even when things went awry. And she had no backup out here in nowhere land, with no place to go if she had to beat a hasty retreat. Then there were the odds she'd have to combat. Twenty-five or so women against her. Her thoughts started to run wild. The first thing she should do when she got to the ranch was find out where the ten thousand chickens were that Kitty Passion had said she had. Find out where they were so she could run to their roosts and let them loose. Then what? Chicken poop everywhere. People slipping and sliding all over the place, herself included. As far as plans went, it was the best she could come up with. Then a horrible thought hit her. She didn't know much about chickens, but she did know they roosted at night. Now, where had she heard that? Well, if things got dicey, she'd just have to wake them up and hope for the best.

"We're here, lady!" the cabdriver said.

Maggie looked out the window. *Nice place*, she thought. Low-slung ranch-style house that looked like it was built out of natural field-stone. Large chimneys sprouted from the sides and roof. She counted four. Fireplaces. Fireplaces were cozy. Homey. Pruned shrubbery, green lawn out here in the desert. Underground sprinkler system of some kind. Rows and rows of one-story buildings, all painted white. Modern chicken coops. The air smelled like chickens. She swallowed hard. She hated the smell.

Maggie paid the driver, adding a generous tip, grabbed her backpack, and got out of the taxi. She could hear voices and laughter as she walked up the flagstone walkway, which was bordered with spring flowers. The voices and laughter were coming from the back of the low, sprawling ranch house. She detoured and headed in that direction, where she was welcomed with open arms as the women swirled around her.

The mood was jovial, the laughter high-pitched. *Almost*, Maggie thought, *verging on hysterical.*

She counted seven open bottles of wine on the long picnic table, along with a dozen or so beer bottles. Obviously, the others had gotten here much earlier than she had. She couldn't help but wonder if that was on purpose.

"Wine or beer?" Kitty asked.

Maggie stared at her host. She liked her, liked the way she'd come to her aid at the Cat & Cradle. She wore no makeup because she didn't need it. Her skin was tanned and flawless; her lashes were long, natural, and curled upward; her lips a natural pink. She herself was drinking ginger ale. She wore cutoff blue jeans and a well-worn T-shirt that said PEACE on the front and the back. Ten-dollar Walmart sneakers graced her feet. She smiled, hugged Maggie, and popped a Bud Light for her.

"I'm not much of a drinker," Maggie said.

"Me either. I'm diabetic."

Maggie wasn't sure what, if anything, she should say to that confession, so she just nodded in understanding. "Are all those low buildings where you keep the chickens?" she asked after she remembered her quasi plan.

"Yep, all ten thousand of them. The other buildings over to the left are where the workers stay. Actually, they're mini-apartments. I have thirty employees. All good people. We need to patrol at night and keep torches lit, so the coyotes don't come out after the chickens. We have wolves and stray dogs that are part wolf. In some respects, it is a hard business, but I'm getting used to it. I actually like it better than working the Vegas clubs. Showgirl to chicken rancher! I get a kick out of myself sometime."

Maggie laughed. She liked this young woman and was having a hard time with the why and the how of her being involved with the rest of the women milling about. And yet . . .

"Do whatever makes you happy, Kitty. That's what life is all about. How did you get involved in"—Maggie waved her arms about to indicate the other women—"all of this?"

"It's a long story. I'm not actually *involved*. It's more like I'm doing a favor for some of the girls. Please don't feel like you have to—"

"Grill's ready!" one of the women shouted.

Whatever she was about to say ended with Kitty running over to the patio, where the grill awaited the thick Kobe-beef steaks that Vegas was known for, piled high on a huge platter.

Maggie blinked, then blinked again. The scene she was watching reminded her of the sisters out at Myra's farm as they worked in sync at mealtime. How many times had she participated in that very action? Too many to count, that's how many. But—and there was always a *but* to situations like this—there was an undercurrent here, a frenzied, almost frantic rush to cook, to eat, to drink so they could get down to whatever it was they were going to get down to and share with her. If she didn't screw things up. She needed to start acting.

Maggie meandered over to the serving table to pick up her plate and cutlery. She smiled, a sickly effort, as she made small talk.

"You look sad," Misty Sanchez said lightly. "This is girls' night. You're with friends here, Maggie. We're all here for you. We meant what we said today at lunch. We'll do whatever we can for you. Always remember, there is strength in numbers."

Maggie nodded and mumbled something under her breath. Misty leaned closer. "What did you say?"

Maggie looked up, tears puddling in her

eyes. "That guy I told you about . . . he fired my brother this afternoon. I found out when I got back to the hotel. My brother, my only living relative, is blaming me. I never should have come here. I'm such a fool. But the heart wants what the heart wants. I'm going home in the morning. He told Jack to clear out his things. And he told him he was going to ban him from Babylon." Sobs shook her shoulders.

"Hey, girls! Come here and listen to this! Tell them what you just told me, Maggie! Never mind. I'll tell them. That rat that dumped Maggie—he just fired her brother this afternoon and kicked him out of Babylon!"

The shocked silence bothered Maggie for some reason.

Kitty turned from the grill, her beautiful eyes narrowed to slits. "Why?"

"Because of me, that's why," Maggie wailed. "Because I was a pest when I asked for answers. I wouldn't go away and insisted on a face-to-face. Jack . . . I think Jack might have said something to him. I don't know for sure. Now he'll blackball Jack, and he'll never get another job in Vegas. All because of me. That man has some serious clout," she continued to wail.

"Well, honey, we have some serious clout of our own," Kate Davis, a tall, leggy redhead, said with spirit.

The others shouted their agreement.

Kitty flipped the steaks. "Where is your brother now?"

"Packing his stuff up. He was staying in one of those apartments that Babylon owns that guys share. Kind of like a dormitory, but with all kinds of privileges. The hotel pays half, and the guys pay half. He didn't even give him twenty-four hours. Just told him to go *now* and to take his sister with him. Meaning me, as I am the sister. What a louse he is. How could I ever have loved someone like that? My God, how?"

That was some pretty good acting, Maggie thought as she blew her nose into a wad of paper napkins. "I just want to go home. Can someone call me a cab? I'll go straight to the airport and maybe get on standby. I don't want to be here anymore. I can't take it. Now my brother blames me and hates me at the same time." She let loose with a fresh waterfall of tears and decided she was almost Academy Award material.

"You aren't going anywhere," the women chorused as they gathered around her and led her to a deep, comfortable-looking chaise longue. Suddenly, there was a glass of wine in her hand and a thick circle of women staring down at her.

"Listen up, Maggie Spritzer, because we are going to tell you a story you are not going to believe. We want and need your full attention here. Do we have it, Maggie?" Lena Adams asked.

Lordy, Lordy, here it comes, Maggie thought. She sniffled and nodded.

"Take the steaks off, Kitty, and get over here!" Lena shouted.

Maggie turned off her tears, and her jaw dropped and her eyes almost popped out of her head as she listened to the women's accounts of their relationships with Dixson Kelly. From time to time, she managed a sputtered expletive or two to show she was into it, along with the women.

"That's why we formed this little club and call ourselves the Dixson Kelly Alumnae Club. We just voted you in as a member. We are going to get even with that son of a bitch. And here is the best part, Maggie. There are more of us. Some of the girls couldn't get here today, because their schedules changed. We numbered forty at last count. That's forty women that bastard conned," Lena said.

"Forty! Did you say forty? I don't believe this! I can't believe this! I do believe it. That rat fink. Am I forty-one?" Maggie let loose with a tortured scream of denial.

"We have a plan."

Thank God someone does, Maggie thought. "What kind of plan? Are you going to kill him? Although killing is too good. He needs to suffer the way he made us suffer, and he has to pay for firing Jack. What's the plan?"

"We are going to set him up, frame him, then rob the casino!" Lena continued.

Maggie almost jumped out of her skin. "You mean like that movie *Ocean's Eleven*?"

"No, no, nothing that elaborate. We have it all figured out. And we have a secret weapon!" Lena said. "And she's standing right over there, our 'hostess with the mostest,' as the saying goes. Kitty is our secret weapon. You know that old saying, 'You always want what you can't have'? Well, Dixson Kelly wants Kitty so bad, he can't see straight. She's stiff-armed him for months now. She has him right where she wants him. Excuse me . . . right where we want him. All we have to do is pick a time and a place and go for it."

"But how . . . the security . . . What makes you think you won't get caught?" Maggie said, dithering. Robbing the casino, even playing a pretend part in it, wasn't something she wanted to think about. Not now, not ever.

"Well, for one thing, Gwen Sanders and Dona Jordan have been dating the two cops who drive the Guarda armored truck with the money. And Erin and Pam are in serious relationships—at least the guys think they're serious—with the two drivers in the backup vehicle. The girls have been picking their brains for months now. We've just been waiting for the right moment, and today, when you walked into that restroom and met Hana, we all knew it was meant to be. We just haven't chosen a date yet. Why aren't you looking as excited as we are?" Lena asked suspiciously.

"I'm in shock, that's why," Maggie sputtered. And she was in shock. Of all the things she had thought they might come up with to get even with Dixson Kelly, this particular method of revenge had never entered her mind. *Well, damn.*

"Do you approve or disapprove?" Kitty asked.

Her voice was so cool and flat, Maggie felt herself shivering.

Be careful, she warned herself. *This is uncharted territory.*

"I'm with you all the way," she said. "Yessiree, I am with all of you! Ooh, I can just see him in prison, some inmate's bitch!"

The women hooted with glee when Maggie finally got her tongue to work.

"He'll get all the loving he can handle on a daily basis, a good-looking guy like him," Misty Sanchez said.

The women laughed uproariously. Maggie didn't know whether she should laugh or cry. Then she did a reality check. How was she going to get out of this?

The wine and the beer flowed; the Kobe steaks and the rest of the food were forgotten. Suddenly, no one was hungry, not even Maggie, who could eat anytime, anyplace due to her out-of-whack metabolism. It didn't take long for her to realize that she and Kitty were the only two women who were stone-cold sober. Her right eye started to twitch, a warning that something wasn't quite right.

Maggie moved to the table and sat down on the bench across from Kitty. "How much money are you guys talking about?" she asked between hiccups.

"Millions."

"What are you going to do with it? How will you divide it? I guess it's the reporter in me.

Like, who would get the most is dependent on who was hurt the most . . . what? Or equally?"

Kitty burst out laughing. "Oh, we aren't going to keep it. Once Kelly is in jail, we'll give it all back."

The reporter in Maggie immediately discounted Kitty's statement, because while those luscious pillow lips of hers were saying one thing, her bedroom eyes were saying something else. "But they'll just let him go then, and they'll pay him a bunch of money for something he didn't do. He wins in the end. Didn't you all think of that?"

"That will be months down the road, and in the meantime, he'll be in jail. No women! That alone is a killer for someone like him. It'll do him in. Then we'll all sell our stories to the tabloids and make our money that way. Now do you get it?"

Maggie forced a laugh she didn't feel. "Awesome. I can see where you all gave this a lot of thought."

"Night and day for months. You know what, Maggie? When Lena first approached me, I said no. Then I met the women and listened to their stories and felt sorry for them. They all truly, truly fell in love with Kelly. Like you, they believed what he told them. They thought they had met their perfect soul mates. Maybe if the guy had changed his MO just a little, it would have been easier for them to swallow, but he handed out the same line to all of them. How he ever kept it straight is beyond me, but he did it."

She's lying through her teeth, Maggie thought. "Burner phones," Maggie said, authority ringing in her voice.

"What? What does that mean?" Kitty asked.

"The way to keep you all straight. Burner phones, no way to trace them. Usually prepaid. A few years ago, I did a story on a guy who was running a scam to bilk people out of their money. A lot of people. The only way he could keep it straight was to assign a phone to each one. He had nineteen that I know of. They were all labeled, and attached to each phone was an index card with notes, along with the phone number. All in all, it was pretty amazing. Did you and the girls ever compare notes as to his phone number? Did you all call his personal cell?"

"I never asked. Hold on." Kitty put her fingers between her lips and let loose with a wild, high-pitched shrieking whistle that got everyone's attention. "Girls! Girls! I need to ask you a question. One by one, tell me the number you used to call to reach Dixson Kelly."

The women rattled off the number they'd been assigned by heart. There were no two that were alike. Everyone asked why, and Kitty explained what Maggie had just shared with her.

The women reacted as one, shouting, "We were nothing but burner phones to that creep,

that skunk, that low-life, bottom-feeding scumbag!" And on and on they went, till they ran
out of hateful names.

"Someone needs to write this down, because
it's one more thing that skunk has to pay for,"
Pam Logan shrieked.

"We should write it down in blood. His!"
someone else shouted.

Maggie just watched as the women went at
it. She hoped they never got their hands physically on Dixson Kelly. Not that he didn't deserve *something* happening to him by way of
retribution.

The big question now was, what should she
do? She, Maggie Spritzer, *Post* reporter. Part of
her wanted the women to succeed simply because she was a woman and hated the way Dixson Kelly had played fast and loose with them.
The other part of her knew she had to tell the
boys what was happening. Or did she? Something simply was not adding up. All this had
nothing to do with RCHood, whoever he was,
ripping off the casinos. Dixson Kelly had had
no part in that theft. That had to mean Kelly
was fair game, since he wasn't involved in any
way with that end of things. Still . . . she wanted
to side with the women because she knew,
could see, how badly they'd been hurt emotionally. They'd become bitter and hateful because of Dixson Kelly. Why shouldn't they want
revenge? She wasn't one of them, and yet she
wanted the revenge for them. Sort of.

Her back stiffened when she heard Hana

Frey say, "So what you're saying is, we were just hunks of fresh meat with a burner-phone number to identify each of us. That's what you're saying, right?"

Maggie didn't trust herself to speak as she looked around at the women, who suddenly all looked sober. She saw tears on every woman's cheeks. She watched as they swiped at them before they came together to start the cleanup, just the way the sisters did back at the farm. She could see the dejection, the rejection, the slumped shoulders. They were going to give up. She could see that the fight was suddenly gone from them.

Suddenly, because she was sober, Maggie found herself standing on the picnic table and screaming at the top of her lungs. "No! Come on! You aren't going to let what I said make you cave in, are you! Come on! Ten minutes ago, you guys had a plan. You were ready to kick some ass and take names later. *You are not hunks of meat and a burner phone.* You are beautiful, wonderful women who have hearts and souls but had the misfortune to fall in love with a badass who gets his jollies from lying to women. I might be new here, but I'm not going to let you give up!"

One of the women at the front of the group snapped, "Who died and appointed you ruler of the universe?"

"You all did when you invited me out here. Chew on that, toots!"

"Wow! You're a spitfire, aren't you?" Kitty

said, smiling. The only problem Maggie could see was that the smile didn't reach Kitty's eyes. While she was beautiful, as was her smile, her eyes were cold and calculating.

"Yeah," Maggie drawled. "That's what my boss calls me."

Chapter 15

Abner trotted down the hall toward the kitchen, from where he heard noises. Phil was up early. He looked down at his watch. Six thirty. He didn't know why he was surprised to see Mary Alice sitting at the counter, with her hands around a mug of coffee, but he was. She looked like she'd been up for a while.

"Good morning, Abner! How did you sleep?" Mary Alice asked.

"Very well, as a matter of fact. I feel right now like a freshwater eel. Something smells good." He looked around to see what smelled so good as he poured himself a cup of coffee.

"Fresh cinnamon croissants right out of the freezer. The orange juice is also frozen. Only the coffee is truly fresh. Mary Alice and I have been talking. We've both been up since five.

I'm not much of a sleeper," Philonias confided.

"What did you talk about?" Abner asked curiously.

"Nothing earth shattering. More like getting to know the flesh-and-blood side of each other. I now know that she likes to walk barefoot in the rain. There is no way I could ever have known that just being cyber friends. What do you want to share, Abner?"

Abner thought about it. "I like walking on the beach as the tide is coming in. I own a lot of beachfront property, but somehow I never get a chance to enjoy it. That's going to change when I get back. What about you, Phil? What does the flesh-and-blood Phil like to do that the cyber Phil doesn't do?"

Philonias smiled. It was a nice smile, Abner thought, but he could see it was rusty at best, as though he didn't smile much and was just trying it out.

"It's not so much what I do, but more like what I would *like* to do. Like you, Abner, I simply never took the time. I plan to do that very soon, if I'm not locked up somewhere."

"What is it?" Mary Alice asked.

"I'd like to own an animal farm. All kinds of animals. The kind no one else wants. I want to give them a good life. I want them warm in the winter, cool in the summer, and to know their bellies will always be full. I donate money to a lot of animal causes, but I want my own. I want to . . . I want to give the animals a bath, clean up their messes. I want to be hands on. I never had a pet as a child, and if ever there was a child who needed a pet, I was that child."

"Why didn't you get one, then?" Mary Alice asked.

Philonias sighed. "It wouldn't have been fair to the animal with what I was doing. I was on the computer almost twenty hours a day. Animals need fresh air, green grass, and room to run and play. Penthouse living is for goldfish."

Abner toyed with the spoon next to his cup and napkin. "Do you have other places like this one, Phil?"

Philonias nodded. "How did you know? Six, to be precise."

"When you leave here, are you going to go to one of them?" Abner asked.

"Yes. I just haven't decided which one."

"I think you should take Mary Alice with you. Just to be sure she's safe. Even though the people I'm with are friends, I'm not sure how they're going to react to the way this all went down and to my . . . um . . . sudden departure, especially since I took her with me. They are going to view it as the ultimate betrayal."

"Wait a minute, Abner. What are you saying here? You want us to be safe, but you are going to stay behind. Is this what flesh-and-blood people do? Help me out here, okay?" Phil said.

Abner drained his coffee cup. He really did not want to talk about this, but he knew he had to. He was the one who had opened up this can of worms. "I don't know about other people, but it's what I am going to do. Whatever happens. I held up my end of the bargain. Or if you prefer the word *commitment.* I also told them from the git-go that I wouldn't be able to break RC's work. I tried. I owed them all that much."

"When you say 'them,' do you mean the Vigilantes and their various partners? Along with Charles Martin, Fergus Duffy, and their pack of old MI-Six operatives, mainly Avery Snowden?"

Abner sighed. Why wasn't he surprised at Phil's knowledge? "You knew, and you never let on? Why?"

"Because that's what cyber friends do, Abner. In the end, cyber friends or flesh-and-blood friends, it's all the same. It always comes down to one single thing."

"Trust," Abner said.

"Exactly. We can't do anything about the past, kids. All we can do is secure the future. And trying to place blame for what is currently going on is counterproductive. I thought that yesterday, with our come-to-Jesus meeting, we put that behind us and that now are just going forward, with the first step being returning all the funds I helped myself to from the casinos. I'm good with everything. What about you two?"

"I'm good," Abner said, and suddenly he realized he really was okay with it all.

"Me too," Mary Alice said.

Phil rubbed his hands together. "I know you

two are going to find this hard to believe, but I am actually looking forward to returning the money, plus interest. I really am."

"That's weird, Phil," said Abner.

"There's weird, and then there's weird. Who else do you know who could make that happen and leave no trail behind? They don't even know it's gone, and then to be put back, and they still won't know. That's genius, if you want my opinion."

"You're forgetting Bert, aren't you, Phil?"

"No. When we're done, he will just think he made a colossal mistake, and he'll knock himself out apologizing to everyone for what he put them through. I'll leave some bread crumbs for him to pick up so he can see where he made his mistake. That's what a flesh-and-blood friend would do, right, Abner?"

"Yeah, Phil, that's what a flesh-and-blood friend would do. Your best bet, Phil. How long do you think it will take us to make restitution?"

"If we start now, we should be done by nightfall, give or take an hour or so."

"And then?" Abner asked.

"Then we part company. But not before we set up new identities so that we can communicate. And, by the way, that special, super-duper phone you have that Mr. Snowden got from the CIA . . . Who do you think designed the prototype that you have in your pocket?"

A chill ripped down Abner's back. His hand involuntarily went to his pocket. He pulled out the strange-looking phone and looked at it. He listened as Phil uttered some gibberish that caused Abner to press buttons on the special phone. In spite of himself, he laughed out loud. "I gotta say, Phil, you outdid yourself here. I didn't have a clue. So you've known all along what's been going on."

"Yep. And now that there are no more secrets between us three flesh-and-blood friends, what do you say we get to work?"

Mary Alice smiled at Phil's tone, grateful that her mentor was no longer angry about her forced betrayal. Abner thought she was pretty in a wholesome way. He rather thought Phil was thinking the exact same thing when he winked at him. *Whoa.*

Maggie waited in line at one of the three bathrooms at Kitty Passion's ranch so she could brush her teeth and wash her face. She'd shower when she got back to the hotel. She had been promised a ride back to town by Hana Frey, and Hana was waiting for her in the driveway. She'd been up all night, even though most of the girls had napped an hour here, an hour there, then were up drinking either more wine or coffee. Good hostess that she was, Kitty had offered to make breakfast, but they had all declined.

Thank God, Maggie thought, as it was finally her turn to get the bathroom.

As she brushed and flossed, she decided that nothing had been decided. As far as she was concerned, the night had been a flop. She had had a bad moment when she had to make the decision on what to tell all the women. She had finally chosen to say that she would take a room at MGM, but she'd said she could stay only one more night, because her money was running out. One of the girls—she couldn't remember which one—had offered to get a room comped for her for three days, saying that in three days, they'd have a fully developed plan to take down Dixson Kelly. Whatever that meant. Now she was stuck with having to relocate.

Since her arrival at the ranch at dusk yesterday, she'd had no contact with anyone, and now she still couldn't do anything, so she was in the dark as far as what was going on. If there was one place Maggie did not like, it was in the dark.

She exited the bathroom, said a few more good-byes, and followed Hana Frey, who had come inside to find out what was taking so long, to the front door, where Kitty Passion was waiting to see her guests off.

"I hope you enjoyed your visit," Kitty told her. "We usually have a little more fun, and last night was a little intense. I'm glad you're going to stay on a few more days. Not to worry. If it takes longer, we'll get everything comped for you. We have a good network. I'll be in touch." The two women hugged each other.

Maggie left the house and headed down the flagstone walkway to the car. She turned around before she opened the door to Hana's Mustang and waved to Kitty.

The ride back to town was quicker than her trip out to the ranch the night before. Hana was a quiet driver as she concentrated on the road she was driving on.

"I'm kind of sluggish this morning. I didn't sleep a wink last night, and my routine is off, so I apologize for not chattering away. I hope you don't mind."

"No problem, Hana. I didn't sleep, either."

"So am I dropping you off at Babylon or MGM?"

"Babylon. I left my luggage with the bell captain. I want to check out my room one last time. I don't care what Dixson Kelly told the desk about kicking me out. I can pitch a fit with the best of them, and do not ever forget I have the power of the pen. I can write a scathing article about the casino and Kelly that will burn the hair right off his head. Don't worry about me. I can find my way to MGM. You just go home and get some sleep. You know how to reach me. Either by text or e-mail."

The rest of the ride into town was made in silence. Maggie waved wanly as she climbed out of the car. She'd never been so glad to rid herself of someone in her whole life. She stood rooted to the concrete under her feet until she saw Hana's car fade from sight. Then she moved faster than she'd ever moved in her life. She literally galloped across the casino floor to the bank of elevators that would take her to the concierge level.

She took the elevator up to the concierge level, where she stopped just long enough to fortify herself with a cup of the hotel's excellent coffee. She eyed an omelet that the cook was preparing and asked if she could have it.

"But of course. I'm making it just the way you've had it in the past. Toast or croissants?"

What the heck. The others could wait a few more minutes, until she fortified herself with some nourishment. Maggie took a moment to wonder what Kitty had done with all the Kobe steaks that had ended up half-grilled and not eaten, along with the rest of the hot food. Not that she cared. Right now, she didn't want to think about anything concerning Kitty Passion, Dixson Kelly, or anyone else. All she wanted was to zone out and have her breakfast, take a shower, grab some sleep, and wake up raring to go.

Maggie finished the last of the excellent gourmet coffee and was ready to leave when the elevator opened to spit out Dixson Kelly, who, Maggie thought sourly, looked good enough to eat. She was suddenly aware of her rumpled clothes, her "I slept in my clothes" look. Damn, the man looked good. She nodded curtly and got up. She knew she didn't have to, but she carried her plate and her cup to the wait station and set them down.

"Are you having a good or bad day, Miss Spritzer?" Kelly asked cheerfully.

And he smelled good, too. Something exotic and yet earthy. One of the girls had said she went nuts over the smell, and she'd do anything he wanted her to do. That was way too much information for Maggie, who had walked away.

"Somewhere in between, Mr. Kelly. Why do you ask?" That was good. Always put them on the defensive.

"You were gone all night, so I just assumed you were . . ."

"Let's not go there. And just for the record, do you spy on all your guests? How do you even know I wasn't here last night?" Her eyes flashed sparks, which had no effect on Kelly.

"Bert entrusted your care to me. I would gladly have arranged travel for you to wherever you went last night, so you didn't have to bear the cost of a taxi. The hotel will be more than happy to reimburse you if you just give me the taxi chit or the amount."

So you can figure out where I went or call the driver to find out? I don't think so, you son of a bitch. Of course, she said no such thing. "No problem. I have a healthy expense account. Nice talking to you again. See ya," Maggie said.

Then she sprinted from the hospitality area to the hall and then on to Charles's suite, where she banged on the door, not caring how much noise she made. Fergus, who had been having a cup of coffee with Charles, opened the door and literally yanked her into the room as he stared out into the hall to see if anyone was with her.

"Kelly is out there in the hospitality area. Call everyone. I have news none of you are going to believe," Maggie said in a jittery voice.

"We also have news you are not going to believe," Charles said somberly, coming up behind Fergus, with a cup of coffee in his hand.

"Oh, crap. This is going to be one of those 'Shoot me and put me out of my misery' moments, isn't it?"

"I'm afraid so, my dear. Let's just wait for everyone to get here. More coffee? Fergus just brought a fresh pot back from the hospitality station," Charles said.

"Why not? I'm wired up now as it is. What's one more cup going to do to me except put me into orbit? Nothing happens in the middle of the night, so what the hell could have gone wrong? I wasn't even gone twenty-four hours."

Neither Charles nor Fergus responded, so Maggie sat down and started to chew on her cuticles, a really nasty habit she had yet to overcome. She was half finished with her coffee when the others started to troop in, in various stages of dress.

Maggie looked them all over and decided they looked worse than she did. She made no bones about saying so. "What's your excuse for looking like you've all been on a weeklong booze bender? Let's hear it, and then I'll share my news."

"Abner's gone. He took PIP with him," Jack said tightly.

Maggie blinked. "What do you mean, he's gone? Where did he go?"

"We don't know. His truck is gone from the parking garage. He also took the batteries out of his personal phone and the special phone. Like I said, he's gone."

"Why? That's not like Abner. Abner is . . . Abner is . . . Oh, my God. You guys set him up and put him to the test, and he chose his hacker mentor over you all. That's what happened, isn't it? Well, isn't it?" she screeched.

"It wasn't quite like that, but yeah, that's pretty much what happened," Ted said.

"And you let him go! Just like that, you let him go!" Maggie screeched again. "Oh, God, you people are so stupid! Don't you get it? If Abner said he couldn't find out who RC is, he couldn't. I've never, ever known Abner to tell a lie. He told you the truth back in the beginning. He warned you all that if it was RC, we were dead in the water. And he had PIP helping him. You made him think you all believed he betrayed you. That's what you did! I see it on your faces! All because Bert got a bug up his butt, made us come here on something he *thinks* happened, and you believed and sided with him. The same Bert who is an emotional basket case, thanks to Kathryn Lucas, his ex-girlfriend. God, how could you be so damn stupid? I don't blame Abner for leaving. I would have, too, if I were in his place.

"Bert is . . . hurting. He's just looking for things to occupy himself because of Kathryn. I tried telling you all of that back at the beginning, but you wouldn't listen to me. I'll bet my job at the *Post* and my yearly bonus that no money is gone from the casinos, and Bert just screwed up. He's just not man enough to admit it, or else he's more stupid than the rest of you. I do not believe this. When did Abner leave?"

"A little before you did yesterday," Dennis said. "He was hopping mad, too. I heard him cuss, and Abner never uses cusswords. And Miss PIP looked like she was ready to chew nails and spit rust."

Sparrow weighed in. "I don't go way back, the way you all do with Abner, but I think he did what he could, and it just wasn't good enough. You all discounted his loyalty to RC, and that was wrong. He said it best when he said that without RC, he wouldn't even be on our radar screen. He wouldn't be a loyal friend. And from all I can see and from what I hear, he is just as loyal as any of you are. So you all have some serious making up to do. That's my opinion."

Harry surprised everyone by saying, "It's too late for making up. He's out there right now, trying to find RC. I think he has suspicions, and between him and PIP, if there's a way to find the man, they'll find him. I don't know what will happen if he and PIP are successful. Sounded to me like Abner burned his bridges when he left here. Serves us all right, too."

Avery Snowden cleared his throat. His pasty English complexion was pink right now. "I don't know how to say this other than to come right out and say it. Those special phones, the ones I got from the CIA, the prototypes, are useless. I just found out a half hour ago, when our mutual friend RCHood sent me a text on my special prototype, saying how silly I was to believe that he, meaning RCHood, couldn't tap into it when he was the one who designed it in the first place for the CIA. Yes, I have egg on my face.

"My contact, the person who got me these phones, assured me they were safe and secure. I was just in touch with him, and while the designer's name is classified, and he wouldn't tell me it, when I mentioned the cyber name RCHood, he went all silent on me. The phones are useless now. That guy is one savvy, smart son of a bitch, that's for sure."

"Does all this mean we're going home?" Espinosa asked.

Jack felt sicker than he'd ever felt in his life. "I don't know. I've been trying to call Bert since last night, but the calls just go to voice mail."

"We have to find Abner," Maggie said as she swiped at the tears rolling down her cheeks.

"What would you have us do, dear?" Charles asked gently. "If you have any ideas, share them with me immediately. We'll jump at anything right now."

"You all should have thought about that when you drove him out. I hope you all think about what is going to happen when Isabelle and the girls find out. I sure don't want to be within five miles of any of you when that happens. Good luck," she bellowed, making for the door just as a knock sounded. She opened it with a flourish to see the nattily dressed Dixson Kelly standing there. She wondered how long he'd been at the door. Then she decided she didn't care as she stomped her way down the hall to her own suite. Let those she'd left behind deal with Dixson Kelly and whatever he had to say or do.

It wasn't until she was in the shower that she realized she hadn't shared her news about the girls and Dixson Kelly.

Maggie toweled dry and slipped into a night-shirt that said HERO on the front. She slid between the sheets and was asleep within minutes.

Chapter 16

Phil closed the door to the computer room and motioned for Abner and Mary Alice to take up positions at two computers opposite the one where he had positioned himself. "Power up, kids!"

The kids powered up.

"Okay, pay attention now. Here comes the tutorial. When I'm done, if you paid attention, you are going to be almost as smart as me. You ready?"

The kids, as Phil called them, nodded.

Fifteen minutes later, Abner and Mary Alice were glassy-eyed.

"That's how you did it!" Abner said in awe. "I'll be damned."

Mary Alice was so speechless, all she could do was shake her head for a moment. "So to undo all you did, we just reverse—"

"No, no, no! It's not that simple. Pay attention now. One false keystroke, and it's all over. Watch, listen, and repeat after me. This is your only test."

They really were kids then, their attention rapt, their eyes wide in awe as Phil led them down the path they were about to embark on. When he was finished, he looked at his star pupils and asked if they understood what they were to do. Both nodded that they did.

"We're not looking for speed here. Remember that. You get stuck or are unsure, shout out, and I'll be there immediately to help you out. Abner, you are going to do The Venetian. Mary Alice, you have MGM. I'm taking Babylon. It's eight ten at the moment. I expect to have Babylon back on track by ten ten. I'm telling you this only to relieve any anxiety you might be experiencing because of your friends. If your buddy Bert logs on at ten fifteen, he is going to be in for the shock of his life. Remember, speed does not count. Make sure the interest is spot on. This has to be *clean*. Hit it, kids!"

Phil tapped furiously, his fingers magical. Out of the corner of his eye, he could see that Abner and Mary Alice were cautiously tapping away. He knew that once they got comfortable with his programs, the speed of their typing would equal his own.

He was excited. He couldn't remember the last time he'd felt so . . . liberated, unless it was when he made his first unauthorized *withdrawal*. Somehow, even though he couldn't remember that moment exactly, he was sure it didn't equal what he was feeling right now, at this very moment.

To admit to having the time of his life would be a gross understatement.

The huge battery-operated clock on the wall said the time was 10:14 a.m. when Phil rolled his chair back from the table and shot both arms high in the air. Abner and Mary Alice stopped what they were doing, hands poised over their keyboards.

"Five minutes," Abner said.

"Me too," Mary Alice said.

The minute Abner and Mary Alice rolled their chairs backward, Phil let loose with a whoop of pleasure that sounded like a war drum. The kids burst out laughing.

"Kids, we just crossed the Rubicon. We need to take a break. I have some excellent flavored coffee that's better than any dessert. Want some?"

Abner and Mary Alice said they did as they trooped behind Phil to the kitchen.

"Damn, that was exhilarating!" Phil said as he ground coffee beans, then prepared the pot. "These past two hours were more rewarding than the day I stole my first nineteen dollars from Babylon. I didn't think anything could beat that moment in time. I was wrong. What about you two?"

Abner grinned. "It's not quite the same for us, Phil. We're just cleaning up your mess. What I personally found rewarding is that the three of us are working together to right a wrong that you committed. That's what friends do for each other. If any of those casinos ever figure this out, one thing is absolutely sure—it will never be made public."

"They'll never figure it out. Trust me," Phil said emphatically. The kids believed him implicitly.

"I bet that's what you said the first time you helped yourself to their money, and yet here we are," Mary Alice said.

"Yes, but by accident. The human factor, which you so aptly pointed out, intervened, Abner. You never did figure out how I did it. Therein lies the difference."

"So we're on target here?" Mary Alice asked.

"We are on target, Mary Alice Farmer." Phil smiled, and the smile wasn't rusty at all this morning.

The guy is having the time of his life, Abner thought. Just the thought made him feel good, which was really strange. For one brief second, he thought of all the friends he'd left behind back at Babylon. And then the anger started to choke him off. He got up to refill his coffee cup to shake away the ugly memory of how he'd exploded. Water under the bridge now.

"Hurry up, kids, if you want to stay on target. We'll break for lunch at twelve thirty. I'll heat up the leftovers. Thirty minutes for lunch and we go back at it. As soon as we knock off the big casinos, the rest will go quickly. If we stay on target, I think we'll be done by six o'clock."

"Then what do we do, Phil?" Mary Alice asked hesitantly.

"I never like to make rash decisions, Mary Alice. Ask me again at six o'clock, and I'll have an answer for you. If you're ready, let's make the world right again." Phil clapped Abner on the shoulder. Abner felt warm all over. He likened the gesture to what a son would have felt had his father given him a pat on the back, even though he'd never experienced that particular feeling.

He smiled up at Phil, who just grinned from ear to ear. "Phil, you are a true Renaissance man!"

"If you say so," Phil said and laughed so hard, his whole body shook. He looked over at Mary Alice, who was giggling, and winked at her.

Whoa again, Abner thought.

Maggie woke up feeling meaner than a bear with its foot caught in a trap. She took another shower, brushed her teeth, and did her best to tame her wild hair. At the latter, she only partially succeeded.

What to do? Should she go to MGM and register for her comped room or stay here? She had to go to Charles's suite and explain what was going on. And she needed to find out why Dixson Kelly had been at Charles's suite. She thought about Abner as she got dressed, tears blurring her vision. She and Abner had a history going way back. He'd always been a true friend. A true-blue friend. Where was he, and what was he doing? More to the point, what was he *feeling*?

Satisfied that she looked as good as possible under the circumstances, Maggie left the suite and headed down the hall to Charles's suite. She banged on the door with her clenched fist. Jack Sparrow opened the door, a wary look in his eye. He stepped aside to allow Maggie to enter the room. To Maggie, it looked the same as it had five hours ago, when she had left to go to her room.

Maggie narrowed her eyes as she looked around at the people she thought of as family, a disgusted look on her face. Her foot was back in the bear trap when she demanded to know what Dixson Kelly had wanted. "And what is Bert Navarro saying? Has anyone heard from Abner, or are you all just writing him off? Because"—and she jabbed a finger at the center of the room—"because if you are, write me off, too. Somebody say something and quick, before I shove my foot up someone's butt. *Now* is good!"

Charles, as their leader, stepped forward. "Mr. Kelly stopped by to see if there was anything we needed. He also wanted to let us know he has been unable to reach Mr. Navarro and wondered if we had been in touch. It was pleasant and cordial, but he left after only ten minutes. And, in case no one told you, the search of his condo in town by Mr. Snowden's people revealed nothing out of the ordinary, with the exception of seventeen more burner phones. Past relationships in which he also assigned phones to his ladies, from what we were able to gather. He appears to keep his MO the same. Clothing, sports equipment, that's all we found in the closets. We've discussed the possibility of trying to gain entrance to the penthouse apartment owned by Philonias Needlemeyer, the man Mr. Kelly met in the Tiki Bar. It's a thread, but we haven't attached it to a needle yet. Mr. Snowden is working on that.

"We have repeatedly tried to reach Bert, with no success. The calls all go straight to voice mail. I feel as bad as you do about Abner. I don't know what to tell you. We didn't do anything differently than we did on other missions. We followed our own rules. Abner . . . although he is one of us, stepped off the grid. He did, Maggie, and it pains me to have to say it. Yes, he did help us. Yes, he did warn us that RCHood would have left no trail of bread crumbs to follow. There is no doubt that he had conflicting loyalties. We should have taken that into consideration and allowed for it. We did not, I'm sorry to say.

"At this time, actually since the moment he walked out of here, Abner has been unreachable. He either took the batteries out of his phones or trashed them. The CIA one-of-a-kind prototype that Mr. Snowden issued to us is junk now. RCHood sent Avery a text telling him he was the one who designed the phone for the CIA. He's been onto us all along. That about sums it up, Maggie. I'm sorry. We all regret the way it went down. None of us wanted things to end up like this."

"Where do you think he went?" Maggie demanded.

"This is just a guess on my part, but since PIP had no money or ID, Abner is probably driving her back to Arizona, after which he'll head back home," Avery Snowden said. "Like I said, a guess. For all we know, he could have headed for Disney."

Dennis stepped forward. "I don't think so. I admit I don't know Abner as well as you all do, but I think I know him well enough to say I think he and PIP put their heads together out of necessity and figured out where and how to get in touch with RCHood. I think they are on their way to wherever he is right now. Or they have already arrived at his location. They found something, a clue, but when they found it, they weren't aware of what it meant. I also think it came *after* the blowup. If I'm right, and it was after, Abner would not feel duty bound to share that information."

Ted shook his head. "You know what, kid? You never cease to amaze me. I think you are spot on here, and that's exactly what happened."

"I think you're on the money, Dennis," Harry said as he winked at him.

Jack Emery looked more miserable than anyone else in the room. "Let's say I agree with you, and I do. Then where does that leave us? Nowhere. Abner is not going to turn in his mentor. I sure as hell wouldn't if I were Abner. I cannot believe how badly this all got so screwed up on a Bert Navarro whim. I don't think I have ever felt as stupid as I do right now in my whole life. Don't look at me like that. You're all just as stupid as I am," he said savagely.

"Have you tried calling him again?" Sparrow asked.

"Yeah, a half hour ago. Call goes straight to voice mail," Jack said.

"Keep trying. Let's give some thought to calling one of the other casinos over there and asking around. Maybe there's a power problem. Does anyone know Bert's counterparts at the other casinos?"

"Yeah, actually, I do. Let me give it a whirl," Jack said, then moved off to make the call in an area that was a little less vocal and hostile.

"I believe you might have something to tell us, do you not, Maggie? You left in such a tizzy earlier, we didn't have time to talk," Charles said.

Her foot still in the bear trap, Maggie talked breathlessly about her night out at Kitty Passion's ranch. And about her move to MGM. "I need to go over there and sign in. But I'll rumple up the bed to make it look like I'm staying there, and then I'll come back here."

"No need for you to do that, Maggie. One of my operatives can step in for you and at the same time browse around to get the lay of the land, in case you are being set up," Snowden said.

Maggie took her foot out of the bear trap and said, "I didn't even think about that. Good catch, Mr. Snowden."

"Maggie, my dear, did you get any sense at all that those ladies were perhaps leading you on, or were they dead serious? Wishful thinking sort of thing. Robbing an armored car just for fun is not something anyone with half a brain would try to pull off," Charles said.

"As serious as a heart attack. Forty or so women with half brains still results in twenty whole brains. They have it all worked out. Trust me, they're going to do it. The big question is, do we do something about it or let them go for it? They said they were going to give it back. True or false? I don't know. Saying it, then seeing millions of dollars in hand, if they're successful, might make them think they could actually get away with it. Make no mistake. They definitely want Kelly to pay for trifling with their affections. You know that old saying, 'Nothing is impossible when it comes to a scorned woman,' and if you multiply that by forty, you don't need to be a rocket scientist to know the outcome."

"What's your role in all this? Did you throw up any red flags?" Sparrow asked.

Maggie sighed and went over it all again, from her story about Jack being her brother and getting fired right down to her torrid pretend affair with Kelly and relocating to MGM. "I think I'm golden. My story was every bit as good as theirs. And I'm the most recent, so it might have carried some extra weight. I'm just waiting for one of the women to get in touch with me to tell me if it's a go, give me the time, date, and so on.

"By the way, if you're serious about getting into Kelly's room, who is going to shut down the video surveillance that's in the hallways? Abner did it the last time. You can't just hit it and steal his phones, unless you rob a few of the other apartments. Ah, already I can see by your expressions that you're feeling Abner's loss. Serves you right," Maggie said bitterly. Her foot was back in the bear trap.

"I didn't know we were going to heist the phones," Sparrow said. "I think Ted and I can handle that, if need be."

Ted nodded, until Maggie shot him a look that froze him on the spot.

Sparrow saw the look and said, "Or not. Why do you want the phones?"

"My contribution to the armored-car gig. I was going to have Abner backstop some text messages to the girls proving Kelly was behind the heist. To solidify my position, in case any of them had second thoughts about me and my sudden involvement."

"I can do that," Snowden said.

Maggie yanked her foot out of the bear trap and said, "Then do it!"

Snowden looked at Charles to see what his orders were. Charles nodded. Snowden and Sparrow moved off just as Jack returned to the sitting area.

"I finally got hold of Bert," Jack reported. "He said power was down, rabble-rousers, a storm, Chinese Internet shot to hell, and about a dozen other things. He's up and mobile again. I brought him up to date. I have to say he gave me a very hard time. He says he is not wrong. He knows what he knows, and someone took the money. He is going to fax me momentarily all his notes. And he is, as we speak, going back into the account and starting over. He's going to call us. It's almost eleven o'clock our time. I'm sure we'll hear something by one, at the latest.

"Listen, I didn't have any breakfast, so I'm going out to hospitality to get some lunch. I need to think. Bert would not budge. He says he knows what he's talking about, and he is not wrong. He was hopping mad when he hung up, in case anyone cares."

"Well, I certainly do not care," Maggie snapped. "This whole thing is nothing but one fiasco after another. This kind of thing never happens when the girls are on a mission. Never!" she said vehemently.

That declaration sent everyone scurrying for cover. If they had been a pack of cats, their tails would have been between their legs.

Out in the hospitality area, Jack was oblivious to the tantalizing odors wafting about. *Some kind of pasta with a garlic sauce*, he thought as he walked over to the sun-darkened window. It looked like another beautiful day out there. He could see Harry's reflection in the window.

"That bad, huh?" Harry said.

"Yeah. I don't know what to do or what to think, Harry. Kind of a first for me."

"It's a hot mess, all right. What is your gut telling you where Bert is concerned?"

"He believes a hundred percent in everything he told us. He's also pissed to the teeth that we even doubted him for a minute. I'm going to tell Charles to hire the best forensic accounting firm in Vegas and have them take a crack at it. Other than that, I am coming up dry. Maggie hit my last nerve with that comment about the girls and how this never would have happened if this were their mission. Is she right, Harry?"

Harry shrugged. "We're not the sisters. Our DNA is a little different. Ask yourself how many times we, meaning us boys, rushed to their aid when things got sticky for them. Kind of apples and oranges. The end result is what is going to count once we get to the finish line. The end justifying the means. All for the betterment of . . . what?"

"Harry . . . an armored-car robbery! All because a bunch of women got emotionally involved with a . . . What should we call Kelly? A lothario, a Romeo, a lover of ladies? They want him to spend ten or twenty years in jail for breaking their hearts! The scary thing here is I can actually see them pulling it off and Kelly doing the perp walk. I'm all for slipping him Lizzie Fox's business card to give him a heads-up. This is just crazy, Harry. And let's not forget that Maggie is now in it up to her eyeballs because she went off the rails. None of that mess has anything to do with why we came here."

Harry fished a handful of seeds out of his pocket and shoved them in his mouth. "I'm going to get some tea. You want anything?"

"Yeah, a Sprite."

"Jack, I know you well enough to know everything you just said is nothing we can't handle. What has your knickers in a knot is Abner. Admit it, and we can go on from there. He's like a brother. The guy does not have a mean or disloyal bone in his body."

"Enough already, okay, Harry? I get it. And you're right. I told you when you appeared out of nowhere that I don't know what to do. I'm trying to think. I want to make this right. Especially for Abner. I just don't know how to do it. Yet. I'm waiting for an epiphany."

Harry walked to the opposite side of the hospitality area to get a cup of tea and the Sprite that Jack had requested. Upon his return he handed Jack his drink and said, "We should pack up and go home."

"If we do that, then we failed. I don't like that word. I never did. It is not a word that I will ever come to like. Our answers are out there. We just aren't looking in the right place." Jack set his glass down and sent off a text to Charles, asking him to bring in a team of forensic accountants. Then he sent off another text to Bert, advising him to authorize the order for Charles. Then he sent off a second text to Charles, telling him to offer to pay double to the firm if they started immediately. "Okay, that's a start. See, Harry? My epiphany is just around the corner. I think I'm hungry now. You want something?"

Harry shook his head and poured another handful of seeds, and some sprouts, directly into his mouth this time. He looked at his watch to see the time.

Both men whirled around at the speed of light when they heard someone in the hall. Charles and Fergus. They both relaxed.

"A twelve-man team will be here within the hour. I've been trying to reach Mr. Kelly, but he is not picking up. Bert okayed the firm and even told me whom to call and whom to ask for. His name carries some weight here. Bert said they can set up shop in conference room three. They are prepared to work through the night, if need be," Charles said.

"Maggie?" Jack asked.

"Texting a mile a minute. To whom, I have no idea. One of Snowden's operatives left for MGM to register Maggie. Ted, Sparrow, and Avery are working on the surveillance. Avery and one of the operatives will do the actual breaking and entering. They're only going to have a thirty-minute window. I say that because I don't think we can keep Mr. Kelly in the conference room with the accountants any longer than thirty minutes. Does Bert plan on bringing Mr. Kelly into the loop, or didn't he say?"

"He didn't say, Charles. He was too busy venting at me and being pissed off at the same time. It's almost time for him to call, so you can ask him yourself," Jack said, irritation ringing in his voice.

Jack risked a glance at Harry, who was studying his cuticles with clinical interest. Jack knew
he was listening intently to the exchange and
would voice an opinion when he was ready, just
not when one would expect him to. Harry was
a strange duck at times.

Time crawled forward as the gang trickled
into the hospitality area to help themselves to
lunch, which the chef had left in warming trays.
Conversation was nonexistent.

An hour past Bert's deadline, Jack's cell
rang. He looked up to see everyone staring at
him. He clicked on and immediately held the
phone away from his ear. The others backed
off accordingly as Bert vented yet again, cursing and yelling and saying he wasn't crazy and
asking what in the damn hell they all did. "All
those hours I put in, all those notes I took, all
shot to friggin' hell, Jack! Are you listening to
me? Everything is different now. It adds up!
Well, that's not quite true. There seems to be . . .
more . . . an overage."

Jack let loose with a wild sigh, as did the others. "What are you saying? *We* didn't do anything. *We* couldn't. Abner couldn't. All he and
PIP were trying to do was figure out how anyone could hack into Babylon's account, and
they came up dry. Take it easy, Bert, or I'm hanging up on you, and if I do, my next phone call
will be to Annie. Are you sure you weren't . . .
um . . . under the weather or drunk when you
did what you did? Seems to me that's what happened, and now that you're operating at a
hundred percent, you can see what you did

wrong. Is any money missing? is all we want to know. So is it or isn't it missing?"

Everyone's eyes popped when Bert let loose with another volley of profanity. "Damn it, Jack! Weren't you listening to me? Now there is *too much money.*"

"Sounds to me like maybe someone is paying back some interest, if what you say is true. If those fancy forensic accountants can figure it out, then maybe Bert was right. Someone *did* take the money, then decided to put it back, plus interest. Makes sense to me, and I'm not a genius. The timing, in my opinion, is priceless," Harry said as he grinned from ear to ear.

"Thank you, Harry Wong!" Bert said tightly. "That's the first thing any of you have said that makes a lick of sense. This is turning into a nightmare."

"Sorry, gentlemen, but I have to leave now to speak with the accountants, who should by now be situated in conference room three with Mr. Dixson Kelly. With your permission, Bert, I'd like to bring him into the loop. Right now, Mr. Kelly is acting like a scalded cat on a slab of ice. It's not fair to the man to keep him in the dark any longer," Charles said.

"Yes, yes, you're right. Go ahead and tell him, and have him call me. We need to talk, anyway, about some other things."

Bert spoke up. "So, Jack, what do you have to say now?"

"Nothing, Bert. How much money are you over that you can't account for?"

"You don't want to know, Jack."

"Now you see, Bert, that's where you're wrong. I do want to know. Look, buddy, we all dropped everything we were doing in our lives and came here to help you. Now how much? Don't make me ask you again."

"Millions. I don't know exactly how many millions at the moment. This makes me look like a first-class stooge. Hell, let those guys you brought in figure it out. I hate this place," he said before he hung up.

Jack shrugged and looked at Harry. "Are you thinking what I'm thinking, Harry?" Not bothering to wait for a response, Jack rushed on. "That guy RCHood took the money. I think that's a given at this point. Somehow or other, Abner found him. I want to stress that Abner found him *after* our blowup and probably by a fluke of some kind. Then, somehow, he convinced the guy to put the money back, plus interest. Abner is honorable that way. That how you see it, Harry? Please tell me you see it that way, too."

Always a man of few words, Harry simply said, "Yep!"

Chapter 17

Maggie stared off into space as she let her mind race. She couldn't shake the feeling that she had missed something along the way. A phrase, perhaps something she'd seen or heard that didn't seem important at the time. Or just a plain old gut feeling that something was *off*. It was rare when she couldn't find an explanation for something that bothered her. The guys always said she was like a dog with a bone, and she had to agree with them. She never gave up until she was 100 percent satisfied with whatever was nagging at her subconscious.

Maggie eyed the plate of peanut butter cookies sitting on the coffee table. She reached for one. She always thought better when she was eating. Three cookies later, she realized it wasn't working this time around. She switched her focus to the other side of the room to listen to what the boys were discussing. She frowned, then jumped up off her chair and ran to the other side of the room.

"Hey! Listen!" she said. "I heard what you all just said, that now there seems to be too much money in the account and it is possibly an interest payment for . . . uh, the loan that hacker took out, right?"

Everyone nodded.

Maggie went on. "I know this is going to sound really, really crazy, but hear me out. Let's just pick a number arbitrarily and go with three million dollars. That's three million dollars no one knows about, okay? We're the only ones who even *think* we know where it came from. Let me stress *the only ones*. You guys following me here?"

The others nodded.

"Okay, moving right along here. All of a sudden, there's a heist in the making. Let's say three million dollars. Wouldn't that be the take on a Monday, after a weekend of gambling, give or take a few dollars? Perhaps more. And perhaps it would match the interest no one can account for. A wash, no? And no one is the wiser. The books balance." Maggie stared at everyone, then laughed out loud at the expressions on their faces. "Okay, who's stupid now?"

"But . . ."

"I don't . . ."

"No!"

"Too much of a stretch!"

"That has to mean . . . Dixson Kelly is actually the one planning the heist, and they're all playing games," Charles said, running with Maggie's out-of-the-blue theory. "It's a setup. I think it was pure dumb luck that you fell in their lap at the café that day. They had to scramble to figure out what to do with you and at the same time try to figure out what you were up to."

"How could Kelly know about RCHood?" Sparrow asked. "Kelly is no moneyman. Unless he's somehow wired into Bert's e-mails and phones. Even then it doesn't work, because Bert found out about RC by accident. More or less."

"What?" Maggie screeched. "You want me to do all the work, and you coast on my coattails? I don't think so! Figure it out. I gave you a possible scenario. Now, either make it work or scrap it. Since you all haven't come up with anything better, my suggestion is to run with mine."

"Bert swears by Dixson Kelly," Fergus said.

"Everyone makes a mistake at some point in their lives. Misjudging a friend's or colleague's character is not uncommon. I think we might have all done that at one time or another. Mr. Kelly might be the consummate actor. If what Maggie is saying is true, then we all made the same mistake Bert made in regard to Mr. Kelly," Charles said.

"We just gave Kelly a leg up by allowing him to sit in with the forensic accountants. Thank God we didn't put him in the loop as yet. Anyone know where he is right now?" Jack asked.

"How could we possibly know that, Jack?" Sparrow asked coldly. "I also want to go on the record right now that I think this scenario is a real stretch. But I'll go with the majority here."

"Good! Good! I think we should all hit the casino floor and do a little recon work. Whoever sees him first, try to entice him up here to the suite. Once we have him under lock and key, we can decide what we're going to do going forward. We all in agreement here?" Jack asked.

The response to Jack's question was a stampede for the doorway. Maggie held up her hand to show she was coming, but first she had to read the incoming text that had shown up on her cell phone. Jack lagged behind to see what it was that was upsetting her.

Hands on hips, he lasered Maggie with his dark eyes. "And that text means what? I can see you're upset. The question is, why?"

"An hour ago, I was asking myself the same question. I was upset then, and I am still upset. I was trying to figure out what I missed. I missed something, Jack. I know I did. I was upset with myself that I let it happen. Usually, I am on top of things. When I can't find a solution or a resolution, it drives me nuts, so I stay with it till I figure it out." Maggie pointed to the text. "This is what got by me. Now, in my own defense, I have to say I had an inkling something was off in regard to Kitty Passion, but she was so awesomely beautiful and nice to me, I brushed it off. And I was obsessed with trying to pull off my story line, so I was not really clicking on all cylinders. Well, shame on me, Maggie Spritzer."

"You want to share?" Jack asked impatiently.

"Well, sure. I'm a team player. Always was, always will be. I think those women were onto us the minute they spotted us at the Cat & Cradle. And, stupid me, I fell for it. Hana was the one in the restroom. Hana is the one I boo-hooed to. Now that I think about it, it was almost as if we were all following a script. The women led me to believe that Kitty was supposed to be Dixson Kelly's next conquest. They said he was pursuing her like mad, but she was holding him off. When they were ready to strike, she was going to seduce him. She was their magic bullet.

"You know what bothered me? I'll tell you. I think Kitty's gay. I'll stake my life and my reputation on that. And there's nothing wrong with being gay. As you well know, some of my best friends are gay. I saw and read her expression every time Kelly's name came up. She wasn't the least bit interested romantically in Dixson Kelly, or any other guy, for that matter. The other girls recited chapter and verse about all their past love affairs, the good ones, the bad ones. Some even talked about old high-school crushes. Not Kitty. She did not volunteer a single thing about her times with Kelly or anybody else. Actually, she looked really uncomfortable, like if she said something, it was going to be all wrong.

"Now that I think back, I can see how forced it all was. For my benefit. How she allowed herself to get involved with that group is something I have yet to figure out. Oh, there is no doubt that she's tied to Kelly somehow. I'm going to go way out on a limb here, but I think she's his sister. Maybe in the end, we'll find out she's the brains behind this whole sorry mess."

Jack's jaw dropped. He struggled to get his tongue to work. "Based on what?" was the best he could manage.

"The eyes. Don't forget, I had to noodle around with Kelly for a whole day and a half. I stared across the table at him for hours. I'd know those eyes in my sleep now. Kitty has the same eyes, right down to the chocolate-brown color. As women, we call eyes like hers bedroom eyes. Bedroom eyes drive guys nuts. That's what all the slick magazines say, anyway. With guys, the color is like a come-hither look. And five bucks says if you run a check on her, you won't find anything on a Kitty Passion. Kitty Passion is a Vegas showgirl name. She probably has some nice Irish name, like Louise, Doris, or Ruth.

"I'll take that all one step further and make yet another wager. No old aunt left her that chicken ranch. I bet it isn't even hers. Either she is renting it or she somehow managed to take it over for a period of time. The reason I say that is there was nothing personal in the house, and I did a walk-through. Not even green plants. Every woman has at least one green plant that she nourishes until the leaves turn yellow, at which point she tosses it out and gets another one. I know this, so please do not argue with me."

"Who's arguing? I'm listening, and you are actually making sense. So what does that text say?"

"Remember what you just said, Jack. The text is from Kitty, and she says she is having dinner with Dixson Kelly tonight at eight at someplace called Chezmarie. She wants me to show up with my brother around dessert time, nine, nine thirtyish. Either she thinks I'm really stupid or this is where she traps me. And you, too, since you are supposed to be my brother. I'm sure they got a good look at you and Harry at the Cat & Cradle. Which has to also mean that Kelly is onto us, too. Boo-hoo again. Too bad, too sad. We need to call a meeting and run this up the flagpole. Get on that, Jack.

"I'm going to run a Google check on one Kitty Passion. Don't get excited, because I already know nothing will come up. We need Snowden and Charles to work on this. And it would be really helpful if we could get Kelly's employment application, along with his military record. And we have no Abner Tookus to do our hacking into databases for us. I have the directions in my pack, so we also need to get a records check on whose name that chicken ranch is in. Bet it's someone who gambles here at Babylon. A high roller for sure. That ranch makes money."

Jack was typing so fast, he felt like blisters were forming on the pads of his fingers.

"This is where we could really use Abner's

expertise," Maggie said sourly. "Better yet, call Bert and tell him to have Human Resources bring it up here on the QT."

Fifteen minutes later, the group was assembled in a campfire atmosphere. Maggie read off the Kitty Passion text. Jack brought them all up to date on Maggie's theory. If they were looking for shock and awe, they got it.

Charles gave voice to what they were all thinking. "The man is pretty good, then, to have fooled Bert all these years. Avery, see what you can come up with. Sparrow, use your clout with the Vegas Bureau and see what you can dig up. I can see it all, but there is one gaping hole here. Help me out. Does Kelly know or not know what RCHood did? Or is this all one big coincidence?"

No one had an answer.

The room turned silent, the only sound the tapping of laptop computer keys. Then, collectively, they started to mutter and mumble under their breath. Paper literally flew out of the copy machine set up in the little workstation that came with every suite. The only distraction came around mid-afternoon, when there was a soft knock on the door. Everybody in the room tensed.

"Bet it's the Human Resources person," Dennis said as he ran to the door and looked out the magic eye. He saw a tall woman dressed in a conservative suit and holding a large manila envelope. He opened the door, snatched the envelope, then slammed the door shut, secured the deadbolt, and slipped the chain lock into place. Too late he remembered he hadn't offered up a tip. As Maggie would say, boo-hoo. The woman's livelihood didn't depend on his five-dollar tip. He ran the envelope over to Charles and handed it over with a flourish.

No one in the room moved or said a word as Charles undid the clasp on the envelope and pulled out a sheaf of papers, which he quickly scanned. The others waited, hardly daring to breathe, for their leader's verdict in regard to Dixson Kelly. Their relief was evident when Charles cleared his throat and started to talk.

"Mr. Kelly's stint in the military, then the CIA is just as Bert told us. Exemplary. No red flags. His employment record here at Babylon when Bert recruited him is just as exemplary. He has a sterling credit rating. Has a condo mortgage and has never been late with his payments. Makes car payments and is never late. Drives a Porsche. Silver in color. This information, by the way, is all due to periodic credit checks. Every employee has to sign off that HR can do this. Mr. Kelly signed off. He has a Visa card that he pays off in full every month. He also has a black American Express card. It's called a Centurion Card. He also pays that off every month.

"He has a robust pension plan, as well as a very nice brokerage account. He never lets his checking account drop below three thousand dollars. He gets a very generous bonus every year, in December, and he instructed HR to send the check directly to a place called Lake-shore Assisted Living in Asbury Park, New Jersey, to pay for his stepfather's living expenses. There is only one negative comment, and that was written by Bert himself. Says he's a womanizer, and he had him on the carpet on three separate occasions, when three different women kicked up a fuss. Kelly said he would try to do better. The last negative write-up was three months ago."

"I was hoping for something a little more . . . dicey." Maggie sniffed. "What about his background, like where he grew up, parents, and so on?"

Charles traced the lines with his forefinger as he read from the report. "Nothing out of the ordinary. Born and raised in Belmar, New Jersey. Mother a teacher. Father a teacher, also, who sadly died early in life. Mother remarried. Has a half sister and a half brother. The brother is a career officer in the marines and at the time of this report was stationed in California. The half sister is much younger. She moved to New York when she was eighteen and worked for an advertising agency. That's pretty much the sum total of what's in here. This has not been updated in the past five years, aside from Bert's negative comments about Mr. Kelly's womanizing and the results of the periodic credit reports. All in all, a report to be proud of."

Maggie's fist shot in the air. "I was right! He does have a sister! I knew it! I knew it! Always listen to your gut, people. It will never steer you wrong. Mr. Snowden, you need to do a check on the half sister and brother. Get everything you can on both of them. Okay, everyone, back to work," Maggie said as she started typing. She looked down at the watch on her wrist. Four forty-five p.m.

At 5:45 p.m., exactly one hour later, Jack Emery whistled sharply to get everyone's attention. "Progress report, people."

Ted opted to go first. "You were right. The chicken ranch is owned by Earl and Helen Bolton. It's a multimillion-dollar business. The Boltons have chicken ranches in Reno and Tahoe. The Boltons are in their seventies and spend half the year in Monte Carlo. And they go on to Macau, then back here for the Christmas holidays, after which they go off again. Vegas is their home base. A foreman oversees the farm here. Ditto for Reno and Tahoe. Sometimes, the Boltons rent out the main house or just let friends who want to winter in Vegas stay there. Before Kitty Passion, someone named Diane Sarrocco was staying there. No other information is available. Nothing comes up under that name, so I assume it's an alias of some kind, just the way Kitty Passion is an alias."

"The sister's name is Clare Andreas," Snowden said. "The brother's name is Steven Andreas. He's a full-bird colonel in the marines. A career officer. Happily married, with two kids in college. Wife is a nurse. Same mother, different fathers. The man in the Lakeshore Assisted Living facility is William Andreas, Dixson Kelly's stepfather. The mother died ten years ago.

"The baby sister is hard to track. She never stays in one place too long. She's a free spirit.

She was a dancer at Trump in Atlantic City, but only for eight months, before she moved on. The last known footprint was Atlanta, where she did a modeling stint at some big designer's show. Nothing shows up after that."

"Nothing on Google for Kitty Passion. I knew it!" Maggie volunteered.

"What about a driver's license? Passport? We need to know what she looks like," Jack said.

"I ran this all by the local field office. So far nothing. I asked them to find out everything they can on the dancers, Kitty Passion in particular. It's going to take a while, but if there's something to find, they'll find it," Sparrow said. He looked at Snowden and asked what he had come up with.

"Working on it. Remember, I have that luncheon on the flash drives from that day at the Cat & Cradle. Let me see if I can bring them up on the computer."

"I need some help here. It's almost six o'clock. That dinner is scheduled for eight o'clock. I'm supposed to show up around dessert time, which would make it around nine or nine thirty. Am I going or not? I never answered Kitty's text. For all I know, she could be checking out that room at MGM. I thought you guys were going to corral Kelly and bring him here. Do I have to do everything?" Maggie groused.

"He didn't respond to my text," Jack said.

"Or mine," Charles said.

"Then we need to sic the big gun on him," Sparrow said. "Have Bert call him and tell him to move his ass up here on the double. I have a question, though. Once he shows up, what are we going to do with him?"

"Good question," Snowden said quietly. "What do you think we should do with him? Think about this. Maybe we should let him take his sister to dinner, then snatch them both when they're leaving the restaurant. We need to think this through. Do you want to sweat them? What's our endgame here?"

"Do you think it advisable to send someone out to the chicken ranch to nose around after she leaves?" Jack asked.

"We have enough people to do that. I could send three female operatives out there. The foreman or the men probably won't think twice about seeing women wandering about. If they elect to cause a ruckus, my operatives know what to do. This is the height of traffic right now, so if you think that's a good idea, I'd like them to hit the road immediately, which means they'll arrive right around the time Kitty Passion is leaving. She'll leave early, knowing what the traffic is like."

Charles looked up from his keyboard and said, "Do it! Have them report in hourly."

"What about me?" Maggie asked without looking up.

"We have three hours to decide, dear. Off the top of my head, the answer is more likely no than yes," Charles said.

She shrugged. What else was she going to do?

*   *   *

Somewhere in Las Vegas, a bell rang at six o'clock. It was a loud, not unpleasant pealing sound. For the most part, people stopped for a second as they tried to reconcile the sound with the gambling mecca they were in. Most just ignored it and went about their business.

Seventy miles away as the crow flies, Philonias Needlemeyer looked at the clock in the kitchen. Both hands were straight up on the number twelve. He missed the sound of the church bell. From his Babylon terrace, he heard it every night. To him it was the signal that the day was coming to a close. All in all, a comfortable thought.

"I guess this is it, kids," Philonias said as he, Abner and Mary Alice left the kitchen and walked outside to the car. "Time to say goodbye. I want to give you both something. Not exactly to remember me by, because I'm the kind of person you never forget. Just a way for you to get in touch, should you ever need me. I want you to remember that, because I mean it." He handed over two phones, one to Mary Alice and one to Abner. "No one, and I mean no one, has this. Nor can it ever be traced. Just want you to know that. I will always take care of you."

Abner was so choked up, he couldn't speak. He felt his eyes start to burn. He squeezed them shut. He nodded. He just knew that any minute now he was going to blubber.

Impulsively, Mary Alice threw her arms around Abner and started to cry. "Everything he said goes for me, too. Phil programmed both our numbers into your phone. Take care of yourself, Abner."

Abner nodded again. He looked at Phil, and he wasn't sure, but he thought he saw tears in the big guy's eyes. He finally found his tongue and said, "Um . . . let's not say good-bye. Goodbyes sound so final. I . . . I want to drive away from here knowing we're going to see each other again. Maybe not tomorrow or next week or next month, but sometime. Let's just say . . . 'See ya.' Does that work for you guys?" he asked anxiously.

Mary Alice's head bobbed up and down faster than that of any bobblehead doll as she shrieked her misery. Phil chewed on his lip and nodded. He held out one massive hand.

Abner looked at the big, meaty hand and grinned. "Uh-uh. Real guys hug. Just don't break my ribs, okay?" he said, trying to wrap his arms around Phil's chest.

Suddenly, Abner found himself airborne, and Phil was laughing uproariously as he swung Abner around like a rag doll. When he finally set him down, Abner was breathless.

"How's that for 'See ya sometime'? Should we say something corny, like 'Don't take any wooden nickels' or 'Don't let grass grow under your feet'?"

"Nah," Abner drawled.

"One more gift, and we're outta here." Phil extended his hand to Abner, who tried to figure out what was clasped in the mighty hand. It looked like a flash drive.

"What's this?"

"That little gift, my flesh-and-blood friend, will make your world right side up again. Go back to Vegas and decide what you want to do. Check it out before you make a decision. See ya," Phil said, sliding into his custom Bentley. Mary Alice scooted around the side of the car and climbed into the passenger side.

"Where you going, Phil?" Like the big guy was really going to tell him.

"I'm going to get a manicure. Gotta keep these treasures," he said, wiggling his fingers in front of him, "in tip-top shape, in case I have to save your ass again."

"Oh, yeah? Well, who saved whose ass?" Abner bellowed as the Bentley roared down the road, leaving a trail of dust in its wake.

"Manicure, my ass!" Abner yelled to the empty surroundings.

Then again . . .

Chapter 18

By seven thirty, the group as a whole was nastier than a group of polecats in a perfume factory. Charles had to commandeer Dennis, who whistled between his teeth so loud that Cyrus went nuclear, barking so loud that everyone had to clamp their hands over their ears.

"That's enough!" Charles roared. "You're acting like spoiled children. Simmer down, and we'll talk. And you, Cyrus, you will confine your comments to one short bark. Do *you* understand me?"

Cyrus barked once, but his heart wasn't in it.

"All of you, do *you* understand me?"

The response he received was heads nodding up and down.

"Good. I love cooperation. I have a bit of news and some suggestions I'd like to share with you. The news is that we cannot locate Mr.

Kelly. Bert is telling us that Kelly asked Pete Justice to cover for him from six to ten this evening. Justice, seeing no reason not to, and given that Kelly is, after all, his boss, said yes. That tells us Mr. Kelly plans to return to Babylon by ten this evening, no matter how the dinner goes at Chezmarie. When he returns here to Babylon, that's when we snatch him. We need someone at the restaurant, either to keep eyes on the sister or pick her up once dinner is over. You all need to make that decision and quickly.

"Maggie will not be showing up at dessert time. I think it's much too risky. She has not responded to Kitty Passion, so that young lady is going to be wondering why. 'Better to be safe than sorry' has always been my motto."

Charles turned his attention to Director Sparrow. "How out of the box would it be for you to order your people at the Vegas field office to do a sweep? By sweep, I mean have your agents pick up all the showgirls who were at the Cat & Cradle and out at the chicken ranch to sweat them, as the saying goes. Have the agents take them all back to your field office and see who cracks first. Is that feasible?"

"Absolutely," Sparrow said. "All I need are the names and addresses. The first shows start at ten. We can pick them up the minute they're off the stage."

"First thing you do once you pick them up is to confiscate their cell phones so they can't call anyone. We're bound to lose a few, but we'll have to live with it. And by the end of the shows, we should have Kelly and the sister in hand. Once you tell the showgirls you can hold them for seventy-two hours without their lawyers present, I think they'll all cooperate. No matter what they did feel or do not currently feel for Dixson Kelly, at this moment in time they will not want to go to a federal prison for nothing more than a bruised and battered heart. Do any of you see a problem with what I just said?"

Cyrus barked to show he understood and was on board, while the others simply nodded.

Sparrow shifted his weight from one foot to the other as he waited for Snowden to print out a list of the showgirls and where they worked, along with their home addresses. He made six copies and handed them over to Sparrow.

"Listen, Director, I saw those women as a whole, and my advice for you to give your agents is this. Tell them not to turn their heads and to keep their eyes on them all the time. Take my advice, or leave it alone. The choice is yours," Snowden said.

"As Countess de Silva is fond of saying, 'This ain't my first rodeo,' Snowden. You can reach me if you need me at the field office. I won't take the van we rented. I'll just hail a taxi. Check in with me."

Cyrus let loose with a shrill bark, then lowered his head between his paws and waited until the next time he was needed for a vote.

"Now what?" Maggie demanded, her eyes on her watch.

"Now we wait," Charles said.

* * *

Abner Tookus parked his Range Rover in the parking lot of a Best Western. He turned off the engine and leaned his head back against the headrest. He couldn't ever remember a time when he had felt so physically drained of all emotion. He was bone tired, and he was hungry. Even when he went through his rough patch with his wife, Isabelle, he had never felt this beaten. He rubbed at his gritty eyes, then wished he hadn't, because his eyes started to burn. He perched his glasses on top of his head and rubbed some more. He needed sleep. He needed food, and he needed peace. Right now, this very moment, he knew he would give up everything he held dear to be able to talk to Isabelle.

That wasn't going to happen, and he knew it. Nothing was going to happen unless he moved his butt out of the car, registered, and checked out the flash drive. Then he could eat and sleep. Only then.

His room was like all hotel rooms, clean, neat, and smelling of air fresheners. He popped a cola from the mini-fridge and sat down at the tiny desk. He plugged in his laptop and inserted the flash drive. All he could see was a blur, until he remembered to put his glasses on. Man, he was so out of it. But he was out of it for only a moment before his eyeballs almost popped out of his head at what he was seeing and reading. When he finally got to the end of what was on the flash drive, Abner started to laugh, his body shaking so hard that he threw himself on the bed and continued to laugh till he was gasping for breath. "Philonias Needle-meyer, you are one crafty, wily son of a gun!" Then he went off on another bout of laughter.

Finally, exhausted, Abner staggered to the bathroom to wash his face and comb his hair. He didn't look any better, but he knew he had to look presentable to go to the lobby and do what he needed to do. Outside his room, he walked toward the EXIT sign over a doorway and walked three flights down to the lobby. It was crowded, and it took him a minute to see where the concierge desk was. He walked over, said that he was a guest at the hotel and that he needed to messenger something immediately to Babylon Casino and Hotel.

Two hundred dollars later, plus cab fare, the packet, with Maggie Spritzer's name on the envelope, was on its way to Babylon Casino and Hotel. He heaved a deep sigh as he trudged his way back to his room. *Shower or not? Not. Leave or not leave? Leave, of course.* He could drive a little farther down the road and register at another hotel. Just in case Maggie or one of the others decided to grill the messenger, and he told them that Abner was staying at the Best Western.

Back in his Rover, he had to fight to stay awake. When he saw a sign for the Starlight Motel, he pulled in, parked, registered, paid cash for one night, and was given a key. He hit the room, locked the door, threw his bag across the room, then flopped down on the bed. He was asleep before his head hit the pillow. The digital clock on the nightstand said it was 8:30 p.m.

Abner woke at five minutes to midnight, fully cognizant of where he was and what had transpired. He hopped out of bed, brushed his teeth, and washed his face. There was no need to get dressed since he had slept in his clothes. He was on the road at five minutes past midnight. He planned to burn rubber and use his smokey detector all the way. If his calculations were right and he drove straight through, he should be back in his loft in twenty-four hours. Give or take.

He stopped at the first gas station he saw, loaded up on gas, hot black coffee, snacks, and cigarettes. He made a mental promise to quit smoking the moment he reached home. For now, he had to do whatever it took him to get cross-country.

After pulling out of the gas station, Abner slipped a disk into the stereo. His two favorites, Bon Jovi and Tina Turner. He realized that he actually felt good. So good, in fact, that he sang along with his favorite artists as he blew smoke ring after smoke ring.

Then he realized something else. At this moment in time, his life was going to be whatever he made of it. No one else, just him.

Chapter 19

The only people left in Charles's suite were Charles, Fergus, and Maggie. Cyrus was there, too. Maggie paced. Frantically, she mumbled to herself, stopping from time to time to glare at Charles and Fergus.

"I need to be out there. I need to do something," she said.

"You are doing something, dear. You're waiting, and you're wearing out the carpet," Charles said quietly.

"It's almost nine o'clock! I should be arriving at Chezmarie about now. This is going to go badly. I feel it in my bones."

A loud knock on the door startled them all. They looked at one another, their eyes wide. Cyrus raced to the door, but he didn't bark. Fergus made his way to the door and opened it.

A bellman held out a manila envelope. "The

desk asked me to deliver this to Mr. Martin's suite. It's addressed to Maggie Spritzer."

Fergus reached for the envelope, but before he could make contact, Maggie, hearing her name, sprinted to the door and snatched it out of the bellman's hand. Fergus offered up a tip, then closed and locked the door. Cyrus went back to his spot on the sofa and went to sleep.

Charles and Fergus watched as Maggie started ripping at the envelope. She stopped in her tracks and held up a flash drive. Frowning, she looked at the tattered envelope she had just eviscerated. Then she smiled, and the smile turned to outright laughter. She held the flash drive up triumphantly.

"What is it? Who sent you a flash drive?" Charles asked.

"Now, who do you think sent it? It's from Abner. He sent it to me. Me! That has to mean he isn't angry with me, just the rest of you guys. Well, let's just see what's on this baby," Maggie said as she slipped the flash drive into her laptop.

Fergus and Charles crowded around her to see whatever was going to pop up. A blizzard of symbols, numbers, and letters flashed across the screen; then the screen went blank for ten seconds. The threesome stared at the screen, waiting, hardly daring to breathe at what was important enough that Abner messengered it to Maggie.

"Oh, my God!" was all Maggie could say. "I don't believe this! Do you believe this, Charles?"

Cyrus barked.

Maggie bent over to eyeball the shepherd. "I know you believe it, Cyrus. I know."

"How do you know Abner sent you this?" Fergus asked.

"Because I know Abner's writing. He half prints and half writes in cursive. Trust me, this is from Abner." Suddenly, Maggie's eyes welled up.

"It's all here. Their whole plan. If we had a mind to, we could turn this over to the local police, and that would be the end of it right now. How in the world did Abner get all this?" There was such awe in Charles's voice, Maggie could only stare at him.

"He didn't. His friend RCHood got it and, for reasons we'll probably never know, gave it to Abner, who in turn sent it to me. Me! Me, because he trusts me. Not you, not Jack, not Sparrow. *Me*!" Tears rolled down Maggie's cheeks as she mourned the loss of her friend through no fault of her own. "Here!" she said, tossing the flash drive to Charles, who caught it expertly in one hand. "Do whatever you want. I'm going for a walk, and I'm taking Cyrus with me."

Cyrus was up and at the door before Maggie could locate his leash.

Maggie kept up a low commentary as she led Cyrus down the hall to the service elevator. "Because you're a dog, we have to take the service elevator. Before we leave here, I'm going to let them know what I think of that particular rule. I do not know where we're going, Cyrus. Just outside. I need some fresh air, and I want to think. Let's get an ice cream cone. I know you like those waffle ones. I always get a brain freeze for some reason when I eat an ice cream cone, but that still doesn't stop me from eating it.

"You aren't listening, are you, Cyrus? And if you are, you don't care. I'm just babbling here, venting, if you will. I feel lower than a snake's belly right now. I want to cry some more, but I don't want anyone to see me cry. How stupid is that? I need to do something, Cyrus, but I don't know what it is I need to do. Just *something.*"

Something literally smacked Maggie in the face when she bumped into Pete Justice. He apologized profusely, asked if she was all right, and walked with her across the casino floor to the door. "I thought you checked out."

"Why would you think that, Mr. Justice?"

"Please, call me Pete." He thought about her question for a minute, then said, "I really don't know why I thought that. Dixson must have said something."

"Speaking of Dixson, where is he? Do you know? We've been trying to locate him with texts and phone calls. They all go to his voice mail. Bert is beside himself, as he's been trying to reach him for hours. The people I came here with are all out here somewhere looking for him."

"He's not answering any of my pages or texts, either. He's due back here at ten o'clock to relieve me. He's never, ever, to my knowledge, been unavailable to Bert, me, or this casino. I hate to say this, but I am worried something happened to him. I'm seriously thinking of calling around to the hospitals and clinics to see if he had an accident or something."

Well, this guy is certainly chatty, Maggie thought. He did look genuinely concerned, however, and she knew for a fact, thanks to Abner, that Pete Justice was not involved in anything that was about to go down. *A nice, likable guy, but a babe in the woods,* was her next thought.

"Maybe he had some personal business he had to take care of," Maggie said helpfully.

"I guess. I have to leave you here and get back on the floor. If you need anything, just call. I really like this dog," Justice said, scratching Cyrus behind the ears. "Sorry about that mix-up with you checking out."

"No problem," Maggie said, leading Cyrus through the door.

It was a perfect evening, Maggie thought as she looked up at the star-studded sky. Not even sweater weather. Almost summer weather.

As she walked along, Maggie wondered what she was doing out here with a dog. She should be back inside, where she could be of help, if need be. She rounded the corner, walked to the end, then turned around and headed back. She stopped twice when Cyrus tugged her to a tree or pole. And then they were back inside the casino, where the slot machines beckoned.

She fished around in her pocket and found a crumpled ten-dollar bill. Knowing she was going to lose it, she straightened it out and slid it into the slot. She waited, pushing the red button again and again, until finally she heard a blasting whistling sound. She looked down at three diamonds and grinned at Cyrus. "What that means to you is that you can have a porterhouse steak if you want it. I just won three hundred fifty dollars!"

Maggie carried the winning slip over to the cashier and asked if the Sunshine Foundation lady worked at night. The harried cashier pointed her in the right direction. "Let's give that little lady a treat, Cyrus. Here. You clamp it in your teeth and give it to her."

Cyrus yipped his pleasure and did as instructed. The little lady beamed and held out her hand. Cyrus offered up his paw, and they shook hands.

Across the floor, by the penny slots, Pete Justice watched Maggie and the shepherd head for the elevators. He'd always prided himself on having good gut instincts, and right now those gut instincts were warning him that something wasn't right. He looked down at his watch. It was almost ten o'clock, and still no word from the boss. He fired off a text and asked for an update. He didn't know how he knew, but he was absolutely certain there would be no updated text coming through anytime soon.

Justice sent off a text to his aide, Artie Ryan, and told him to take over for twenty minutes. Justice was going to the Tiki Bar for a ginger ale. All he wanted to do was sit down in a dark corner and try to figure out what was going on and how it involved him, *if* it involved him. His gut was telling him that whatever was going on was serious. He carried his drink to the far end of the bar, sat down, and closed his eyes, but not before his phone chirped that a text was coming through. *So much for a quiet twenty minutes*, he thought when he saw that the text was from Bert, asking if Dixson was back. He hoped his succinct *no* would end the matter and he could relax. He was way too tense. Way, way too tense.

Ten o'clock came and went. Justice was back on the floor, having relieved Artie Ryan. His gaze swept the casino floor; he was hoping for a sighting of his boss.

Nothing.

Director Sparrow of the FBI was proud of himself and had turned himself into a pretzel to pat his own back at how quickly he'd put together a team of agents to hit the casinos and bring in the showgirls for questioning. Admittedly, there had been a lot of shrieking, wailing, cursing, and shouting, with the agents simply flashing their gold shields. No one in authority had intervened when they saw the agents holding up their shields and the huge yellow block letters on the back of the Windbreakers, clearly proclaiming them to be FBI special agents. Their matching ball caps, along with their guns, had confirmed that they were indeed federal agents.

Right now, Sparrow was standing in the middle of a living nightmare, making him wish with all his heart that he was back in Charles Martin's suite.

The women had been separated, eight to a room, with three agents overseeing them in each. Sparrow whistled between his teeth for silence, with no results. The women were caterwauling so loud, his ears hurt. There were feathers everywhere, along with glitter and rhinestones. He winced when his feet crunched down on some oversize rhinestones that had come off their costumes. He sneezed as he plucked a feather that was sticking to his eyebrow. He looked over at the agents and asked them why they hadn't allowed the women to change.

One of the agents said, "Because the directive said, 'ASAP and no excuses.'"

One of the women was screaming about how much she'd paid for her costume, which was now ruined. "The goddamned FBI better pony up, like, right now. *Now!*" she screeched at the top of her lungs.

The others chimed in, and from there on in, it was pure bedlam. Then, as if members of a chorus, they started to chant, "We want a lawyer! We want a lawyer! We demand a lawyer!" The chant turned into an earsplitting scream.

Sparrow weighed his options. He had none. These women were never going to shut up, and he knew it. Because he was always an agent, and was now the director of the FBI, Sparrow was never without a gun. He yanked it out from the back of his pants and brandished it in the air.

It had absolutely no effect on the screeching hellcats. Sparrow clenched his teeth and fired into the ceiling tiles. The room went so silent, Sparrow thought he'd lost his hearing for a second.

"You all need to be quiet now, or the next bullet goes into one of your kneecaps. Whose? I'll just pick one of you at random and, *poof,* your dancing days are over," he said. "Now, please, give me your undivided attention."

Feathers sailed across the front of his face. He brushed at them. Purple feathers! He thought about pocketing one of them so he would always remember this moment in time.

"Do any of you know why you're here?" He really didn't expect an answer, so he wasn't surprised when the room remained silent. "Okay, here's a clue. Does the Dixson Kelly Alumnae Club ring any bells? Before you respond, I want to remind you that it is a felony to lie to an FBI agent. Now, who wants to go first?"

No one wanted to go first. The women tried to huddle closer to each other, but their feathered wings and foot-high, rhinestone-encrusted headpieces kept getting in the way.

"Take those damn things off," he ordered.

"What? What?" the women screamed in unison.

"So you can see our naked bodies! That is not going to happen, Mister FBI Agent! These wings are sewn onto the costume!" one of them said.

Properly chastised, Sparrow looked around at his agents, who were trying to look everywhere but at him. Gun in hand, Sparrow waved his arms about. "Okay, I did not know that. Let's be clear on something right now. No one wants to look at your naked bodies. Let me repeat that. No one wants to look at your naked bodies. So this is what we're going to do. We're going to bend your wings, and then you are all going to sit down on the floor and fold your hands. Legs straight out in front of you, like you used to do in grade school, at story time. That will give me a clear shot at your kneecaps. I'm ready to listen to what you have to say about your . . . club. Talk!"

A brash blonde with glitter on her impossibly long eyelashes looked straight at Sparrow and said, "We do not know what you are talking about, Mr. Director." A cloud of pink and purple feathers circled upward. The other dancers agreed with her that they didn't know anything about Dixson Kelly or a fan club with his name on it.

Sparrow sighed. He looked over at the three agents, who still had their guns in their hands. "Tell you what. Guys, take these women down to a holding cell. Start the paperwork, but there's no hurry. We have about seventy-one hours to go. I'll check the other rooms to see if those women are more willing to cooperate. By the way, there are no bathrooms in the holding cells. I need you to know that. Make sure you put that in the paperwork, Agent Connors. We don't want any he said, she said comments later. I apprised them of the fact that there are no bathrooms in the holding cells. Feel free to give them *all* the water they want."

The women started to hiss and snarl among themselves. Finally, a luscious redhead tried to raise her arm, which was covered in glitter.

"Assuming we might know a *little something*, will you let us leave here if we share it with you?" she asked.

"Now, that depends on what that *little something* turns out to be," Sparrow said, tongue in cheek.

"So we have this little club. So what!" the redhead said. "We bash Dixson Kelly for breaking our hearts. It makes us feel better. There's nothing wrong with that. We didn't harm anyone."

"Didn't you leave something out?" Sparrow asked as more feathers, yellow this time, floated up and about.

"Well, it goes without saying, we all hate his guts. You being a man and all, plus being the director of the FBI, I thought you would figure that out on your own. Can we leave now?" a silver-haired dancer said.

"I'm talking about the plot, the plan, whatever you want to call it, that Kelly and your pal Kitty Passion, aka Clare Andreas, hatched to heist the armored car with Babylon's money in it," Sparrow said.

The women as one tried to get up, but their feathered wings got snarled together, and they were forced to remain in place. There were feathers everywhere. Sparrow thought he looked like a rainbow, as the feathers stuck to his sports jacket and trousers.

"Are you going to confirm or deny?" Sparrow roared.

"We want a lawyer!" the blonde with the glitter on her eyelashes bellowed in return.

"Well, of course you do." Sparrow turned to the agents and said, "Put them all in a holding cell. If they give you any trouble, shoot them."

"Yes, sir!" one of the agents said.

Sparrow bolted from the room as he tried to pluck the feathers from his clothing. He stepped into a small, cramped office that was empty and pulled out his cell phone. He gave Charles an update on what had just transpired. He could hear Charles's suppressed laughter and winced. He turned serious when he listened to Charles tell him what Abner had sent Maggie.

"Well, if that's the case, then I can leave my agents here to take care of things and head back to Babylon."

Sparrow poked his head in the door and motioned for one of the agents to step outside.

"First things first. For God's sake, don't shoot anyone. What I said in there was pure theatrics. Second, find them some clothes and don't let them out of your sight," Sparrow instructed. "Even though we can legally hold them for seventy-two hours, we'll let them call their attorneys in the morning. But don't do it until you check with me first. Let the ladies cool their heels until then, and I guarantee they'll be falling all over themselves to get out from under. And get someone to clean up those damn feathers and that other junk. The place looks like a bordello."

"Yes, sir."

"You did good, son. You did good. All of you will get a good report. You need me, call."

Sparrow walked outside and into the cool evening air and took deep breaths. He did not envy the agents, given what the rest of the night held in store for them. As he walked along, trying to hail a taxi, he couldn't see the people turning to look at his back and the trail of feathers that were being plucked from his jacket and pants by the gentle breeze. If he had seen the people staring, he wouldn't have cared.

"Women!"

Chapter 20

Jack Emery knew that he looked like half the tourists in Las Vegas, so he wasn't overly concerned about his quasi disguise as he leaned up against the side of a plate-glass window so he could keep his eyes on the door of Chezmarie, where Dixson Kelly and Kitty Passion were dining. He yanked at his baseball cap and settled it lower on his forehead as he talked on his cell phone to Charles Martin. As a disguise, he realized it was on the pitiful side, but it was the best he could come up with on his own, without the benefit of Alexis Thorne's red bag of tricks.

"I'm good so far, Charles. They should be finishing up shortly. Harry and Dennis are several buildings away. I can't see them, but I know where they are precisely. Any news?"

"Avery's female operatives out at the chicken

ranch are on the way back to town. They came
up dry. Aside from several changes of clothing—mostly casual wear, shorts, jeans, that kind
of thing—there is nothing in the house to indicate anyone plans on staying there. As Maggie said earlier, at first glance, to her it all
looked temporary. Little to no food in the refrigerator, the bare essentials in the bathroom.
The women spoke to the foreman, who, they
said, was quite chatty. He said his orders have
always been not to interfere or mingle with
anyone staying at the house. He also said he
has always been given the name of the current
guest for mail purposes.

"The woman who stayed there before Kitty
Passion was someone named Diane Sarrocco
from Summerville, South Carolina, along with
her daughter, Lisa Pepin, and Ms. Pepin's young
son. Mr. Pepin, the daughter's husband, was to
be a later arrival. Those guests are personal
friends of the Boltons. They stayed for two
months and left. Very nice people. A week
later, Kitty Passion showed up. He said the only
time he knows when she's there is if she throws
a party, like she did a few days ago. He can't be
sure, because he minds his own business, but
he thinks the party people are the same each
time."

"So," Jack said, "where are Snowden's operatives now? And where is Snowden?"

"The operatives are on the way back. I don't
know where Avery is. He hasn't checked in as
yet. Maggie got antsy and took Cyrus for a walk,
and she ran into Pete Justice on the casino

floor. They talked for a few minutes, and no, he has not heard from Kelly, either. Neither have I. Bert checked in, and he is furious at being unable to contact his number one man."

"Ted and Espinosa?"

"Pretending to gamble. They're scouting the casino floor for anything that seems odd or out of place. Just a minute, Jack. Director Sparrow is reporting in. His agents rounded up the show-girls, and they're being held at the field office." A minute later, Charles said, "I understand there was a bit of a to-do with the women, but for now it's all on lockdown. Of course, they are all demanding lawyers. I think that's about it. What do you plan on doing, Jack?"

"I'm going to do my best to stay with Kelly, but this cab situation stinks. There's no way, with this never-ending traffic, that I can suc-cessfully follow him. It would be great if Avery's people could somehow make it at least halfway here so we could switch off if I lose Kelly. There are hundreds of people milling about in the streets. Harry and Dennis are on Kitty Passion. She drove here from the chicken ranch. The question is, is she going back there after din-ner or staying in town? We never did find out if she has a place here. How did that get by us, Charles?" Jack said fretfully.

"I'll have Maggie get on it right now."

"Since Kitty drove in from the ranch, she might give Dixson a ride, drop him off some-where. Or he might decide it's a nice night and opt to walk to wherever he's going. It's ten o'clock now, so they should be coming out soon."

"Unless they left by the back door, through the kitchen. That's what they always do in the movies," Charles said, with a chuckle in his voice.

"No actual egress. I checked earlier. Deliveries are through the front door. Space here is at a premium. He has to walk through the front door. Anything else?"

"Not at the moment. The minute you have eyes on, call me. We need to make a decision. Hold on. Hold on, Jack. I have a text coming in from Avery."

Jack waited, tapping his foot impatiently, until Charles's voice came back on the line.

"Avery said he has a hunch that Kelly is going to go by his own condo. According to the street map I have here, Mr. Kelly could walk to his home from Chezmarie, and that might be why he chose that particular restaurant. But why would he do that when he is supposed to relieve Mr. Justice?"

Charles's voice was now as fretful sounding as Jack's. "Here's the address, Jack. Remember it, as I know you can't write it down. Just in case Mr. Kelly gets away from you. Avery will be waiting for you all. Let's hope his instincts are right."

Jack broke the connection and shoved his phone into his pocket. He looked at his watch. He fought the urge to run into Chezmarie and physically drag Dixson Kelly outside so he could beat the hell out of him. Wishful thinking.

Jack blinked, then blinked again. Straight in his line of vision were Dixson Kelly and Kitty Passion. The couple moved off to the side to allow a party of four to exit through the same door. From where he was standing, it looked like the two of them were deep into an intense conversation. From what he could see from where he was, neither one looked happy. He looked around, hoping Harry and Dennis were seeing the same thing he was seeing.

Jack was starting off, trying to do his best to remain invisible, when it dawned on him that what he was doing didn't feel right. He stepped out of the way and leaned against a brick building. He brought his phone to his ear so people wouldn't give him a second thought or glance. What they were doing was all wrong. He questioned himself, replayed all that Charles had confided.

If this were the girls' mission, what would they be doing right now? How would they handle Kelly and Kitty Passion? He needed to think and think fast. What was it that was bothering him? What? The girls always had it going on, and they didn't make mistakes, and on the rare occasion when something did go awry, they somehow turned that something to their advantage. Maybe because they were so tuned in to one another, so united. That was the word he wanted, *united. We're scattered. You can't run any kind of operation if your people are scattered. Even a dumb-ass fool would know that.*

The phone already in hand, Jack pressed the

number three on his speed dial. Charles picked up on the first chirp.

"Just listen, Charles. Call everything off. Have everyone return to the hotel. That includes Ted and Espinosa. Now. Do it *now!*"

Jack jammed the phone into his pocket, turned around, and sprinted off, going down side streets and alleys to avoid the crowds. Thirty minutes later he was in front of Babylon, winded and breathless. Still breathing hard, he entered the massive building and headed straight for the casino floor. The sound level was deafening. He hated the intense looks he saw on the gamblers' faces. Didn't they know the house always won? Obviously, they didn't care, or else they had money they didn't care about. He shook his head to clear his thoughts as he made his way to the elevator.

Charles's suite was crowded, almost to the point of overflowing, when the door opened, courtesy of Maggie. Cyrus yipped his pleasure at seeing his master.

"Harry and Dennis are ten minutes out. Five now," Maggie said. "What's going on, Jack?" she hissed. "You have everyone in a tizzy here, and I do mean a tizzy."

"Yeah, I know. That's why we're all here. We're going to correct the situation right now, just as soon as Harry and Dennis get here. What time is it?"

"Almost eleven. Is the time important?" Espinosa asked.

"Maybe yes and maybe no."

Someone knocked sharply on the door. Maggie and Cyrus both ran to it, with Cyrus winning easily. He barked happily as he greeted Harry and Dennis.

"What the hell is going on, Jack? We were *that* close to snatching Kitty Passion when Charles called. I almost didn't answer. We had her in our sights," Harry said. "We saw her go into a condo complex and enter one on the first floor. We were about to do a snatch and grab when Charles's phone call came."

"Yeah, what's going on?" Dennis asked. "We had it all lined up. It was perfect. I doubt we'll ever get a better shot at her. And the best part was there was no one around."

"Look, everyone calm down and take a seat," Jack said. "I had a good shot at Kelly myself when it hit me. We've gone about this all wrong. Well, not really wrong. When it blew up with Abner, and we need to take responsibility for that, we lost our way. When we get back to D.C., we'll make it right with Abner.

"I realized when I started to tail Kelly that it wasn't feeling right, so I stopped and asked myself what the girls would do. For starters, the thing with Abner never would have happened if they were in charge. That's when we got scattered. *Scattered!* We did not pull together. We did not unite. Each of us had our own idea, and in the back of all our minds was Abner. Are you all following me here?"

Heads bobbed up and down.

Jack went on. "We didn't let Charles form a plan for us. We were listening to Bert instead of Charles, and I want to be the first to apologize for that. We should have done more due diligence. As an example, we didn't know Kelly had a sister, even if she's only a half sister. We didn't know whether she had a place to stay in town. We didn't know she didn't own the chicken ranch. We should have had all that information at our fingertips. Even with PIP and Abner doing the scut work, we fell short.

"I don't think it's too late to fix this. But from here on in, we do not take our orders from Bert. From this point on, no one leaves this room until we have a concrete plan of action, and I don't care how long it takes. Now, let's run all this up the flagpole and see what we come up with."

Abner Tookus flipped down the visor and pressed the remote that would allow him to enter the parking area that came with his converted loft. He was home. Home sweet home, though without Isabelle. Still, he was home. Even he had to admit he had made good time, having taken full advantage of his radar detector. For the most part, he had relied on his GPS and the detector and had driven eighty miles an hour. It was still a mystery to him how he hadn't been pulled over for speeding. The thing was, he never drove over the speed limit, just the way he never smoked. And yet he'd done both. He shook his head at his disbelief before he gathered up all his trash—the cigarettes, the coffee, and some soda cups, along with snack bags of cookies and chips. He dumped it all in a trash can next to the elevator, even the radar detector. His speeding and smoking days were officially over.

On the elevator ride up to the loft, Abner realized that he should have picked up his mail. Not that he ever got much, but he didn't like it to accumulate. He conducted all his business these days electronically. Oh, well. Tomorrow was another day.

Abner stood statue still when he stepped into the foyer of the loft. He closed his eyes as he sniffed. He could smell Isabelle's perfume and the lavender scent she sprayed the loft with. He looked at the coatrack and saw her yellow slicker with the matching hat. She always said she felt like a duck when she wore it. He smiled, but it was a less than valiant effort. He dropped his backpack and kicked off his Nikes. Then he headed for the kitchen to pop a bottle of root beer before he settled down in his favorite chair, which was right next to Isabelle's chair. He felt more lonely than he'd ever felt in his life. His eyes started to burn. He didn't even have a phone to call anyone. Then again, whom would he call? No one, that was who, so why was he even thinking about making phone calls? He wished he hadn't thrown out the cigarettes. He could use one right now.

The phone Phil had given him buzzed. He could feel the vibration against his leg. He pulled it out and grinned when he said, "Don't tell me you miss me already?"

"Nah. I just called to welcome you home.

Mary Alice and I were talking, and we both decided you are probably feeling kind of lonely right now, so we called to cheer you up. You okay, pal?"

"Yeah, I'm okay. A little tired. I'm not even going to ask how you know I'm home. Where are you guys?"

"We're wherever you want us to be—thirty thousand feet in the air, the middle of the ocean, down under, in the desert. It doesn't matter, because we're talking. Did you take care of business?"

"I did, and then I left. I was just sitting here wondering what I'm going to do with myself now that I'm more or less a free agent. Guess I'll look for a job one of these days."

"Sooner or later, something will fall into your lap, probably sooner than you think. For now, just kick back and sleep around the clock. Your body needs it. Spray some lavender on your pillow. It helps."

Abner laughed, his first genuine laugh in days, because Isabelle was so into lavender, it was comical. She was forever spraying everything with the scent, because she said it was comforting and calming. "Is there anything you *don't* know, Phil?"

The big man laughed, a great booming sound. "Well, my friend, we're going to hang up now so you can get some rest. We'll be in touch. And, Abner, I'm glad you made it home safe and sound. Good thing I called ahead to all those trooper stations to alert them you were headed their way."

"And all it cost him was a couple hundred thousand dollars for the troopers' widows and orphans fund." Mary Alice giggled.

"You didn't . . ."

"See ya, Abner."

"Well, I'll be damned!" Abner slugged back the rest of the root beer and headed for the bedroom. He hit the shower, lathered up in lavender suds, washed his hair with lavender shampoo, then dried off with a lavender-scented towel before he hit the bed, which smelled like Isabelle and lavender.

Abner could have sworn that he heard someone whisper, "Sweet dreams," before he fell into a deep, restful sleep that lasted fourteen hours.

Chapter 21

The guys went at it tooth and nail, with everyone having a different opinion as to how to handle the situation, which had gotten so off the rails. Even Cyrus couldn't seem to make up his mind whose ideas he should endorse with his one-vote bark.

Jack took the floor and held up both hands for attention. "Hear me out here, please. This is how I think we have to look at things right now, at this moment in time. I have lost track of the texts and calls I've placed to Dixson Kelly. He has not responded to any of them. Nor has he responded to Bert. I think that pretty much tells us he has no intention of cooperating and that he *knows* what is going on.

"Right now we do not know where he is for certain, although we think he's at his own condo.

While we think he went to his condo in town, and the sister we didn't know he had went to the condo Maggie discovered she had in town, neither of those suppositions is carved in stone. It is at least possible that when Maggie did not show up for dessert, they decided to leave and are at some airport right now. Ten minutes ago, I sent off a text to Pete Justice, who, if he is telling the truth, has not heard from Kelly, either. He asked me what was going on. I told him I would get back to him. Bert told him via a text that he was the man in charge for now, and he was relieving Kelly of all his duties. That's what we *know for certain*. We have to decide what to do and do it quickly." Jack directed his attention to Maggie and asked her what she had.

Maggie looked around at the gang, each one of whom looked like he was about to hang on every word that came out of her mouth. "Not much, but something. Clare Andreas, aka Kitty Passion, shares the condo she has in town with an airline stewardess named Sabrina Abernathy. The only name on the deed and the mortgage is Abernathy's, not Passion or Andreas. The condo is for sale at a greatly reduced price . . . for a quick sale. I checked Abernathy's Facebook page, and there was a lot of stuff on it, girl stuff, but at her age, which, if she is telling the truth, is thirty-five, you'd think she'd be a little more circumspect.

"First of all, she is a Brit. Divides her time between here and London. Said she broke up with her gal pal a while back and put her home up for sale to get out from under. The Facebook post does not name Kitty/Clare. I am assuming Kitty/Clare is the gal pal. Said she served an eviction notice on Kitty/Clare. Her last posting was yesterday, about eighteen hours ago, when she announced she would be flying the London to Hong Kong route from now on. The last thing she said on her post was she was sorry she had blinders on and she was so very sad that people—I guess she meant Kitty/Clare—were so ruthless. That's it."

"So are we saying Kitty is staying in the condo illegally?" Fergus asked. "After she was evicted?"

"I have no idea. I would guess she has a key. Maybe she returned there tonight to pack up her stuff. Maybe she's moving in with her brother. I don't know," Maggie said.

"We would have that information if you hadn't called us back here," Dennis said. "We should go there now and pick her up. She's probably in for the night."

"Or getting ready to take it on the lam with her brother, if that hasn't already happened, seeing as how he isn't here at Babylon, either," Ted said. "Every minute we sit here sucking our thumbs is a minute they can use to head for the hills. They have to know we know something. Don't think for one minute one of those showgirls or some of them that weren't rounded up have not been in touch with someone. You know how women like to stick together. No offense, Maggie. It's just a pure fact, and us guys have to live with it."

Sparrow held his arm up for attention, a fierce look on his face. "Oh, man, you guys are *not* going to like hearing the text I just got."

Cyrus barked to show he was in agreement even before he knew what he was agreeing to.

"What?" Harry growled. When Harry growled, people invariably paid attention. People even paid attention when Harry whispered.

"Those women we're holding—they're all represented by the same law firm."

"Director, you did say, did you not, that you could hold those women for seventy-two hours without benefit of counsel?" Charles said, his voice dangerously cold at what he was hearing.

"It's true, but as we said earlier, a few of the women could have evaded our net when we swooped in. Being women, they did what they had to do—call their lawyers. The group's attorneys—that's plural—just showed up ten minutes ago at the field office, breathing fire and brimstone. You know what this town is like. These people take care of their own, and let me tell you, those women have the best of the best. By morning, this will be a goddamned circus," Director Sparrow said.

"What law firm is it?" Jack asked, virtually certain that he knew the answer even before he asked the question.

Cyrus yipped to back up his master's question.

"Lizzie Fox represents half of them, and

Cosmo Cricket, her husband, represents the other half."

Cyrus was so devastated at the news, he covered his face with both paws as the others cursed out loud at this revolting turn of events.

Jack drew a deep breath. When he finally expelled the air, it sounded like a gunshot. He looked at his watch. "I don't see any solution other than to pick up Kelly and the sister, if they haven't already left. The question is, where to take them if we're successful?"

"How about that room at MGM that the girls comped for me?" Maggie said. "Mr. Snowden gave me both key cards. He said there is a sitting room, kind of like here in this suite, so the room should accommodate all of us. I can leave now and head to MGM to wait for you."

"Sparrow and I will take Kelly, assuming he's at his condo," Jack said. "Harry, you and Dennis pick up the sister. Snowden, split up your team, with half as backup for me and Sparrow and the other half as backup for Harry and Dennis. Charles, you, Fergus, Ted, and Espinosa be our lookouts at MGM. Hit the casino floor and keep your eyes on the main door. Maggie, of course, will be waiting at the room. Our mass departure from here will *not* go unnoticed. Everyone clear on their positions?"

Cyrus reared up and let loose with an unholy bark. He scratched frantically at the carpet, growling deep in his throat.

"I didn't forget you, big guy. I know you want to bite someone on the ass, and you will get that opportunity, I promise. You're going with Charles and the guys."

Cyrus ran to the door and waited even before Jack was finished with his monologue.

The gang left one by one, with Charles and the boys the last to walk through the door. Charles fastened the leash to Cyrus's collar. "Let's be clear, Cyrus. You do not bite anyone's arse until we give the okay. You understand?"

Cyrus yipped once to show he got it.

It was almost midnight when the crew took to the street. Inside the casino, where there were no clocks, the gaming was in full swing, with blinding neon lights, along with the shrieking bells and whistles and a few shouts from hysterical winners. For all the gamblers knew, it could be four o'clock in the afternoon, as far as they were concerned. Outside, it was a different matter. The crowds on the streets had thinned considerably, mostly due to the light, chilly, misty spring rain that was falling. People did not want to be wet and cold while sitting on a stool in an air-conditioned casino, even if they were winning.

The chilly mist didn't bother Jack or Sparrow as they half jogged and half ran, because both men were extremely physically fit. It took them only twenty minutes to reach Dixson Kelly's condo. They were barely panting when they stood to the side to stare up at all the lighted windows.

Jack looked out at the mess of traffic on the street, mostly taxis, clogging the street. "Good thing we decided to hoof it, or we'd still be sitting out there, cursing the driver."

"I could never live here," Sparrow said.

"Me either. Cyrus wouldn't like it. He hates concrete. He likes green grass and trees."

"Me too." Sparrow laughed.

"Doorman building. How do you want to play this?"

Sparrow laughed out loud. "This badge gets me in anywhere I want to go. Just follow me."

"I'll need to see your key card, gentlemen, before I can open the door," the doorman said politely and respectfully when the duo approached him.

"Will this do, young man?" Sparrow said, whipping out his ID.

"I believe so, sir. Anything I can do for you? Is there going to be any trouble? This is a family building."

"I certainly hope not. Wait, there is one thing you can do. Have a taxi waiting with the motor running. Can you do that?"

The doorman's eyes were wide as saucers when he said, "I believe so, sir."

"Do not use your cell phone until I tell you to. We clear on that?"

"I believe so, sir. I mean, yes, sir. You have made yourself crystal clear. I will not use my cell phone."

"Good! Good! I'll be sure to give you a glowing report. Now, please, open the door. By the way, how many of the tenants returned in the past few hours? Any strangers or anyone with the tenants you didn't recognize?"

"Not many. No, no strangers. It's a slow night. The people who live in this building are not gamblers. Well, maybe they are to a certain extent, but what I meant was they come home at night, like other people with regular jobs. Let's see . . . Who came in? The Ellisons around nine thirty. They were out to dinner. Mrs. Ellison isn't much of a cook, according to Mr. Ellison. John Stephens came in with his suitcases. He was away on a business trip.

"Then the two architects came in a little while ago. They were arguing about something that went wrong on a project. Then Mr. Kelly came in all in a lather, huffing and puffing, and didn't even say good evening. That's not like him, and he is never here, anyway. Once in a blue moon. Oh, yeah. The Olivers, with their four kids, came in right after Mr. Kelly. One of the kids had a recital, and then they stopped for ice cream. That's why they were so late coming home. Tenants like to chat. That's it so far."

"Have any of the tenants left the building in the past hour and a half?"

"No, sir. Like I said, it's a slow night."

"Okay, you can open the door now. Have that cab ready."

"Yes, sir. You got it, sir." The doorman opened the plate-glass door with a flourish. Sparrow and Jack stepped through.

"That was almost too easy," Jack said.

"He didn't say Kelly went back out, so that has to mean he's still up there in his condo.

What do you suppose he's doing?" Sparrow asked.

"A wild guess on my part would be he's packing. I think he knows we're onto him. Then again, maybe the guy is just sitting there, waiting for us, with some cockamamie story to try out on us."

"What do we do if he doesn't open the door? This is your show. I'm just along for the ride," Sparrow said.

"I remember Snowden saying the only way out was through the front door. I can pick a lock with the best of them. But first we knock. The only thing I'm having a problem with is, what if he calls the sister and alerts her before Harry and Dennis get there? Hell, he might have already done that. It's also possible that he's going to take the fall all by himself and let her get off scot-free. You know, big brother stuff."

"No, I'm not buying that one. A stretch in the federal pen is serious stuff. Call Harry or Dennis and ask where they are and what they're doing," Sparrow said.

Tongue in cheek, Jack said, "Now, why didn't I think about that?"

"Probably because Cyrus isn't here to do your thinking for you," Sparrow quipped. "Well, what are they saying?"

"They're actually outside her door. She must have gone to bed. No light shining through the magic eye or showing under the door. Dennis is going to try picking the lock, so we're

going to wait to see what happens. Believe it or
not, Annie taught him how to do it, and how to
crack a safe. If Kitty/Clare has an alarm and
she turned it on, then we're in some serious
trouble. I'll keep the line open, so the minute
they're in, we bang on Kelly's door, and whatever happens. Unless you have a better idea."

"Works for me," Sparrow said.

"So we wait."

Less than a mile away, Harry successfully intimidated the condo building's doorman with
his special gold shield. Once they were through
the door, they opted for the stairwell, as opposed to taking the elevator.

"Just a minute, Dennis. I want you to check
the mail room roster to see whose name is on
eight-oh-nine. I think we both know Maggie is
going to want to know."

Dennis sprinted forward to look at the mail
roster behind a glass frame. His index finger
traced the numbers while Harry studied and
committed to memory the schematic on the
wall. "Okay, what I am seeing here is Abernathy slash Andreas."

"Okay, then, let's head for the stairs to see
what we can do." They entered the stairwell
and walked up to the eighth floor. "By any
chance, do you know how to pick a lock, kid?"

Dennis straightened to his full height and
preened for a moment. "Actually, Harry, I do
know how to pick a lock. Annie showed me.

She also showed me how to crack a safe. When she was satisfied that I had mastered the technique, she gave me my very own lock-picking kit. She said to always carry it, because you never know when it will come in handy."

Harry gaped at his protégé. This kid never ceased to amaze him. "What about the alarm?"

"We didn't get that far. I know nothing about alarms. So what if it goes off? No big deal. We'll have her in hand, so we can force her to turn it off. She'll probably be half-asleep, anyway. Let's just do it!"

"Do not make any noise, kid. It's almost midnight, and people are asleep. Try for quick and fast."

Dennis dropped to his knees, squinted, and then went to work with his picklock. "Beats me," he whispered, "why people live in these swanky places and use the cheapest locks on the market. Guess they think their security systems will save them. Or they're counting on that doorman not to let anyone who doesn't belong into the building. Dumb. Okay, I did it. All we have to do is turn the knob and walk through the door. You want me to go first?"

Harry looked over at Dennis and shook his head. "Stealth is required right now. Do you remember the layout of the condo from the schematic we saw when we were in the stairwell? It's the same one that was in the mail room."

Dennis nodded.

"I'm going to head straight for the bedroom. You stay here by the door but inside. *If* there is an alarm, and *if* it goes off, I'll hustle her to wherever it's located. It goes without saying she's going to try to get away, so be prepared."

Dennis stepped to the side to allow Harry to enter the condo. He followed him into the dark of the foyer. A faint glow of a night-light shone off the living room. The foyer, where the alarm should be, showed only a picture of some kind. No alarm pad. He heaved a sigh of relief. Then he started to wonder if perhaps it was in the bedroom, but he doubted it. People wanted an alarm by the door so they could immediately either arm or disarm the system while they were either coming or going. He took a second to wonder how he knew that. Probably had read an article on alarm systems at some point, and it had stuck with him. He was, after all, a reporter, and he read constantly to keep his faculties sharp and his information base updated.

He was about to disobey Harry's orders when he heard a squeal, then a thump, then some colorful cursing. He froze in his tracks. More yelps. He ran toward the bedroom but stopped in the doorway. A small night-light was on. He couldn't be sure, but he thought Harry looked frazzled in the dimness. He looked at the bed, where it looked like a woman had been sleeping peacefully. The bedcovers told another story.

"She put up a fight," Harry said flatly. "I had to use some extreme measures. There is no alarm. Is that right?"

"Right. Right. No alarm," Dennis said, his eyes on the woman on the bed.

"Find her clothes, whatever she took off when she got in bed. We need to dress her."

"But she's . . . I don't know. . . . I never . . . Harry, she's . . ."

"Naked. I know. That's why we have to dress her. Move, Dennis!"

Dennis moved. To the bathroom. Where he found a small pile of clothing and a pair of spike-heeled shoes studded with rhinestones. The kind of rhinestones that were on the cowgirl boots Annie loved and wore almost every day. He bent over to pick up the clothes with one eye closed. Unmentionables. A bra that was all lace. With his foot, he tried to shoo it over to the tank top that was next to a pair of spandex capri pants. He reared back when he saw something else. Strings. He bent over to peer more closely. *Oh, jeez. Oh, Lordy, Lordy.* Should he touch them? Touch what? Three strings. *Jeez, Jeez, Jeez.*

"Uh, Harry!" he called out.

"C'mon, kid. Move it. We don't have all night, and Jack is pitching a fit. What's the problem?"

Dennis looked down at the pile of clothing and started to move it all with his foot toward the bedroom doorway. "Listen, Harry, I think you should wake her up and let her dress herself. I never . . . I don't even know how . . . how these three strings work. I never put a bra on a woman."

Harry stared at Dennis for thirty long seconds. In his life, he'd never seen anyone look more miserable. Then he looked down at the pile of clothing. He decided they should take the clothes over to the bed and try to put them on. Well, this would certainly make for interesting conversation when Yoko got back. Then again, maybe not. If the kid was refusing to dress the woman, that left only him.

"Tell you what, let's . . . uh . . . just forget the underwear and go with the rest. Between the two of us, we should be able to manage it, doncha think? I don't like this any more than you do, but we have to get her dressed to take her out of here. Maggie didn't say anything about her sleeping in the nude. Who does that?" Harry asked fretfully.

"I don't know, Harry. This . . . this is all new to me. How can they call three strings underwear? I wonder how they figure out what the thread count is."

"Shut up, Dennis. I'll take the pants, and you take the top. Just yank it over her head. Oh, crap! This is that stretchy stuff. You need to *pull and tug.*"

"Yeah, yeah, they call it spandex, and once you get it on, it fits like a second skin. I saw that on a commercial."

Harry and Dennis tugged and pulled, then tugged some more.

"She's hippy. How the hell did she get these on all by herself?" Harry muttered as he gave the waistband another yank.

"Women dance around and jiggle to get them on. No, I don't know that firsthand. I saw it on a commercial," Dennis babbled, his face beet red with all his exertion.

Harry closed his eyes and waited a few seconds, until his breathing returned to normal. He made a mental note to himself to check Yoko's drawers when he got home, and if there were any such items, he would dispose of them and pretend the dojo was robbed.

"We need her cell phone, all electronic devices you can find, her purse for sure. Make it snappy. I'm going to wake her up, and she's going to be ready to go another few rounds. We might have to gag her because of the security cameras in the hall. But once we get her into the stairwell, we'll be okay. Her car keys should be in her purse. We'll dump her into the trunk and hope for the best. Oh, shit. Someone is ringing the doorbell. Watch her, Dennis, while I check it out."

Someone at the door! "Holy Mother of Jesus," Dennis said as he blessed himself. He looked down to see Kitty/Clare reaching up to grab him by the throat. His eyes almost popped out of his head when he realized that this woman got the drop on him. Oh, no, that wasn't going to happen, not under Harry's eye. Or his eye, either.

Dennis reached for Kitty/Clare's wrist and knocked it out of the way. "Listen to me, lady. You try that again, and I'll slice your tits off. In case you haven't noticed, we didn't put your bra on, in case it came to this!" Dennis hissed.

"I'd like to see you try that! You dressed me! You saw me naked! You pervert! Who are you? Who is that crazy Chinese guy who knocked me out? Let me go, so I can kill you. Damn perverts. This is my home, my castle. I'm supposed to be safe here."

"None of your beeswax. Now, shut up and stand up. I meant what I said about . . . earlier, and if they aren't real, they're going to leak all over the place. I'm not going to tell you again, so get the hell up right now!"

That was when Dennis saw Harry and Snowden grinning from ear to ear and the two female operatives smiling as they took in the situation. He suddenly felt so light-headed, he almost blacked out. He'd performed to their expectations. In his eyes, it didn't get any better than that. *Woo-hoo!*

"Gag her," Snowden said.

One of the female operatives ran into the bathroom for a washcloth. She returned and shoved it into Kitty/Clare's mouth. The quasi showgirl fought like a tiger, kicking out and struggling, but to no avail.

"You got a plan, Snowden?" Harry asked.

"Yeah, more or less. We know where she's parked. We dump her in the trunk and head out to MGM, where we'll be just another drunken party returning to her room. Standard operating procedure here in Vegas. What that means is no one will pay the least bit of attention to us. So, yeah, that's the plan."

"Guess I can live with that," Harry mumbled. Harry eyeballed Dennis. "Did you get everything?"

Dennis held out a designer duffel bag and hefted it to show it was full. "We're good, Harry. Let's go. This place gives me the creepy-crawlies."

"I'm proud of you, kid. You handled yourself well tonight."

Dennis felt his chest puff out. Praise from Harry Wong just made his day. In this particular case, his night.

Chapter 22

J ack used his clenched fist to thump on Dix-son Kelly's door. He peered into the magic eye but couldn't see anything, any sign of movement. What he could see was dim light off to the side, probably from the main living area. He waited a full two minutes before he thumped his fist again. When nothing happened, he got out his mini lock-breaking kit, the same one that Dennis carried, and went to work. He heard the tumblers click in the first minute. *Cheap lock,* he thought.

Sparrow motioned for Jack to step aside. Gun in hand, he stood in the open doorway and said, "FBI, Mr. Kelly! Show yourself. Don't make me do this the hard way."

Kelly appeared from a dim hallway, glass in hand. "Gentlemen! Welcome to Casa Kelly. You should have called first. You're calling on me with a gun in hand! Not nice. Not to mention breaking and entering. The last time I looked, that was against the law. What are you doing here?"

Jack stared at the security chief, who was dressed casually in creased khakis and a white button-down shirt, the cuffs rolled up to mid-arm. His gold Rolex glowed in the light of the lamp he'd just turned on. He had a highball glass in his hand.

"Half the world has been trying to reach you all evening, actually the better part of the day. Bert, Pete Justice, Charles, Maggie, me. You didn't get back to any of us, so we all got worried. We'd like you to come with us," Jack said.

Kelly eyed both men over the rim of the highball glass. "Is that an order or a request? Just for the record, this is my day off. On my day off, I do not do anything I don't want to do. Occasionally, I will stop by the casino to check on things, but I really didn't feel like doing that today. I'm asking you again, why are you here, what do you want, and why do you need a gun? Oh, and let's not forget your little breaking-and-entering caper. I would really like an explanation, gentlemen."

Cool as a waterfall. Urbane. Slick. The guy must have nerves of steel, Jack thought to himself. "Let's cut this civility bullshit and get on with it. Just in case you don't know, all those luscious ladies you had relationships with, the members of the Dixson Kelly Alumnae Club,

they're being held at the local FBI field office.
I'm sure you know, being ex-CIA and all, that
they can be held for seventy-two hours without
benefit of counsel. They were rounded up about
two hours ago by my partner here, Director
Sparrow. Your half sister, Clare Andreas, aka
Kitty Passion, was just picked up about fifteen
minutes ago. What that means to you is, you
lose, and we win. You won't be robbing the Babylon armored car anytime soon. We have all the
e-mails that your half sister sent to a hacking
guru, a bundle of others she sent to the members of the Dixson Kelly Alumnae Club, and
dozens more to you, apprising you of the progress in regard to the heist. How's that for
starters?"

Dixson Kelly laughed. To Jack, it sounded
forced. "I understand from Bert that you're a
lawyer. If that's true, what are you charging me
with, seeing as how you're asking me to accom-
pany you out of here? For receiving and sending e-mails? For having relationships that
didn't work out? Research for a work of fiction
featuring a heist? Research, gentlemen, for a
book I'm working on. Check my computer. All
eleven chapters are on it. Happens every day
of the week, gentlemen. Where is the crime?
Who did what?"

Jack's stomach curled itself into a tight knot.
He must really be slipping. The guy was writing
a book or was pretending to. He should have
figured on something like that. Perfect cover.
Kelly was right. To a point. There was no crime.

Yet. He opted for silence and let Sparrow have the floor.

"Mr. Emery isn't charging you with anything at the moment. I am, however, going to take you into FBI custody for questioning. Since you already know the drill, then you know I can hold you for seventy-two hours. Hold out your hands, Mr. Kelly." Sparrow whipped a pair of flexicuffs from the pocket of his Windbreaker and tossed them to Jack, who fastened them securely, giving them an extra tug for security.

His eyes narrowed to slits, Kelly eyed Jack. If looks could kill, Jack knew he'd keel over any minute.

"I want it on record that I have said nothing. I want a lawyer. My lawyer's name is Cosmo Cricket. Law firm is Cricket & Fox. Where is my sister?"

"In our custody. And she's talking. Don't worry. You'll see her soon enough," Sparrow said.

"Well, that's a lie, if I ever heard one. If you had my sister, then you would know she won't say one word without a lawyer present, so let's cut the bullshit right now."

"Jack, see if you can find a jacket and drape it over his shoulders. We don't need any questions from late-night looky-loos. The man might want to come back here someday, so no sense ruining his reputation at this point in time."

Jack took his time in Kelly's bedroom as he tried to see everything there was to see, which to his mind was nothing. He found a tweed jacket and marveled at the softness. *Cashmere*, he thought. *Pricey. Designer quality.* Jacket in hand, he walked over to a desk that was perched in a small alcove, which was probably supposed to be a dressing area. He scooped up the laptop and the letter lying on the desk. Kelly's resignation letter, with today's date on it. He carried both out to the living room, laid them on the end table, and asked Kelly where his cell phone was. Kelly clamped his lips shut.

"Oh, well, we have all your other burner phones." As Jack said this, he made a lightning move and yanked the phone out of Kelly's pocket just as Kelly raised his leg to kick out at him. Jack nimbly sidestepped the kick and waved the cell phone and the resignation letter in the air. "Going somewhere, Kelly?"

"I want a lawyer. From here on in, you can ask him anything you want to know. I also want it on record that I did not give you permission to take my belongings. The letter you have in your hand, my phone, and that laptop belong to me. And that I cooperated and explained about my novel and research."

"Yeah, yeah, yeah," Jack said as he draped the designer jacket over Kelly's shoulders, once again marveling at its softness.

Sparrow opened the door to see three attractive women standing there, looking at him. Jack caught the wink Kelly bestowed on the women. "We good?" he asked.

"We're good," one of the females said as she returned Kelly's wink.

"Avery . . . uh . . . *borrowed* a van. It's double-parked outside the main door," Jack said.

Kelly stiffened and refused to move. "You aren't taking me to the field office. Where are you taking me?" he demanded.

"You'll find out when you get there," Jack snapped. "You give us any trouble, and it's lights out for you. Walk slowly and look straight ahead."

"Screw you!" Kelly bellowed.

One of Snowden's operatives, who could have doubled for a young Christie Brinkley, leaned forward and locked her lips with those of Kelly, who suddenly went limp.

"Good kisser," the operative said with a giggle in her voice. "So, a fireman's carry, or do we do the drunk thing?"

"We do the drunk thing. He's too heavy to carry," Jack said before running down the hall to catch the elevator.

"Gotcha. We left the engine running in the van, and the door is open. We slipped the doorman a hundred bucks to keep his eye on it. And we also told him to dismiss the cab he had waiting for the two of you, and gave him another fifty for the cabdriver. Once we get out of the elevator, it's a short haul across the lobby and out the door to the van. Anyone seeing us will just think we partied a little too hearty," the blonde said. "We'll just repeat the process once we get to MGM's parking garage."

"He's coming around," Sparrow hissed.

Luscious lips moved and again locked her lips with Kelly's. Jack rubbed his hands over the back of Kelly's neck, and Kelly went limp all over again.

Somehow, they managed to get Kelly across the lobby and out the door and into the van. Luscious Lips handed the doorman another folded bill before she scrambled into the van.

"Burn rubber!" she commanded the driver, who did just that. The occupants slipped and slid across the van, then back again, as the driver tore down the road to take a corner on two wheels.

"Where in the hell did you learn to drive?" Sparrow bellowed as he tried to right himself, only to fall back against a lovely redhead with an exquisite smile.

"Daytona!" the driver bellowed in return. "It's a requisite to work for Mr. Snowden."

Twenty minutes later, the driver of the *borrowed* van took the ramp leading to the MGM parking garage at forty miles an hour. She raced down the length of the floor; then, her tires screaming, she tore up another ramp at the same speed. When she finally slowed enough to pull into a parking space, the occupants of the van all slid forward. That included Dixson Kelly, who was once again awake and who swore viciously. Jack clipped him alongside the head and told him to shut up. Kelly did his best to head butt Jack, but Jack moved quickly enough to avoid what would have been a punishing blow, what with all of Kelly's weight behind it.

"Stuff something in this guy's mouth," Sparrow ordered as he dragged him out of the van.

Jack took off his necktie and jammed it in
Kelly's mouth.

Two of Snowden's operatives, Jack, and Sparrow formed a cordon around Kelly as they led
him to the elevator. They all heard the squeal
of the van's tires as the third operative prepared to return the *borrowed* van to its rightful
parking space. Before she climbed out, she
placed a folded hundred-dollar bill under a
clip attached to the visor.

Maggie was standing in the open doorway of
her comped room, motioning for them to
hurry. Kelly did his best to drag his feet, until
Jack socked him in his midsection. He doubled over, making it easier to drag him down
the hall. When they reached the door, Sparrow
gave Kelly such a hard shove, he literally flew
across the room, to land almost at his sister's
feet. She scowled at him, then started to rant,
until she saw Dennis approach her, his face full
of menace.

Jack looked over at Harry, who whispered,
"I'll tell you later, but even then, you won't believe that kid. Now what?"

"I say we dillydally a little till the two of them
get comfortable with the knowledge that they
are not going anywhere but here and that we
hold their fate in our hands. I'll have Maggie
order us some room service, coffee, pizza, sandwiches, whatever. It's all on the house when
the room is comped." Jack motioned for Maggie to come closer and asked her to order the
food, which she promptly did.

"Someone should call Charles and the others and tell them to come up here now," Jack said as he stared straight at Dixson Kelly, who stared right back at him. "I'm going to call Bert and tell him what's going on."

Snowden volunteered to make the call to Charles and Jack said he would call Bert later.

Jack looked over at Kelly and said, "Anything you want me to pass on to your boss other than to tell him you're resigning effective today? Actually, yesterday, since that's the date on the resignation letter I have here."

"I want a lawyer," Kelly said.

"I also want my lawyer," Kitty/Clare said.

"Well of course you do. I would want my lawyer, too, if I were in your position. Here's the thing, Mr. Kelly, that is not going to happen. So just settle in and remain quiet."

Jack stepped out into the hall to make his call to Bert. He stopped the call when he heard the elevator ping, and the boys stepped out. Cyrus literally flew down the hall, to skid to a stop. He put his paws on Jack's shoulders and stared at him. Then he growled.

"Yeah, yeah, I know. You didn't get to bite some badass's ass, right? Well, we still have time for that, and your chances of making that happen are better right now than when you left here. Go inside and *guard.*"

Cyrus raced off, but not before he let loose with a few joyful yips of pure pleasure.

The boys looked at Jack expectantly.

"Well?" Charles said.

"We got them both. We're taking a break. Maggie ordered some sandwiches, coffee, and pizza. Those two need to sweat a little. The only word the two of them seem to know is *lawyer*. I just stepped out here to call Bert. Go inside, and I'll be inside in a minute."

The phone call to Bert was short and to the point, with Jack doing all the talking. All Bert could manage to get into the conversation was a few ripe curses that he'd been so wrong about one of his hires.

Jack ignored him and said, "Look, I gotta go. I'll update you later, when . . . we're on our way to the airport." He broke off just as Bert started to rant on. Jack sighed. Life was never easy.

Jack stood at the door to Maggie's comped suite. He took several deep breaths to calm himself. For some reason, his thoughts went to Abner. He felt so depressed, he took another deep, calming breath. Abner was one of the good guys. When he explained everything, he hoped the computer whiz would forgive him and the others. If he had to grovel, he would grovel. If he had to kiss his feet, then he would kiss his feet. Whatever it took, he would do it.

Jack squared his shoulders and opened the door just as the elevator pinged to allow a group of tipsy revelers fresh from a win at the craps table to make their way down the hall. He wondered how much they had won, not that he cared. It was just something to think about to get Abner out of his mind.

The suite, while nice and comfortable, could not compare to the suites they'd had at Babylon. It was crowded. It looked to Jack like either they were waiting for him to start whatever it was that was about to go down or they were waiting for him to give the go-ahead. He looked over at Charles for direction. Charles shrugged, as much to say, "This is your gig. Run with it."

Jack decided to run with it. He motioned for Cyrus to join him. "Guard these two. If they even twitch, you get your wish."

Cyrus, ham that he was, stretched luxuriously before he trotted over to the two bound prisoners sitting on the floor. He let loose with two yips and then bared his teeth as he let loose with a ferocious growl to show he really wanted to bite someone's ass.

Jack at that moment decided a few little lies on his part wouldn't hurt and just might move things along. He cleared his throat. "I want the two of you to listen to me very carefully. First things first. You are not going to be released, nor are you going to be arrested. That's too good for you two. Second, this dog—his name is Cyrus—is a trained killer. On command, he will go straight for your throat, rip it out, and hang on till you bleed out. Now, having said that, Cyrus does have one *little quirk* that he refused to give up during his military training. Sometimes he just has to bite someone's ass. In this case, it will be your asses.

"Third, we want a written, signed confession statement from the two of you. Your relocation address will depend on how cooperative you both are. Oh, fourth, and last, Cyrus is good in that position for just fifteen minutes. Then he starts to salivate, and from there on, it's his ball game. Right, big guy?"

Cyrus barked joyfully to confirm all Jack's lies.

"Okay, someone get ready to record their confessions so we can print them out for signatures. Maggie is a notary, so everything will be legal. She said everything is all hooked up and ready to go. So, *go!*"

Kelly went first. His tone was conversational. "I told you, I did not do anything. My sister did not do anything. I'm writing a book about a Vegas heist. Nothing like *Ocean's Eleven*. This is the real deal. My sister was helping me since she's into all things digital and electronic, whereas I am a Neanderthal. She enlisted the aid of a mentor, who showed her the ropes about hacking so she could become the professional she is. That's what those e-mails are. I admit to knowing that the showgirls formed that asinine club and making it all work for me. Besides not being able to take revenge on me, they agreed to help my sister when she presented the project to them. It's called research. Authentic research. How else can a person get a book published? That's my story, and I am sticking to it. It's up to you to prove otherwise."

"It's my story, too," Kitty/Clare said.

Jack wondered if he was the only one who had noticed how shaky and trembly Kitty/Clare's voice sounded.

"Let me clear something up here," Maggie said as she waved a sheaf of papers in the air. "That novel you claim to be writing, all those chapters . . . All I found was nine separate files that claim to be chapters one through nine. It's a one-paragraph chapter. Then there are two other files with gibberish. I don't know if you consider them chapters or not. One through nine are basically just notes."

"It's my outline. My guide," Kelly said defensively, one eye on Jack and Maggie, the other eye on Cyrus. "That's how you write a book."

"That's pure bullshit, and you know it. Clock's ticking, Mr. Kelly. Miss Andreas, do you want to go down with your brother, or do you want to tell us what you all were really planning? Don't start with that lawyer business again, either. That is not even on the table," said Maggie.

Kitty/Clare licked at her dry lips as she stared up at Dennis, who was hovering over her. "We did not commit any crime. We, meaning me and the other girls, were helping my brother. He promised us all a share of the book's proceeds and a share of the movie he said they would make. There's no crime in that."

"To a point, you're right," Jack said. "What we didn't show you were the texts and e-mails from your mentor, RCHood, where you confessed to what you were going to do. He drew you into his web, pretended to help you, and now he's gone. If you aren't getting it, he let you hang yourself. His legacy is this pile of incriminating evidence, which will, if given to the proper authorities, ensure a nice long vacation in a federal penitentiary. You'll be old and gray when you get out. Assuming someone doesn't get to you first.

"See, we're looking out for you, because we know what will happen to the two of you if we cut you loose and turn you over to the feds. You know how Vegas works. Ah, I see by the look on your face that you know what I'm talking about. Your best bet is to cooperate with us and confess. The clock is still ticking, but not for long," Jack said.

Maggie stared hard at Dixson Kelly. She remembered how delicious he'd looked in his pristine white shirt, Hermès tie, and designer warrior suit when she'd first set eyes on him. He looked nothing like that now. Right now he had a beaten look, which he was trying desperately to cover up.

Kitty/Clare spoke hesitantly. "Speaking hypothetically, just suppose my brother and I agree to give you a confession, not that we are guilty, but to put an end to this . . . this silliness. Should we agree to do that, hypothetically, what's in it for us? Since no crime was committed. That part is true and not a hypothetical."

"Save your breath, Clare. These people are

not here to help us. They're here to help themselves. Open your eyes and look around. Do
you see a Mickey Mouse operation here? I sure
as hell don't, so just shut up already. This
whole thing has teeth."

Jack looked at his watch. Two minutes and
counting. "Cyrus, stay alert and pay attention."

Maggie held out her recorder. "Last chance.
Time is almost up."

"If I sign it, will you let me go?" Kitty/Clare
asked.

Her voice sounded so pitiful, Jack almost
laughed out loud.

"Absolutely!" the occupants of the room
said as one.

"Okay, okay, I'll sign it, but it's bogus. I just
want out of here. Dix, sign the damn confession so we can get out of here."

"Are you out of your mind? You can't believe anything they say. You are such a fool,
Clare. Why I ever listened to you in the first
place is a mystery to me," Kelly snarled.

"Time's up, guys! They're all yours, Cyrus!"

That was all Cyrus had to hear. He was up on
all fours. He eyed the situation just as Dixson
put his bound wrists up over his face for cover,
then rolled over flat out. It was exactly what the
shepherd wanted. He pounced and bit down
and then hung on for dear life. Blood spurted
in all directions. Kitty/Clare started to cry and
shriek her misery. Kelly bellowed at the top of
his lungs. Ted smacked him on the side of the
head and told him to shut up.

"Get that goddamned dog off me! All right, all right, I'll sign your frigging confession, but I'm signing it under duress, and I am going to put that in the confession, too. I need a doctor! That damn dog better have had his rabies shot," Kelly bellowed.

Jack grimaced. "He's due for one next month. I'm sure you'll live, Kelly. Your ass might be sore for a few weeks, but I guarantee that you will live. At least if your fan club doesn't get ahold of you. Roll over, sit up, and write out the confession. You, too, sweet cheeks."

The moment the brother and sister signed their names to their confessions, Maggie quickly notarized their signatures, fixed her seal, dated it, and said, "I think this is all Lizzie and Cosmo will need to cut those women loose. We're in the clear, guys!"

Kelly couldn't keep the surprise off his face. "You know my lawyers?"

Jack looked at Kelly for a moment, then laughed out loud before saying, "Get with the program here, Kelly. Who do you think they named their kid after? I'm Little Jack's godfather."

"Son of a bitch!" Kelly exploded.

Jack laughed again.

"They're all yours now, Mr. Snowden. We're done here," Charles said.

"Wait just a damn minute," Kitty/Clare shouted. "You said you would let us go. We want to go by ourselves. We definitely do not need an escort."

"Oh, but you do, my dear," Charles said.

"You lied! You goddamn lied to us! That's . . . that's . . . unspeakable. Dixson, say something!" Kitty/Clare shrieked at the top of her lungs.

"I did warn you. Will you please just shut up! You're giving me a headache," Kelly snapped.

"Take two Aleve," Dennis said helpfully.

Kelly could only stare at the young reporter as he recalled the big man in the Tiki Bar telling him the same exact thing. That was what had started this whole megillah. He wished now that he had two Aleve to take.

Ah, well, this was Vegas. *You win some, and you lose some.* Only to himself would he admit that he had never *really* thought he was going to get away with his plan.

When Snowden and his people departed with Kitty/Clare and Dixson in tow, the comped MGM room was silent. So silent, no one wanted to shatter the stillness.

"Plane will be ready in thirty minutes," Dennis finally whispered as he stared at an incoming text. "Wheels up in ninety minutes, so we need to move quickly."

The group scattered and scrambled.

Jack was the last to board the private Gulfstream. He stood on the tarmac and looked around, wondering if it was true what they said about Vegas.

What happens in Vegas stays in Vegas.

He ascended the stairs and before he entered the plane, he stood on the top step and offered up a sloppy salute to the town he hoped never to see again.

Only one loose end. And he'd make it right when he got back home or die trying.

Just one loose end.

No mission was considered complete until all the ends were tied in a neat bow.

Just one loose end.

Epilogue

Two months later . . .

Isabelle Flanders Tookus snapped the lock on her battered briefcase, then turned around to look at her husband, who was sitting at the kitchen counter, staring into his coffee cup. "I'm leaving now, Abner. Don't wait up for me. I'm going to be late. In fact, I think I might take a trip to Outer Mongolia and never, ever come back." She waited a few seconds to see if Abner would respond. He nodded when she poked at his arm.

"You did not hear a word I said, Abner. Look at me! I mean it, Abner. Look at me. See that bag over there by the door? I'm leaving. I can't live like this anymore. I *won't* live like this any longer. When and if you get your act together, call me."

Abner swiveled his stool around to face his

wife. "Why? I asked you to cut me some slack. I asked you to give me some time to work through some issues that I have. You said you would, and now, just like that, you're leaving. Again, why?"

"Don't even go there with me, Abner. I'm done talking. I've had it with you. Go look at yourself in the mirror. I dare you! You look like a skid-row bum. And you smell! That beard, if that's what it is supposed to be, is pitiful. You've been wearing those same clothes for a week. I repeat, you smell!"

Abner's arms flapped in the air. "You don't understand."

"Oh, I understand, all right. More than you know. I'm the one who has been running interference so you could revel in your own misery. I know everything that happened, thanks to my friends, who thought I should know. I'm sick and tired of lying for you. You need to own your own misery. I will not forsake my friends while we all sit around, waiting for you to get over your snit. When was the last time you picked up the mail or took out the trash? Two months! When was the last time you left this loft? Two months! I'm telling you this, so you don't have to tax your brain. You're all but brain-dead. The only thing you aren't doing yet is drooling. Good-bye, Abner."

Abner heard the door close. He moved his head slightly to see if the bag by the door was gone. It was. His wife was gone. He needed to think about that. She'd told him to do something. What was it? Then it came to him. Isabelle had said he should look in the mirror. Maybe she'd left him a message scrawled in lipstick on the mirror. He frowned. *Isabelle doesn't do things like that.* She'd said he smelled. And something about the mail. She was also sick and tired of waiting for him to drool. Shit! He wished now he'd paid more attention to what his wife had said.

Isabelle was gone. The bag by the door was gone. Ergo, his wife had left him because she was sick and tired of waiting for him to drool. How goddamn stupid was that? Abner thought as he shuffled toward the bathroom so he could look in the mirror.

It was a pretty bathroom, big enough for two people on a busy morning. Isabelle had decorated it. It wasn't girly girly, nor was it manly. It was just plain old pretty, with misty green towels, luscious ferns on pedestals. Abner looked around and finally looked in the mirror. Then he looked around again to see who had followed him into the bathroom. He looked back at the mirror and realized he was looking at himself. Nothing in the world could have prepared him for what he was looking at. Nothing.

Son of a bitch! No wonder Isabelle had left him. How in the hell did he get like this?

Abner moved like a whirlwind as he reached for his razor and went at it. The moment he could see his actual skin, he rooted around in one of the vanity drawers till he found a pair of scissors. He started to whack at his stringy hair. He'd always cut his own hair, because no one could cut it the way he wanted it cut. Abner leaned forward to peer at his reflection. He saw himself and was pleased.

Abner spent thirty long minutes under his seventy-two pulsating jets as he rubbed and scrubbed to get the stink off him. He lost count of the times he washed his newly shorn head. He then turned the master knob from fiery hot to icy cold, then back again and again, until he thought he would black out.

He stood dripping wet on the bath mat as he contemplated his next move. *Dry off. Dress. Mail.* He had to get the mail. He didn't give a good fiddler's fart about the mail, but obviously, his wife did. Therefore, he had to get the mail. *Then what? Drooling.* He swung around and brushed his teeth for ten long minutes. Then he flossed. After that, he used up a half bottle of Listerine. The minty kind. He splashed on some woodsy, citrusy aftershave that Isabelle had said drove her nuts. He suddenly realized he felt pretty good. He got dressed in jeans, sneakers. He rummaged around in his drawer and finally settled on a deep purple Izod shirt, another gift from his wife. Purple was her favorite color.

Abner walked out to the kitchen. He felt better than good; he felt like a million bucks. He made a fresh pot of coffee. While he waited for it to drip into the pot, he decided to get the mail, which was so important to Isabelle.

Outside, Abner looked around at the colorful pots of flowers that seemed to be everywhere. He did some mental calculations. It had to be the end of June, close to July. According to Isabelle, he'd been in a stupor for two whole months. Sixty-one days! How was that possible?

At the mailbox, he noticed a fussy-looking little man walking toward him.

"Mr. Tookus?"

"Yes."

"You are one hard man to get in touch with. I've been out here every day for the past two months, hoping to see you. No one answered that bell thing you have going on by the garage door. You didn't answer any of my letters, e-mails, or texts. I had no phone number to reach you. Nelson Carter," the fussy little man said, holding out a fragile, bony-looking hand. Abner was careful not to squeeze it too hard.

"Is there someplace we can talk?" the fussy little man asked.

"About what? Why have you been coming out here every day for two months? Who are you?"

Carter withdrew a slim wallet from his jacket pocket and held it up for Abner to see his picture and the letters *CIA*. "I work for the Central Intelligence Agency, out at Langley. Can we go inside now? I don't much care to discuss business outdoors, and I really could use a cup of coffee, if you'd care to offer me one."

"Yeah, sure," Abner said, totally forgetting to pick up the mail as he led the man through the garage to the elevator that would take them to the loft.

Once they were seated at the kitchen counter

on bar stools, coffee cups in hand, Abner waited for whatever was about to happen.

"I'm going to get right to the point, Mr. Tookus. You came to me highly recommended, so highly, in fact, that I have a hard time believing you are as good as the person who recommended you said you are. That person also said there was no one else in the universe who could fill his shoes but you."

Abner started to laugh. The sound was rusty. Obviously, he hadn't laughed much lately. "Do we mention names here? Or do we just go with 'I think I know who you are talking about,' or however you want to put it. You spooks are a whole other breed. I get that."

Carter allowed himself a small smile. "Let's just say my . . . uh . . . spook decided to leave the agency on rather short notice. He recommended you as his replacement. He . . . actually insisted. I took that to mean . . ."

"Your agency would feel his full wrath or something like that if you didn't do what he said." Abner chuckled.

"Exactly. The powers that be insist you come to work for us. Name your price. It's not an office, nine-to-five kind of job, as I'm sure you know. However, you will have to join us out at Langley for ten days or so. That's because we need to brief you. We will also schedule a video conference with your . . . uh, predecessor. So, Mr. Tookus, what do you say?"

Abner drained the coffee in his cup. He didn't know what to say. *Yes? No? I have to talk to my wife, but she left me. I need to talk to the boys, but they are no longer talking to me. Yes? No?*

"Sure. Why not? I'm at loose ends here. When do you want me to start?"

Carter didn't miss a beat. "Tomorrow morning, six a.m. Don't be late."

Abner walked Nelson Carter out to his car, a nondescript black Nissan sedan. They shook hands.

Abner didn't know if he should laugh, cry, dance a jig, or howl at the blazing sun. Instead, he ran like hell back to the garage and the elevator and the special phone Phil had given him. The problem was, he couldn't remember where he had put it. Not a problem, he realized when he heard it ringing inside the bread box, where he must have thrown it. He was laughing so hard, he could barely talk. So he listened.

"You take the job?"

"Yeah," Abner gasped. "I start tomorrow. Should I say thanks?"

"Not necessary. What are friends for? Listen, kid, I have something to tell you. Mary Alice and I are getting married. The day after Thanksgiving. We want you to come to the wedding."

"Now, why am I not surprised? I'm happy for you, Phil. What kind of present can I possibly give you? Man, you have the whole world."

"You want to give me a present? If I tell you what I want, will you promise to give it to me?"

"Absolutely. If I can."

"I want you to be my best man. Is that too much to ask?"

Abner was so choked up, he could barely speak. "No, no, it's not too much to ask, and I accept. I'm honored that you asked me. And flattered. Just tell me where and when."

"Day after Thanksgiving. Las Vegas. The Elvis Presley Chapel."

"Return to the scene of the crime, eh?"

Phil laughed. "One more thing. Don't wait too long before you mend all those fences you pounded into the ground. See ya, kid."

"Yeah, see ya, Phil. Hey, give Mary Alice a hug for me. I'm happy for you, Phil."

What a day, and it is only nine thirty in the morning. First, my wife leaves me, and then I'm offered a top gun job at the CIA, and then I'm asked to be best man at the wedding of one of the richest men, not to mention the smartest man, in the world. Yep, a hell of a day so far.

He hoped the day would stay as good as it was when he made his entrance at the BOLO Building to mend his fences.

But before he did another thing, he had to call his wife.

The moment he heard her voice, he laughed. "Thanks for the kick in the tail. I needed that. Please tell me you didn't buy a ticket to Outer Mongolia."

"They were sold out." Isabelle giggled. "Want me to come home early?"

"Oh, yeahhh."

Be sure not to miss #1 *New York Times*
bestselling author
Fern Michaels's new Sisterhood novel!

CRASH AND BURN

*The Sisterhood: a group of women from all walks of life
bound by friendship and a quest for justice. Armed with
vast resources, top-notch expertise, and a loyal network of
allies around the globe, the Sisterhood will not rest until
every wrong is made right.*

The women of the Sisterhood are united by their
mission to help those unable to help themselves.
But now they've encountered opponents who
share a unique bond of their own. The law firm of
Queen, King, Bishop & Rook—the Chessmen—
has been a formidable force in Washington, D.C.,
for decades. And Sisterhood member Nikki
Quinn's new case has made her their prime target.

Nikki has agreed to represent Livinia Lambert as
she files for divorce from her domineering, greedy
husband, Wilson "Buzz" Lambert. Buzz, currently
Speaker of the House, fears the scandal will
scupper his presidential plans, and intends to
make life extremely difficult for Livinia—with the
Chessmen's help. The Chessmen may play dirty,
but the Sisterhood play smart. For too long, the
Chessmen have believed themselves above the law
they pretend to serve, but there's no statute of
limitations on the Sisterhood's particular brand
of justice—or their loyalty . . .

Turn the page for a special sneak peek!

A Zebra mass-market paperback and eBook
on sale in January 2017.

It was early. Just barely past seven in the morning, when Alexis Thorne carried her cup of steaming coffee, the first of the many she would consume on this blustery early-October day, over to the huge, plate-glass window and stared down at the nearly empty parking lot. Her BMW was the only car in the lot so far that day. She sipped at the hot coffee just as another vehicle, Nikki's bright red Jeep Cherokee, swerved off the street and into the parking lot and came to rest next to hers. She smiled to herself. As was always the case, she and Nikki were the first ones into the office, beating each other out by a bare minute or two. She laughed out loud when she saw Nikki look up at the window and snap off a salute. Alexis did the same, unsure if Nikki could actually see her past the glare of the bright, early-morning sun on the window.

Alexis continued to watch her boss as Nikki sprinted across the lot like a gazelle. Alexis was holding out a matching mug of coffee when Nikki blew into the firm's kitchen. "Beat you by seven minutes, boss."

"Traffic was a bear this morning. Bumper-to-bumper two lights back, and I even left ten minutes early this morning. Hmmm, this is good."

"New coffeepot," Alexis said, giggling. "What's on the agenda today? Anything earth-shattering?"

"Not on my part. I have a ten o'clock appointment this morning. I don't even know what it's about. Mitzi said the woman refused, yes, absolutely refused to discuss with her why she wanted the appointment. Very mysterious. My new girl is due at eight-thirty to finalize her divorce. I plan to leave at noon if nothing else comes up.

"Listen, Alexis, we need to talk here. I really want to make you a partner in the firm. Why do you keep fighting me?"

"Because you have already done enough for me. You pay me way more than I'm worth, and we both know it. I'm happy with the health benefits. This is *your* firm, Nik. Yours and yours alone. I know what you had to do to get to this point, and I'm not going to take any of that away from you. If the day ever comes when I think I deserve a partnership, I'll let you know. Another thing—I really, really do not want to be perceived as the firm's token black partner. I know full well that you and the other associates don't look at it that way, but there are lots of other people who will."

"If anyone ever deserved to be a partner, Alexis, it's certainly you. Without you at my side, we never could have handled those two class-action suits. You did more than I did, and you know it. You need to be rewarded for all your hard work. Because of those two big wins, we suddenly became the go-to firm for class-action suits. That's the reason I'm hiring this new girl. And I have two more I'm considering."

"One more time, Nik. You did reward me with that super-duper end-of-the-year bonus that made my eyeballs pop out of my head and let me buy that monster sitting in the parking lot. I don't need or want anything more. Can we stop talking about this now?"

"Sure. For now. Doesn't mean I won't keep trying, though. By the way, you are coming out to the farm tonight, right? With all the guys in New York on some secret gig, you can leave your car here, hitch a ride with me, and come in with me in the morning. Does that work for you?"

"Absolutely. A hen party and not a rooster in sight. My kind of party. Did you call everyone?"

"Everyone other than Maggie, since this meeting is about her. Don't look at me like that, Alexis. You know as well as I do that we all need to talk this through. The others agree."

"It's not that I disagree, Nik. It's more like . . . oh, I don't know . . . maybe I'm feeling disloyal or something. Uh-oh, you better check this out. There's some drama going on down there in the parking lot. I think it's your new associate. And is that her husband? The one she's divorcing? She's got a lip-lock on him like you wouldn't believe. Or . . . is that guy someone she had waiting in the wings?"

Nikki ran over to the window to look down at the parking lot. "That's the soon-to-be–ex-husband. I have to say, this is, without a doubt, the strangest case of divorce I've ever handled. You know who he is, right?"

"No, actually, I have no idea. Should I?"

"He's Jeffrey Lambert, son of the current Speaker of the House, Wilson 'Buzz' Lambert. Jeffrey Lambert started up that software company called Lobo, the one that just went on the stock exchange at the beginning of the year. If you believe the hype and the media, the guy has money blowing out his ears.

"He wants to give Amy half, and she won't take it. She settled for a set of assorted bedding, some dishes, a Crock-Pot, and a few other odds and ends. It got a little contentious at our last meeting. She doesn't want anything. It's weird. They actually love each other, but they are not *in* love. They're both agreeable to the divorce and want to remain friends. Will that work? Who knows? If I had to guess, I'd say *probably*, but only because he will be on the West Coast and she'll be in the D.C. area.

"Actually, Myra said she could stay in our safe house. You remember, the one that belonged to Marie Llewellyn, the woman who got the Sisterhood off the ground in the first place when we defended her. We keep it up and use it when needed. Amy is all set. She's going to be a great addition to the firm. I can feel it in my gut."

Alexis nodded. "Looks to me like they're both crying. I'm not getting this."

"Me either. This is how Amy explained it to me. She said they were like an old comfortable shoe and a warm sock. They found each other in college, at a time when they each needed someone. She said there was never any passion, just contentment. She wanted more, and so did he, but for five years, neither one wanted to rock the boat. Once Amy passed the bar exam, and Jeffrey got his company off the ground, they became a little more vocal about their needs, wants, and expectations, and, for better or worse, this is the outcome."

Alexis nodded. "I think they're coming in now, and they're holding hands. Why is he even here?"

"Because he has to sign off on the divorce. He absolutely insisted on setting up a trust fund for Amy. Margie is handling all of that. He needs to sign off on that, too. Amy balked, but he shut her down and said he wouldn't agree to the divorce unless she agreed to the trust. He finally wore her down."

"Is there a lot of money involved?" Alexis asked.

"Oh, yeah," Nikki drawled. "The number of zeros is enough to make you dizzy. Amy no more needs to work than Annie does. Not that she is likely to touch any of the money in that trust. That guy is right up there, nipping at Mark Zuckerberg's heels. You know, the Facebook guy."

"Just when I thought nothing else could surprise me, I hear something like this. You better get moving. By the way, I just realized that since you're leaving at noon, I'll have to drive myself out to the farm. I have two late-afternoon appointments back-to-back. And the more I think about it, I might even be late, depending on traffic. Don't start without me."

"No problem. You want to meet the new associate?"

"It can wait. I need another cup of coffee before I'm ready to face strangers. Good luck with the Bobbsey Twins."

Nikki found herself giggling all the way back to her office. Before she did anything else, she turned on the gas fireplace in the casual seating area, which she preferred to use rather than dealing with clients, at least the ones she cared about, over her massive, shiny, cold desk. She knew that Mitzi Doyle, her office manager and notary public, would have a pot of coffee on the coffee table before her clients made their way to the office. Before that thought could leave her mind, Mitzi, a motherly gray-haired woman, appeared, tray in hand. "Anything else, Nikki?"

"Nope, I'm good, Mitzi. Thanks. By the way, hold my calls, and I'm planning on leaving at noon. You can reach me at home, if you need me. You can show the Lamberts in now."

They were such a nice-looking couple, Nikki

thought, as they all shook hands and seated themselves. Amy was petite, a ball of fire with blond hair and eyes that were laser blue. Jeffrey was tall, ripped, with dark, untamed, curly hair, and puppy-dog-brown eyes. Both of them had killer smiles, which they didn't show often enough, at least to her knowledge. "Coffee?"

"I think I have already had my quota for the day," Jeffrey Lambert said. Amy nodded as she kept trying to shred her fingers, which refused to remain still in her lap.

Nikki poured herself a cup of coffee and leaned back. "You both look so nervous. Why is that? You ironed everything out weeks ago. We spoke on the phone, and you both assured me that things were on track. It's okay if you have changed your minds. It happens more often than you know."

"It's just that . . . neither one of us has ever been divorced. I guess it finally hit us that this is the end of . . . of . . . our being together. We won't be cooking any more meals together or meeting up to eat something on the run at the end of the day. No more movie nights. No more sharing our day's experiences. Togetherness will be just a memory, and I find it sad, but, no, I haven't changed my mind, and neither has Jeff. We are going to go through with the divorce. Just tell us where to sign, so Jeff can catch his flight back to California." Nikki cringed at the jitteriness she was hearing in Amy's voice.

Nikki made a big production out of leafing through the folder on the coffee table in the hopes that she was covering up what she was suddenly feeling. She didn't know why, but she didn't have a good feeling about this divorce. Finally, when she realized she couldn't stall any longer, she placed the papers in front of the young couple. "My notary is on the way in, so it will be just another minute."

Amy Lambert went back to shredding her fingers, while her husband, for the moment, stared at the Jackson Pollock paintings on the wall. Nikki thought he looked more nervous than his wife. She felt her sudden uneasiness ramp up a notch. She let loose with a soft sigh the moment Mitzi and her notary stamp appeared. Seven minutes later, everything was in order, and the Lamberts were on their feet, waiting to shake Nikki's hand.

"Amy, I'll see you on the first of November, when you report for work. I was going to have you meet up with Alexis Thorne this morning, but her calendar is full. So when you get here for your first day of work, ask for Mitzi Doyle, the woman who just notarized your divorce papers. She's also our office manager, and she'll take you down to HR so you can get all of that out of the way. That's when you'll meet with Alexis.

"Everything at the house is ready for you. You'll have to do some grocery shopping, but that's about it. Is there anything else I can do for you before you leave?"

The Lamberts shook their heads and tried for smiles, which never quite made it to their faces, much less their eyes.

"Well, then, I guess this is good-bye, Mr. Lambert. Don't worry about Amy. We'll take good care of her."

Out in the hall, Nikki leaned up against the wall as she struggled to take a long, deep breath. *Something's out of kilter* was all she could think of to explain her sudden attack of nervousness. Long ago, she'd learned to pay attention to such feelings. She pushed away from the wall and headed straight for the door whose plaque said the office belonged to Alexis Thorne. She rapped softly, turned the knob, and peeked into the room. "Good, you're alone. I have to say that was one stressful meeting. And yet nothing happened. We were up to speed on everything. Smooth as silk, as they say. I had this crazy set of feelings, almost a panic attack. I don't know why. Some days, and this is one of them, I hate being a lawyer."

"What's happening?" Alexis asked.

What was happening was that Amy Lambert was licking at her lips. There was so much she wanted to say to this fine young man who was still her husband until a judge stamped her divorce papers. But the words wouldn't come, and even if she had known what to say, she seriously doubted that she would have been able to give voice to them. And to her eye, it looked like Jeffrey was having the same problem.

"Amy, if you . . . if you ever need anything, anything at all, promise you'll call. You know

I'm not just saying the words. I mean it. I think you know me better than anyone on earth, even better than my mother knows me."

Amy's head bobbed up and down. When Jeffrey walked out of Nikki's office to go to Margie Baylor's to sign the trust agreement, he was also walking out of Amy's life. At that moment, she had at least a two-minute window of time to change her mind. If she wanted. The door opened. Scratch the two minutes. This was it. She clenched her teeth so hard, she thought she might have cracked a tooth. *Don't cry. Crying is a sign of weakness. You can do this. You're a big girl now. Right now, Amy Jones, you are on your own. I should have told Jeff I was taking back my maiden name. Why didn't I do that? Why? Probably because I thought it would be like pouring salt on an open wound. How could I tell him that I don't want to be associated any longer with the name Lambert—not because of Jeff, but because of his father and those around him?*

Damn, she should have left when Nikki left. There was no reason for her still to be standing there, and yet, there she was. She whirled around to search for her purse, found it, and slung it over her shoulder. From somewhere deep inside, she managed to drag out the words. "Let's not say good-bye, Jeff. Let's just go with 'I'll see ya.' If I find the law isn't for me, I might hit you up for a job at some point. Don't forget to send me a Christmas card." She was stunned at how blasé her tone was. Mind over matter. She almost faltered at the strange look she was seeing on Jeff's face. *Move! Just get the hell out of here. Move. Don't think. Go, for God's sake.* Earlier, on their way into the building, Jeffrey had warned her that the office might be bugged and to be careful with what she said.

How she got to the lobby, she didn't know. And then she was outside, with the fierce October wind bent on attacking her as her hair blew in every direction. She walked around the building to the employee parking lot and her sad little gray Honda Accord, which had 140,000 miles on it. She'd insisted on driving it cross-country because she knew she would need a car to get around once she reached her final destination. Jeff had insisted on driving with her and refused to take no for an answer, saying he would fly back. Jeff had wanted to buy her a new car, a fancy high-end Mercedes, but she had declined his generous offer. How noble she was, how proud. She'd gone into the marriage with nothing, and that's how she was leaving it. She had no intention of touching the money in the trust fund. She had her pride.

Amy wrestled with her wild mane of hair as she tried to pull it back into a ponytail. Finally satisfied that she could see, she started the engine. It purred to life like a contented cat. As she was typing in the address to her new, albeit temporary, home on the portable dashboard GPS, a gift from Jeff, she saw a shiny black Lincoln Town Car drive past her and park next to a bright red Jeep Cherokee. As she waited for traffic to slow, she watched the car in her side mirror, saw a man in a dark suit wearing a chauffeur's cap get out and open the passenger door in the back. She gasped as a tall, handsome man with snow-white hair, despite his relatively young age, got out and strode forward. "Damn!" Amy fumbled with her cell phone and pressed the number one on her speed dial.

"Pick up, Jeff! C'mon, pick up." And then she heard his voice, and she calmed down.

"What? You're missing me already?" The words were lame-sounding, but still music to her ears.

"Listen to me. I was leaving the parking lot, and your father was just arriving. He's entering the building now, Jeff. *Now.*"

"Are you sure?"

"Of course I'm sure. I even recognized his driver. Your father, the Speaker of the House, is now in the building. Okay, I'm outta here. Have a good flight, Jeff. Send me a text when you land, so I know you arrived safe and sound."

"Okay, *Mother.*" It was meant to sound funny, and it might have come across that way if the tone hadn't been so brittle and brusque. Amy didn't bother to respond. Wilson "Buzz" Lambert, the Speaker of the House of Representatives, was not her problem. Not any longer. He was Jeffrey's problem. She would never forget the day Buzz, of all people, called her a gold digger, among even other less-than-flattering names. Never.

Amy cracked her window, then slid a CD into the portable player that Jeffrey had installed for her. She smiled. She loved Bon Jovi. So did Jeff.

Scratch Jeff. She had to stop including Jeff in her thoughts. It was just her now. *Amy Jones*. She felt a momentary thrill of excitement at her maiden name. *Amy Jones. Look out, world, here I come—a little late to the game I intend to be playing, but I'm here now. And when the game is over, the whole world will know about who I am and how I won.*

Jeffrey Lambert, CEO and principal shareholder of Lobo, son of the Speaker of the House, Wilson "Buzz" Lambert, was thinking almost the same thing as his now ex-wife. *I'm here now, inside the building, and what do I do?* Such a stupid question he thought as he ended his call with Amy and scrawled his signature to finalize the trust fund he'd set up for her. Sweat beaded on his forehead. He suddenly felt stupid to have thought he could get in and out of Washington without meeting up with good old Buzz.

"Is there any way I can leave here beside through the door I just came through, Ms. Baylor?"

Margie Baylor banged down on the stapler, looked up, and pointed to a door to the left of her office. "That door will take you to the outside corridor that leads straight out to the parking lot."

Jeff's mind raced. He wished he could take the time to explain to this nice lawyer, with the panicky look, why he was acting like he was, but he simply did not have the time. "I don't want to go to the parking lot. Is there another way?"

"I'm sorry, but that's it. You could take the steps or the elevator to the basement, walk up one flight, which will bring you inches from the revolving door at the entrance. There's usually a line of cabs waiting. Well, maybe not a line of cabs, but at least one or two. Is everything all right, Mr. Lambert?"

"No, everything is not all right. I understand my father is in the building, and I want to avoid him. He's a pretty forceful kind of individual and is probably right now trying to intimidate your receptionist and your office manager with his bluster. Look, I just need to get out of here!"

Margie laughed. "Our people do not know or recognize the word *intimidate*. We're women! I assure you that if anyone is going to be intimidated, it will be your father. Nikki trained us well. Like I said, we're women!" She pointed to the side door, and said, "Go!" Jeffrey didn't need to be told twice. He literally flew through the doorway.

"Never a dull moment at the Quinn Law Firm," Margie mumbled under her breath. She pressed a button on the console and spoke quietly. "I need you to take these papers over to the courthouse and have them filed. I'd like you to do it *now*, Judy."

"Yes, ma'am, I can do that. There is someone here to see you. He doesn't have an appointment."

Margie's mind raced. She knew who it was. "And what is our rule here at the Quinn Law Firm, Judy?"

"The attorneys only see clients with appointments. Mr. Lambert is insistent, Ms. Baylor. He asked me to tell you he is the Speaker of the House."

"All our clients are treated equally. One more time, what is our rule here at the Quinn Law Firm, Judy? Tell the Speaker to make an appointment." That said, Margie hightailed it out the same doorway Jeffrey Lambert had just gone through. She did exactly what she told Jeffrey to do. She rode the elevator to the basement and walked up a flight of steps to the lobby and was through the revolving door in minutes. Outside, a cab was at the curb. She climbed in, and said, "Take me to the courthouse." She leaned back against the cracked leather seat. Sometimes, you just had to do things yourself. It was important to Jeffrey Lambert to have the trust documents filed today. As his attorney, it was her job to make sure it happened.

This whole thing—the ever-so-friendly divorce, the unwanted trust, and the Speaker of the House showing up at the eleventh hour— was enough to boggle her mind, and yet people said the law was boring. She sniffed. Those people didn't know anything about the all-female Quinn Law Firm. Not a damn thing. Nikki's mantra, to which they all subscribed, was "Take no prisoners."

*   *   *

While Margie's cab crawled through traffic, Buzz Lambert was railing at her secretary, demanding to see the head of the firm.

"I'm sorry, *Mister* Speaker, but rules are rules. I have a job here that I love, and I want and intend to keep this job. I will, however, call Ms. Quinn to if she has time to meet with you. Take a seat, please," said Judy.

"Don't you dare tell me what to do, young lady. It works the other way around—I tell you what to do. Is it necessary for me to remind you who I am? I need to get back to the Hill."

"No, sir, you have already told me four times who you are. But it just doesn't matter. You are not my employer, and you do not set policy for the Quinn Law Firm. Now, either you sit down or you leave, or I will be forced to call security. How do you think that is going to look on the evening news? I can just hear the news anchor. 'And now a story about the Speaker of the House, Buzz Lambert, being escorted by security out of the building housing the Quinn Law Firm. Calls to the Speaker's office asking for comment on the incident have not been returned.' I am calling Ms. Quinn now."

Buzz couldn't believe that this slip of a girl was telling him, the man two heartbeats away from becoming the president of the United States, what to do. And yet, here he was, sitting down. He seethed like a fire-breathing dragon as he waited.

"Ms. Quinn instructed me to escort you to

her office. She said she can give you five minutes, not one minute longer, as she has a client who is always prompt and is due to arrive momentarily. Here at the Quinn Law Firm, we do our best not to keep our clients waiting. Follow me, sir."

Nikki was standing in the open doorway to her office. She nodded to Judy that she should return to her own office, that she could and would handle things from here on in. "Mr. Speaker, I'm Nikki Quinn. This is my firm. I don't care who you are or why you're here, but do not ever try to bluster your way in here and try to intimidate my employees. We do not tolerate that kind of behavior. You have five minutes, so talk fast. I have a client who is due to arrive any minute."

"Where's my son? Where's that gold digger he married? Jeffrey's mother told me they were getting divorced and that you were handling the divorce."

"I have not the slightest clue as to the current whereabouts of your son. I assume that he has finished what he came here to do and has departed. Likewise for his wife.

"And as a lawyer yourself, you should know that I cannot discuss my clients' business with you. This might sound trite, but I would bet dollars to donuts that you have your son's phone number and access to a telephone. Perhaps you should try calling him to find out where he is, instead of coming here and disrupting my law firm. I think we're done here, Mr. Speaker."

"This isn't the end of it, lady," Buzz blustered. He couldn't remember the last time anyone had talked to him like this blond floozy. Even men didn't dare talk to him like she had.

His face red and mottled like the old bricks on the building, Wilson "Buzz" Lambert turned on his heel and marched down the hall, his back ramrod stiff.

The fine hairs on the back of Nikki's neck moved. So her gut was right, and right now her gut was telling her that the Speaker's words were true. This wasn't the end of the Lambert divorce, not by a long shot.

Books by Bestselling Author
Fern Michaels

Available Wherever Books Are Sold!
Check out our website at **www.kensingtonbooks.com**